D1519657

WASHED IN BLOOD

Heaven's Guardians MC - Book 1

by: ASHLEY LANE

Cover Design

Pink Elephant Designs

https://www.facebook.com/pinkelephantdesigns2

Editing

Miss Bliss Author Services

https://www.facebook.com/groups/missbliss2019

Proofreading

Paige Sayer Proofreading

https://www.facebook.com/paigesayerproofreading/

Nothing but the Blood of Jesus

Words and Music by Robert Lowry (1826-1899), Published in 1876

It is the blood that makes atonement for the soul.

Leviticus 17:11

DEDICATION

For my husband, Michael.
You save me every day.
I love you.

And to my Deddy.
Thank you for preordering my book.
Please skip the end of chapters 10, 13, and 16.

WASHED IN BLOOD

CHAPTER 1

TWENTY YEARS EARLIER

An ear-piercing scream breaks through the haze surrounding me and dread fills the pit of my stomach. *Doe?* An animalistic roar escapes the confines of my chest as I tear through the destruction surrounding me. *Fuck, baby—where are you?* "Doe!" Her name leaves my lips as a desperate plea, but I jerk to a halt when I realize the cops and paramedics around me are unfazed by my outburst.

I scan the room, spinning, frantically searching for her—for any sign of what's happening. A flurry of activity surrounds me, yet no one looks my way. My mind spins, a hurricane of thoughts, images, voices. *The fuck is going on?* A wall of police block the entrance to the living room and I move closer to them, stepping over shards of broken glass as I go. As I get closer, their hushed mumblings become clear and my mind whirls as their words filter through.

"Six 9mm rounds to the chest, kid never had a chance." A detective in a wrinkled suit stands by the door jotting notes in a small spiral notepad.

"Any idea what time the coroner is coming?" a huge tank of a cop asks.

The detective shakes his head before looking down at something in the middle of the police huddle. "Nah. Let the paramedics call it. Injuries not compatible with life. The girl took one to the upper chest, they're loading her up now."

Kid never had a chance. Injuries not compatible with life. My heart pounds against my chest and I look down to see my hands are covered in thick, crimson blood.

A phone rings, and when the officer steps away to answer it, I'm allowed my first glimpse at the carnage lying before me. On the living room floor, my lifeless body is littered with bullet holes; the carpet beneath me, saturated with blood that pours from the wounds in my chest. The same pattern from the spray of bullets bloodies my shirt. *No. NO! Th—this can't be happening. This isn't how it's supposed to end!*

The living room has been torn apart. Frames that were once hanging, have come to a mangled rest against the floorboards. Shattered and broken, right where they belong. The images of smiling, happy children behind the glass were nothing more than the printed result from an internet search. Lies to add to the facade of a nonexistent happy family. Furniture is overturned and ripped cushions are scattered across the dirty carpet along with piles of debris.

A commotion outside distracts me from the demolished room. As I approach the door, her tortured screams grow louder and despair courses through me. *Girl took one to the chest. God, please. No.* I drop my head, steeling myself for a scene I know is going to rip my soul to shreds. With one last deep breath, I attempt to calm my racing heart before I grip the door knob. Head down, I step outside.

Chaos surrounds me as police struggle to get handcuffs onto the wrists of my murderer. My foster father bucks wildly against the officers who attempt to subdue him. "It was self-defense! Little fuck attacked me first!" My body trembles at the lies coming from his mouth.

That piece of shit. He's trying to pin this on me. He—he fucking raped her! And he's trying to pin it on me. I take a charging step forward, but the sounds of Doe's screams cause my body to freeze. I turn in time to see her tear stained face being loaded onto a stretcher. The top of her shirt is stained with blood, but her arms are extended toward the house as she fights the paramedics. *Stop fighting them, baby, please. Let them help you, God please.* "No! Please! Save him, you have to save him!" Tears threaten my eyes, my heart breaking with her pleas. She wants them to help me, but I'm already gone. Drawn like a magnet, my feet take me toward her, but like trick rooms in a carnival house, the world around me melts away.

What the hell is going on? All traces of my foster home and my street are gone. Instead, I'm in the middle of a ramshackle warehouse. The walls are lined with closed doors; I have no idea which way is out. I start toward the closest one when my eyes catch on a door several paces away. It's cracked. Logic tells me to run, find an exit and get out, but a haunting whisper urges me to stay.

Careful of the broken down pieces of machinery, I make my way to the door and press my fingertips against it. I wince when the hinges creak loudly as the door swings open. Mold and decay linger in the air and my shoes stick to years of filth and waste that coat the floor. A small, barred window is covered in a layer of dust and grime so dense, I can't make out what's on the other side. In the far corner of the room, a single chair sits facing an old metal bed where a worn mattress lies atop a rust covered frame. From the ceiling, a dim light bulb hangs from a thick cord, it sways slowly back and forth even though the air is eerily still.

Hesitantly, I walk toward the bed to get a closer look. Bile rises in my throat at the sight of the deep crimson stains absorbed into the mattress. My eyes catch on a pair of handcuffs hanging from the bed frame. *Jesus Christ. The hell is this place?*

Frustration builds as I attempt to piece together where I am, and what the fuck is going on. Gripping my hair, I tug harshly and turn back in the direction of the door. My body freezes, fear holds my muscles captive. In the chair that was empty moments ago, now sits a man, and he's staring right at me.

"Hello, Kingston."

The hairs on the back of my neck stand on end and my chest heaves as my fight-or-flight kicks in, triggered by the fear pumping through my veins.

The man is wearing a crisp black suit complete with a black shirt and tie, he looks like a made man. His square jaw and high cut cheekbones contribute to his malicious appearance. Finally meeting his eyes, I suck in a breath and find his sinister gaze already fixed on me.

"Wh—who are you? How do you know my name?"

Still and unmoving, he eyes me. I shake my head hard. *Is he real?* He must be a figment of my imagination.

"I assure you I am very real indeed." When he answers my unspoken question, my body goes stiff. "Do you know what happened today, Kingston?"

My lips pinch together. *I know what happened. First, I found out my girlfriend was raped by our sick fuck of a foster father, then I was murdered. Now I've lost my fucking mind.*

"I died," I grit out, though I don't quite believe it yet.

Hands clasped in his lap, he nods. "Yes. You died. But more than that, you died defending an innocent life, isn't that right?"

I scoff. "Yeah, but what did it get me? I was supposed to fucking protect her, and I didn't. I failed, now I'm dead." Regret and self-loathing threaten to choke me. "I—I don't even know if she's going to be okay. She could..." I can barely finish the thought. "She could die, and it will be *my* fault," my voice cracks. I don't know who the hell this weird, creepy dude is, and here I am pouring out my heart and soul to him. *Shit, I'm losing it. You're fucking dead, King. This isn't real.* I squeeze my eyes and count to ten hoping that when I open them, he'll be gone.

Nope, still here.

His crystal blue eyes glow, taking on an ethereal sheen. A slight smirk plays across his lips. "You caused me to lose a bet today, Kingston."

My jaw clenches. *What the fuck is he talking about?* "What do you mean *I* caused you to lose a bet? Dude, I don't even know who the hell you are." Frustration builds as I pace the filthy floor.

He stands, his torso bending in a slight bow before he takes his seat again. "Forgive me for not

14

introducing myself, my name is Azrael. You can think of me as a liaison of sorts."

I narrow my eyes, skeptical as he continues, "Many years ago, a prophecy was foretold. A boy, not a child, yet not a man, would face a choice. No matter the path chosen, the outcome would have a ripple effect that would alter the lives of countless others."

A growl vibrates in my chest as my fists tighten, fingernails bite into my palms. He's speaking in fucking riddles and I want answers. "I don't understand what the hell this has to do with me."

Ignoring my outburst, Azrael stands from his seat and paces toward the blood-stained bed. "At the time, we were only seeing in black and white, dark and light. I wagered the darkness within you would ultimately win. If that had come to pass, today would have had an extremely different outcome. Surprisingly, something we weren't anticipating happened. Instead of one overpowering the other, light and dark joined. They fused together to become a burning inferno of fierce, protective rage." He continues pacing before he stops in front of the window and faces me, obviously waiting for me to comprehend what he's saying.

I open my mouth to speak, but a shocking pain radiates through my chest and takes me to my knees. Clutching at my chest, I groan as shockwaves tear through my body, causing my heart to stop momentarily before it starts thumping again. When I drop my hands, they're coated in blood—my blood. A faint beep echoes through the barren room; I search for the source of the noise, but silence takes over.

Unfazed by my condition, Azrael continues, "I was sent here today to inform you that *He* is not finished with you. He has plans you have not yet fulfilled."

From my position on the floor, I gaze up at him, the noises surrounding us grow louder by the second. Voices float through the air and the faint beep returns, louder this time.

Azrael starts for the door, and panic surges through me—I still need answers. "Wait! Who? Who isn't finished with me yet?"

He waves a hand through the air, wisps of smoke trail from his fingertips. "Your meaning will become clear in time. For now, it's important you remember these four things, Kingston. Not all Demons you encounter in your life will be bad. A Bullet doesn't always hit its intended mark. Stay vigilant for Angels, and always keep a Patch close, you never know when you'll need one."

As the room fades, the commotion inside my head becomes so loud my vision turns black around the edges.

"Just as a shepherd leads his herd, you too shall lead. Find them, guide them. Be patient, Priest, and you will be rewarded. Until then, *Guard Heaven...*" With those cryptic words, he opens the door, flooding the room in white light.

I bring my hand up to my eyes in an attempt to block the glare, but at the same time electricity courses through my system, forcing me back into reality.

"We've got a rhythm!"

"At least we were able to save one of them," someone says.

"Damn. The girl?"

"It was just too much. Her body couldn't take it. We were able to save the baby. She's a micro preemie, only twenty-six weeks gestation, so she has a tough road ahead."

I fight to open my eyes, but my body is too weak.

Her body just couldn't take it... Darkness pulls me under, and I pray it's death coming back to take me with him. There's nothing left for me here. Because like a flame needs oxygen, I needed her. But now she's gone, and so am I.

WASHED IN BLOOD

CHAPTER 2

WILLOW

Present Day

The pain in my stomach started as a dull ache, now it's a persistent stab. A glaring reminder of how long it's been since I last ate. Three weeks ago, my only goal was to escape. Get out and start over. I didn't realize how hard the starting over part would be.

My reality check came when countless applications were filled out to no-name diners and seedy motels, only to be denied the second they found out either, A: I had no form of identification, or B: I was pregnant. That's right, folks. Forget that I'm a hard worker, willing to work any shift for almost any pay—

a bun in the oven equals a boot out the door. So here I am, Willow James, twenty years old, homeless, pregnant, and on the run from my abusive husband. Ready my mother of the year award, will ya? *God, how did this become my life?* I don't even know how to *be* a mother. How could I? That's what happens when you're born to a sixteen-year-old orphan who dies in childbirth, leaving you an orphan yourself. I was doomed from the start. But I was also a fighter. Born at twenty-six weeks, doctors didn't expect me to live. Despite the odds, I survived.

So, how did this become my life? Not willingly, that's for sure. I'm no stranger to being homeless. As soon as I turned 18, I was out the door and thrown to the wolves. Not a dime to my name, I had the clothes on my back and what little I could fit into my backpack. The first week was the hardest. Being alone at night, sleeping under bridges... it's definitely a place I never wanted to wind up in again, but here I am. By the end of the second week, I'd come to learn that living on the streets was more about *who* you knew, rather than *what* you knew.

Making friends when you're homeless, even with other homeless people, isn't an easy feat. Everyone was protective of their territory, and I was an outsider. So instead of risking my life trying to make friends, I decided to go at it alone.

Back then, I opted for the traditional homeless route. I loitered outside grocery stores and popular interstate exits, begging anyone who would listen for a scrap of change. But I soon discovered most people were cruel and unforgiving. They'd sling hateful slurs or snide comments, not once thinking I had no other options. It was a rare occasion for anyone to look at me, let alone throw me a shred of food or spare change.

I was the rabid dog everyone avoided for fear they'd catch some deathly disease. Women clutched their purses close to their chest as they averted their gaze, not daring to meet my eyes. Mothers pulled their children closer as though I was some kind of sick and twisted predator, ready to pounce on unsuspecting victims. But men were the worst. They'd approach me with a kind smile and cash in hand, seeming every bit the helpful stranger. But as soon as my hand would reach for the measly dollars, they'd snatch them away and ask me how bad I wanted it.

After six months on the streets, I had a change of luck. One night as I was scouring the trash cans behind an old '60s themed diner, I was cornered by three college kids who'd had one too many at the sports bar down the street. After my time on the streets, my body had withered away to almost nothing, I never stood a chance against them.

My saving grace was the owner of the diner, Mr. Warren, who heard my screams. He acted fast, told his wife to call the police while he grabbed his baseball bat and ran outside just as the punks were pulling off my pants. He lost his mind, screaming like a wild man and swinging his bat at them as they ran away. Mrs. Warren took one look at me and broke down in tears. Without knowing me at all, they took me into their home. They fed me, bathed me, and gave me a place to sleep for the night. It was more than I could have hoped for. The next morning, I woke and gathered my things, ready to leave. I was stunned when they offered me a job. Four months later, Vince walked into my life and swept me off my feet. He charmed my desperate heart, and I became a puppet on his string. Six months later, we were married and moving to New Mexico for bigger and better opportunities.

The minute the ink was dry on those papers, Vince peeled off the mask he wore like a second skin and revealed the devil underneath. Still, I longed for what a life with him could mean. I was more than willing to endure the fires of hell if it meant finally getting the things I'd dreamed of all my life. Love, children, a family of my own. I thought we could make it work. If I tried hard enough, I could change and be who he wanted me to be. All I needed was a little time.

Then, everything changed. The day I missed my period, I knew I was pregnant.

At first, I was excited to tell Vince I was having a baby. Color me a fool, but I thought a baby could be the answer to it all. The answer to a thousand whispered prayers in the dead of night. But instead of a blessing, it was another curse better left unsaid. Telling Vince about the life inside me was one of the worst mistakes I'd ever made. He was livid. Positively enraged. It took five pregnancy tests to prove I wasn't lying to him, but still, he was convinced the baby wasn't his. Who else's would it be? I was hardly ever allowed to go anywhere without him. How he thought I had the chance to screw another guy was beyond me. It pissed me off and caused me to forget my place. A place he had taught me was right where I belonged... beneath him.

That night, he beat me within an inch of my life.

It's a miracle my baby survived. And if I wanted to give it a chance, I had to get the hell out of there. I may not know *how* to be a mother, but I will die to protect the innocent life growing inside me. And if that's what it takes, I'm ready and willing to pay the price.

Beaten to hell, I left that same night. I waited until the drugs and alcohol he pumped into his body took effect, then I packed a bag and ran. I walked for hours before I stopped outside a deserted truck stop to figure out my next move.

As an older gentleman was leaving, coffee in hand, his eyes widened when they landed on my weary body resting on the curb. He offered a kind smile but no words as he climbed into the tall cab of his truck. Once the engine was running, he reached across and opened the passenger door, staring at me expectedly.

His eyes held no judgement as they touched on every bruise, every scar, and every mark on my frail body.

For several long minutes, I contemplated my choices. The man could have been a murderer, or a rapist using his Mr. Rogers look as a front, but I was out of options.

He never asked any questions, never spoke a word. But his eyes told me everything. To him, I was not invisible. He saw me; and he cared.

It was rather ironic that our journey ended in Colorado. This is where my life began, seems fitting this is where I would end up. I've been back in Colorado for twenty-one days, and all I have to show for it are failed attempts of finding a way to provide for myself and my unborn child.

It's past dark when I start my walk toward the deli in town. The owner is insistent that each day starts with new bread, so when the day is over, anything left in the case is thrown out. Lucky for me, I was raised on the *'waste not, want not'* motto.

After I get dinner, I need to find somewhere to bunker down for the night. Homeless in Colorado in January means cold days and even colder nights.

As I head down the back alley behind the deli, I pass a shiny black Escalade idling next to the curb. Steam billows from the exhaust pipes, and though I don't see anyone inside, it urges me to stay vigilant as I approach the dumpster, ready to scour any wasted edibles. Just before I open the lid, the rear entrance of the deli flies open, slamming against the building with a loud crack. With a squeak of fear, I drop to a crouch and scurry behind the dumpster.

"No… please! I swear to God, I'll get the money!" The man's garbled voice pleads.

My hands shake as his fear becomes my own.

"You've already had your chance to get the money. The boss gave you double what he gives others. You knew the conditions. Now it's time to pay the price." The second voice is unfeeling, cold—menacing.

"No… listen—" his voice shakes. I recognize it as Mr. Guidelli, the man who owns the deli. "I just n—need to get it…" He pleads again, "The safe. It's in my safe."

"We've already been by your house tonight and your safe doesn't have shit; though your wife was very accommodating… 'fraid we might've left her in a bit of a mess," the second voice implies.

I force back the vomit creeping up my throat. My eyes burn with tears and I do my best to steady my breathing, but my heart is about to pound out of my chest.

Mr. Guidelli releases a wounded, broken scream that sounds more like a battle cry. "What did you do to her? I'LL KILL YOU! I'LL FUCKING KILL ALL—"

POP.

POP.

POP.

Gunshots pierce the night, firing in rapid succession, they cut off Mr. Guidelli with brutal finality. The sound so violent and brash, a scream is released from my lungs before I have a chance to smother my mouth.

"What the fuck was that? Go look around. The boss can never find out we were here—no witnesses..." the cold voice continues with mumbled curses before footsteps fade away.

Both pairs of shoes disappear from my view underneath the dumpster. When the deli door slams closed, I take my chance to bolt and run in the direction of the woods across the street.

"There… Get her!"

I scream, pushing myself to run harder, and just as I crest the opening of the woods, I trip and fall to my hands and knees. When I turn to look over my shoulder, one of the men has his gun trained on me. I take in every detail of his fierce, menacing face and dark eyes in the quick seconds I have before I'm back up and running into the thick woods. When a gunshot blasts behind me, I release a shrill cry of terror. *I can't die, not like this.*

As soon as I'm covered by the safety of the trees, I scramble into the thick overgrowth. The guy chasing me is huge, no way will he be able to follow me in here. I squeeze through a narrow gap between two trees. It's so dark, and with the moon covered by thick grey clouds, I don't notice the steep decline.

I lose my footing and slide down a ravine, tumbling through broken branches and loose stones. Cradling my stomach, my thoughts are only on my precious baby. I pray to any God who's listening… *Please, keep my baby safe.*

When I reach the bottom, my bones ache and my muscles are weak. I pause for the shortest second, listening for any sign the men are still following. Silence lingers, broken only by the eerie howl of a wolf. *I need to hide.* Further ahead, moonlight peeks through the clouds onto a fallen tree as though it's a sign from above, leading me to relative safety. I scramble forward, almost tripping over the stump. I barely hold in my cry of relief when I see the tree's hollowed out carcass. *I can fit in there.*

Still clutching my stomach, I stay low and keep as quiet as possible. When I finally manage to wedge myself inside, I shove my bag beneath a pile of dead leaves and brush away the inches of snow to reach the ground underneath. I grab handfuls of dirt and rub it over my face and arms. *This is what they do in survival shows, right?*

After what feels like hours, adrenaline wears off and I'm fighting to keep my eyes open. The wind blows with an unforgiving force, bringing a flurry of snow with it. *You have got to be kidding me.* I burrow deeper into the tree hoping to shield my body from the brunt of the snowstorm.

The sun rises and sets until I lose count of the hours and days. I should leave and try to find food and better shelter, but fear overrides every other emotion. I need to protect my baby. I did not survive Vince, and every odd stacked against me only to die at the hands of a couple of thugs.

God, if you can hear me, please send help.

WASHED IN BLOOD

CHAPTER 3

PRIEST

Three days later

"Yo, Prez. You got a minute?"

Bullet, my sergeant at arms and tech-security man stands at the door. I wave my hand at him to come in as I move the ledgers and papers I was going through to the side of my desk. In his hand is the GPS tracking device he set up a few months back. On the screen, a blinking red dot. He takes a seat in the leather chair opposite my desk and glances at the paperwork.

"You busy?"

"Just looking over some financials for Sinners. I'm pretty sure that little fucker that Angel just hired has decided to keep a little extra before putting peoples' cash in the register. You'll need to pay him a visit and remind him who the fuck he works for."

Bullet leans forward as I push the paperwork across the desk. His brows knit together in anger. "The fuck? He's only been there a couple weeks."

I nod, trying to rub away the beginnings of the headache. "Exactly. And since him, we haven't hired anyone new. Fuckin' kid, obviously stupid if he's stealing from us and thinks he won't get caught. Be sure to relay that he's fired when you deliver our message."

He gives me a chin lift, letting me know he's got it handled before he reaches forward and lays the device in his hands onto my desk.

"What you got?"

He shrugs. "It's probably nothing but the land surrounding the back of the club had a wire tripped three nights ago. It was the same night as that big snow storm, so I figured it was a fallen tree. I didn't notice it until now, but there's a slight heat signature showing on the corner of camera nineteen. Probably an old deer that was struggling to make it through the winter. Thought maybe we should go put it down and reset the wire that was tripped." He folds his arms over his chest, waiting for my reply.

Bullet earned his road name honestly and can put a bullet in a person quicker than I can try to reason whether or not they deserve it. When it comes to an animal, that hard as steel man turns into a big pile of mush.

Fucking shit. I sigh, I won't be able to talk him out of putting the animal out of its misery. "Alright, Mother Teresa, why don't I come with you… in case you need back up?"

He flips me off, but he knows he's a little bitch when it comes to animals.

"I'd hate for any of your tears to show up on the infrared cameras. I'm tryin' to protect your manhood."

He laughs outright. "Fuck you. I can't help it if I'm the only one around here who still has a heart."

I don't reply because we both know it's a lie. None of us have hearts anymore. They've been gone for years.

I head across the room to the coat rack and grab my flannel lined leather jacket. The guys gave me shit for getting a lined jacket, but I don't give a fuck. We live in Aspen. They can laugh their fucking asses off all they want, but they'll freeze their dicks off while doing it. It's early January now, so we're lucky if the days stay in the thirties, and nights are even worse, barely reaching the low teens.

We exit my office and turn down the hall that leads into the main room. Some of the doors we pass are closed, but the ones that are open show rooms that look like a fucking frat house, not a place where grown ass men live.

As we make our way toward the wooded area of the forest, I drop my head to avoid the chill in the air. According to the GPS, the wire that was tripped is about a mile out from the clubhouse. Bullet is a certified fucking genius. After a close call a few months ago with some local kids and a gang initiation challenge, he rigged up a perimeter wide system. If a wire is tripped, heat signature cameras in that area will alert us to the location. Though we can't always make out exactly what it is, we are able to tell if it's walking on four legs or two. If multiple heat signatures are detected, we have a problem.

It takes us around twenty-five minutes to reach the location. While Bullet gets to work repairing the wire and resetting the cameras, I shine my light at the ground, searching for signs of a wounded animal. Bullet said it had been three days since the beacon went off, and with a fresh layer of snow that's fallen since then, I wonder if it's worth freezing our asses off out here. Whatever it was, it's probably dead.

After a few minutes stumbling through the overgrowth and storm damage, I come to a fallen tree. At first glance, I don't see anything out of the ordinary, but on closer inspection, it's obvious *someone*—not *something*—has been here. My flashlight stops on an old, ratty backpack, a half-eaten piece of moldy bread, and a rotten apple core. My stomach clenches and adrenaline flows through my veins as I piece together what I'm seeing. *Holy fuck. Someone is living inside there.*

Pulling my gun from the holster at my back, I squat down and remove the backpack from where it's wedged in the opening of the hollowed tree. I keep my gun trained on the opening while shining my light inside. A young woman comes into view, and my heart that moments ago I was sure didn't exist, pounds against my chest.

Minutes feel like hours as I work quickly, hooking my arms under hers to drag her small body from the dead tree stump. When my skin makes contact with her cold flesh, I'm certain she's already dead. There's no way she could survive being out here for three hours in this weather, let alone three days.

Urgently, I pull her small wrist from where it's tucked underneath her and place my fingers against it, searching for any signs of life. Shock courses through me when I feel the faint but steady beat of her pulse.

I pull her into my lap and shout until my throat is raw. "Bullet!"

Seconds pass before he's standing over me, gun drawn and aimed at an invisible threat in the darkness. I shine my light on the woman's body, highlighting the dire state she's in.

He drops his gun and leans down; confusion knits his brows. "The fuck is that?"

I move my arm slightly, angling it toward the ground and maneuvering the light to shine it on her dirt covered face. Her head lolls to the side, the action so sickening, bile rises in my throat.

Bullet leans in for a better look and stumbles back once he sees. "Oh fuck. Oh shit, it's a woman... holy shit."

Moving to my knees, I cradle the dying woman in my arms. "Help me, I have to save her."

He moves forward, attempting to take her from my arms. A burning, obsessive rage washes over me and I pull her against my chest, snarling at him like a deranged psychopath. "Don't touch her!"

Clearly stunned by the vehemence in my voice, Bullet jerks back suddenly and falls on his ass in the dirt. "The fuck, Priest? You asked me to help..."

Christ, the fuck is wrong with me? Fear and anguish torture my mind, tearing at my once cold heart. "Just... help me stand. I don't know what's wrong with her, and I don't want to risk hurting her further by handing her to you." I'm positive he knows that's a load of shit, but he nods and gets to his feet to help me stand.

As soon as I have my footing, I start in the direction of the clubhouse. "We have to get her back. *Now.*" Her pulse is so low I'm worried she won't make it, but I have to try. She fought this long, I can't let her die like this.

While we rush back, Bullet shrugs off his jacket to drape it over her as I break into a sprint. I growl low in my chest hating the sight of his clothing covering her, but she needs the warmth. Distracting myself from my barbaric thoughts, I shift into Prez mode and shout out orders. "Call Patch. I want him at the clubhouse when we get there. Tell him he's got ten-fucking-minutes, or I swear to God I'll kill him. Tell him he needs fluids, antibiotics, whatever the fuck else he needs when dealing with hypothermia and starvation."

Bullet grunts with a "Yep" and "Got it" to my every command. "Anything else?" He continues jogging beside me as we get closer to the clubhouse.

"Call Angel, he's at Corrupt. Tell him to go to the nearest store and get every heating pad he can find. I want them in my room and warm by the time we get there." I have no idea if that's what needs to be done, but with her frigid skin against mine, my only thought is getting her warm.

He brings his phone to his ear, and after a few short seconds he's barking orders at Angel. In that split second, I'm reminded again why I'm thankful for these men who became my brothers by choice.

We make it back to the clubhouse in record time and burst through the back door so violently I'm surprised we don't find ourselves on the receiving end of a few bullet holes.

"The fuck is goin' on?" Demon, my best friend, and Vice President of the club rushes toward me. Per his usual self, he's pissed and has an eat-shit look on his face, but when his eyes drop to the woman in my arms, he goes still. "Who the hell is that?"

Without a word, I push past him and make my way through the main room and down the hallway. When I reach my bedroom, Angel is already there, sweating and breathing hard. He must have busted his ass to get here in the time I had given. As he plugs the last heating pad in, he looks up at me from where he's crouched on the floor. When his eyes lock onto the woman in my arms, his face drains of color so fast I worry he may pass out.

"Turn 'em on low. I don't want to warm her up too fast." I contemplate holding her until Patch arrives, but instead, I place her on the heated pads on the bed. It's not until she's laid out that we're able to make out how truly emaciated she is. She can't be more than five feet tall, and from carrying her, I know she's severely underweight. There's no way she weighs more than a hundred pounds. My stomach sinks when I realize it's highly likely she won't make it.

A commotion in the hallway drags my focus to the door where Patch is standing, a large duffel bag in one hand, and his go-bag in the other. He moves past the other men in the room and makes his way to my bed. To my shock, he doesn't falter when he sees the broken woman, instead, he drops his bags and starts shouting orders. "Priest, get me two bowls of warm water and as many clean rags as you can find. Demon, help me get her jacket and clothes off, they're soaked.

I need to find a vein and get fluids started, then I'll check for injuries."

At the thought of my best friend laying a finger on this woman, the monster from the woods that had been silently waiting inside, comes back with a vengeance. Rather than rushing to follow Patch's commands, Demon doesn't move a muscle. It's almost as if he knows exactly what's going through my mind. When I make no move toward him, he steps forward and reaches for her shoe.

Before I can control my rage, I have him slammed against the wall.

"The fuck?" Spittle flies from the sides of his mouth as he shoves me back in an attempt to dislodge my forearm that pins him to the wall.

My voice is menacing. "Don't touch her."

He looks at me like I have a goddamn screw loose, and for all I know, I do. I don't know what the hell is going on inside my head, but I don't want anyone near her. The only reason I'm allowing Patch to touch her, is because he'll do everything in his power to save her.

Patch, having had enough of me pissing over my territory, and needing what he's already instructed, loses his patience. "I don't give a fuck who brings the water and who helps me get her clothes off, but do it now or I'm going to lose her."

After throwing a scathing look my way, Demon bolts out of the room in the direction of the kitchen while I rush to Patch's side and help him get her jacket off. I turn to throw it across the room and notice the other men still standing there staring... at my woman. *My woman? What the fuck?* I scrub my hands down my face and shake my head hard. *What's happening to me?*

"Get the fuck out. Tell Demon to knock before he comes in, and I'll meet him at the door. No one else in or out unless I specifically say so." Angel and Bullet nod, and without a single word or second glance at the woman on the bed, they leave.

When we get her clothes off, we see what we're dealing with. The woman is practically a skeleton wearing skin. The outline of every rib clearly visible. Patch glances at me; it's the first time I've seen genuine fear in his eyes. *He can't save her.*

He takes a deep breath and looks into my eyes, silently telling me he'll do everything humanly possible for her. I give him a nod. I know he will, not only because he's a doctor, but because of the demons from his own past that still haunt him today.

"There was a bag of moldy bread and rotten apples next to where I found her. She probably had them in her bag and tried to make them last as long as she could."

The horror on his face is tangible. "Jesus Christ. What the hell was she running from that this was a better option?"

"No fucking idea." I had the same thoughts when I was carrying her back to the clubhouse. Whatever her situation is, I'm going to find out what drove her to this. I don't care who she is, or what she's done, my gut is telling me one thing—she belongs to me. She was mine from the moment I dragged her body from that rotted out tree. *What the actual fuck Priest? Mine. My woman.* I don't even know if this girl *is* a woman. *Now is not the time for my dick to be getting hard for some fucking girl.*

"Fuck!" Patch curses, struggling to get an IV started. After the third failed attempt, he straightens and takes a deep breath, gathering his composure before he moves from the bend of her elbow to her hand. When he's finally able to find a vein, he flips the clamp and the fluids start to flow into her body.

Two bags hang from a hook on the headboard. One is fluids to rehydrate her emaciated body. "What's in the smaller bag?"

Not making eye contact, he works quickly to get supplies out of his bag. "It's a broad-spectrum antibiotic. It'll do a good job at keeping any infections at bay until I can run her blood and find out what we're dealing with. Until then, this will hopefully keep her from turning septic, if she already isn't."

A sharp knock on the door echoes through the room and I rush over, knowing it's Demon with the water and rags. I crack the door open and he hands them to me without trying to come in. "Yell out if you need anything else," he says without meeting my eyes.

After I give him a chin lift in thanks, he turns to take a seat against the wall across the hall. Angel and Bullet are already seated with their heads hanging low. Bullet looks up at me before I close the door, the rage forming behind his eyes is mirrored in my own, and the promise of retribution gives me a sudden burst of adrenaline. Whoever did this to her, or caused this to happen, will pay. No sin will remain unpunished.

Using one bowl to wet the rags and another to rinse them, Patch cleans over the wounds on her body before applying a thin layer of antibiotic ointment to her scrapes. Some of the larger, deeper wounds he covers with dressing and bandages. Close to an hour later, all her wounds are cleaned and covered, and Patch sets to work drawing her blood.

With the vials of blood stored safely in a small medical cooler, he gives me one last look before he stops at the door. "I'll head on back to the hospital now and run these myself. Once they come in, I'll come back with whatever medication she needs. You remember how to change the fluid bag when that one empties? She'll need at least one more after this."

I nod. "Yeah, same as when Demon was shot last year."

"That's right." He pauses with his hand on the doorknob. "I turned the heating pads off. Now that she's inside and getting fluids, her body should do the rest naturally, I don't want her to overheat. Keep an eye on her temperature and call me if she spikes any kind of fever."

I tip my chin up and ask, "How long before you have the results?"

"It's hard to say. I'll put a rush on them, but it could be a few days."

"Let me know if there's anything you need that you can't get without raising too many flags. I'll make sure it's done."

"Will do, Prez."

I stop him before he leaves. "Can you catch them up on what's going on? I don't want to leave in case she wakes. Tell 'em I'll be out to discuss what happens next when we know what we're dealing with."

He gives me a chin lift and closes the door behind him.

A surge of protectiveness smothers me when I stand by my bedside. The woman's pale face is marred by a few small scratches and the tinge of a purple bruise beneath her eye. *She fell down that ravine.* It's the only logical explanation for the cuts and bruises that cover her body. I allow my eyes to travel down the length of her legs, pausing on her bandaged knees, mentally seeing the sores underneath. I focus on her full, pale lips, slightly parted to allow little puffs of air to be released with each quiet breath. I move a strand of blonde hair from her forehead and when my fingertips brush across her brow, I feel the warmth already returning to her body.

Over the back of my chair, my Heaven's Guardians hoodie hangs. It's the one I wore yesterday and still carries the scent of my cologne. Maybe that will calm her since I'm the one who found her... *Or maybe I'm turning into a fucking pussy.* I laugh at myself, wondering when the fuck I decided my scent was in any way calming—to anyone. Laying my hoodie over her, I watch for any sign she's about to wake, when there's no response, I pull the blanket up to her chest and step back.

After switching on a lamp, I flick the overhead lights off. I take a seat in the leather chair in the corner of my room, and I watch her sleep.

I've seen a lot in my life, and I've witnessed the horrors some women have endured at the hands of the men who claim to love them. If this girl has experienced anything like the thoughts playing over in my head right now, I won't rest until the bastard responsible is buried six feet under.

I lean back in my chair, my eyes on the unknown woman. I don't know how she ended up in the forest, but one thing is absolutely clear. Nothing will hurt her again. I'll protect her with my life.

WASHED IN BLOOD

CHAPTER 4

WILLOW

Three days later

W hen I open my eyes, I'm no longer in the woods. Instead, I'm in a huge bed. Panic coils in my chest as a muffled sob slips from my trembling lips. *How did he find me?* I grip the dark grey blanket that's covering me. *This isn't Vince's.* The actions that led to me hiding in the woods come back to me and I jerk up. Splintering pain bursts through my skull, and I moan before I lie back on the pillows.

Closing my eyes, I take stock of my body. I cradle my flat stomach, holding what I hope is still the life inside me. I rub my thighs together, searching for any wetness—there is none. Hope blooms in my chest. Maybe God doesn't hate me after all, and has finally listened to my prayers. Maybe this time will be different.

I wiggle my fingers and toes and move my arms and legs to assess the damage from falling down the ravine. Other than my head, no pain seems too substantial; I must have avoided any serious injuries. After giving myself a little pep talk and focusing on the fact that I'm no longer diving into dumpsters, or hiding in hollowed out tree stumps, I open my eyes again.

The room I'm in is barren and clean. A large, dark cherry wood dresser with a mirror above it, matches the wooden bed I'm lying in. There are two doors, one I assume leads to either a bathroom or closet, and the other must be the door out of here. Not a streak of light peeks through the deep red curtains drawn across two large windows to my right. I can't tell what time of day—or night—it is, and I have no idea how long I've been asleep.

I continue to survey the room and jolt when I find a man sleeping in a dark leather chair in the corner. My body trembles in fear as I take him in. He's huge. Even with his legs bent they still take up several feet in front of him. Starting at his feet, I catalogue his appearance. Black boots, black jeans, black V-neck t-shirt, and tattoos. Lots and lots of tattoos covering both of his olive toned arms. I raise my eyes to his face and my breath catches in my throat. He's beautiful.

High cheekbones come down to a stubble covered square jaw. His dark hair is shaved on the sides, and the longer hair on top is ruffled and messy, as if he's been running his fingers through it. Is this one of the men from the alley? *Why would they help me?* My stomach drops and my heart races as the possibilities of who he is run through my head. Beads of sweat form on my brow, and a shiver of fear shoots down my spine. I need to get out of here. Now.

I reach to pull back the covers when there's a light tug on my hand. *Wha*— With an inhale, I raise it slowly to find an IV attached to a line that leads to a small bag of fluid hanging from the headboard. I tug slightly on the line but wince when it doesn't pull free. I'm about to yank it out when a large, tattooed hand grasps my wrist to still my movements.

Screaming, I scramble back on the bed, but his grip is tight and he effortlessly holds me in place. I struggle to free myself, my screaming instantly muted when he opens his mouth and speaks, "Easy, baby, easy. No one is going to hurt you here. You're safe now, you're okay." Dark blue eyes search mine as I try to calm my beating heart.

A wave of nausea washes over me, making me lightheaded and dizzy. I swallow thickly, my tongue sticking to the roof of my mouth. I can't pass out, I need to stay awake and coherent. Who knows what this guy will do to me if I'm not able to defend myself.

He crouches down beside the bed, his gaze locked on me, not a shred of anger visible. "My name's Priest. I'm the President of Heaven's Guardians Motorcycle Club. I found you in the woods three days ago. Do you—Can you tell me your name?"

My body trembles and the man's brows draw together in concern. "Are you okay? Are you in any pain?" There's an urgency to his words, and when his hands start running over my shoulders and down my arms, I freeze. He moves down to my legs, squeezing slightly at my knees and ankles, watching my face. I realize he's waiting for a wince of pain, or a sign that I'm hurt somewhere. *Why does he care?*

I shake my head, letting him know that I'm fine.

His face visibly relaxes but his body still seems wound tight. "Can you tell me your name?" he asks for a second time.

Uhh–think, Willow, think! My eyes flicker between his steady gaze, nothing but a genuine sea of blue staring back. I know absolutely nothing about this man, but my gut is telling me to trust him. Unfortunately for me, my gut has been wrong before, *the bitch.* And it cost me greatly. I know I *want* to trust him, so I weigh up my options and decide to give him half truths for now… on some things at least. I don't know if my baby is alive yet, but for now, that secret stays with me.

When I finally reply, my voice comes out scratchy and hoarse. "My name's Willow. Willow Jane."

His smile is genuine, showing off straight white teeth. "And how old are you, Miss Willow Jane?" A blush creeps up my neck and heats my cheeks. I pray he doesn't notice, but when his smile grows noticeably wider and he releases a quiet chuckle, I know he did. "Uh, I just turned twenty a few months ago."

A look of relief crosses his face, his breath rushing out. "Well, Willow, it's nice to finally meet you. You've been asleep for a while. Do you need anything? Water? Bathroom?"

As soon as he mentions water, a switch is turned on. Or more like a faucet. Clenching my thighs, I shift my legs as the fullness of my bladder makes itself known. My face burns with embarrassment once again as I nod.

He lets out another small chuckle at my expense, enjoying my embarrassment. "Yeah, I figured you'd be about to burst, you had two full bags of fluids." His face turns serious. "I can take your IV out now. We took it out after you finished your last bag, but you spiked a fever and needed another round of antibiotics. You finished those a few hours ago, Patch said there's no need to keep that in."

I give him a wary look. "Do you know how to take it out? And who, or what is patch?"

He scratches at the stubble on his jaw. "Club doctor. His real name's Evander Cruz, he works at the hospital in town. Patch is his road name."

I scrunch my nose, confused. "Road name?"

His eyes widen as though I've just told him I'm not human, then a smirk tugs at the corner of his lips. "You've never watched any motorcycle shows on TV, like *Sons of Anarchy*?"

I'm not sure how to tell him I was a prisoner in my home and wasn't allowed to have a TV or phone, so I shake my head and leave it at that. My bladder is about to burst, but he makes no attempt to step back or lead me to the bathroom.

He leans against the wall with a hand shoved into the pocket of his jeans. "A road name is a name we earn within the club. Sometimes it's something we do that's stupid, or something we're good at. Either way, once it's declared there's no changing it."

I drop my feet off the bed, readying myself to stand as he continues, "I promise you, you're safe here. I won't hurt you, and I know what to do with the IV, I've had to do it before for my Vice President."

With my hand over the blankets on my lap, I consider everything he's saying. Is his real name Priest? In the grand scheme of things, does it really matter? *He's not Vince.* I remind myself that not all men are like the monster I ended up with.

47

Finally, I agree, only because my need to go to the bathroom is becoming harder to ignore. "Okay, just be gentle, please."

A gorgeous smile lights up his face. "I'll do my best, sweetheart, though telling a biker to be gentle is like telling a wolf not to howl."

Even though he jokes about it, I don't feel a thing as he removes the tape from around the IV before steadily pulling it out. He covers the hole with a small bandage before I spot even a speck of blood.

With a hand under my elbow, he helps me to my feet. "Here, let me help you to the bathroom, then I'll go get you something to drink."

When my legs are free from the covers, I flinch. I'm only wearing underwear. *Where are my clothes?*

"Ah, shit. Let me grab you some pants." He paces over to the dresser on the other side of the room. "Your clothes were soaked and you were hypothermic," he rushes to explain before returning with a pair of black sweatpants. After helping me stand, he drops down to crouch in front of me. "Put your hands on my shoulders so you don't fall."

When I place my hands on his shoulders, he trembles at my touch. Looking up at me, his face softens and his voice lowers to a husky whisper. "Now step in, baby."

One at a time I slip my legs into the pants he's holding for me, all the while trying to ignore the way my stomach clenches at hearing him call me baby. All I ever heard from Vince was *bitch, whore,* and *trash.*

With a heavy sigh, I return my focus to Priest as he drags the pants up my legs. I gasp when his thumbs graze the skin on my thighs ever so slightly, leaving goosebumps in their wake. When he stands, I try to avoid his eyes, hoping he doesn't notice my reaction to him.

When I finally meet his gaze, his hooded eyes tell me he absolutely did. After tying the pants in place, we both stand for a moment, a heavy silence lingers between us.

I have no idea what he's thinking, but I'm confused as fuck. *What am I doing?* Yes, he's freaking gorgeous, but I don't know who he is, not really. I need some space away from him to clear my head, and to think of a plan that will get me far away from this place. There's no way any guy in his right mind will stick around to take care of a pregnant, homeless woman who's on the run.

Priest steps back and points to the door on the far side of the room. "The bathroom is through there, I'll set a towel out for you when I come back with your water. Whenever you're ready, come find me. I'll introduce you to everyone and we'll get you something to eat."

Holding the hoodie to my chest, I nod. "Okay."

He turns to walk away, but before he can get too far, I grab his wrist. When he stops, his eyes drop to where my hand holds his. I release him immediately, bowing my head toward the floor. I don't want him to see the fear I know is painted across my face.

Had I ever dared grab Vince like that, I would have paid for it. He would have either backhanded me, or broken my wrist depending on his mood.

When I peek back up, confusion clouds his eyes. He must notice my sudden change, but I don't try to explain it. The less he knows the better.

He raises a brow, reminding me I stopped him. "You okay?"

Cringing, I fold my arms across my chest. "I just wanted to say thank you… for everything you've done."

His hand clasps the back of his neck, eyes clenching briefly in pain. "I made a promise to someone a long time ago that I would always protect her. Circumstances out of my control made that impossible. Today, you gave me a chance to honor her memory."

I give him a small smile and head into the bathroom. With my back pressed against the closed door, I wonder who he made that promise to, and where she is now. Whoever she was, he loved her. I've always hoped to be worthy of a love like that, but I'm trash and no one loves trash.

It would do me good to remember that.

WASHED IN BLOOD

CHAPTER 5

PRIEST

I close the door to my bedroom and stand in the hall to regain my composure before I walk out to see the guys.

Willow doesn't completely trust me, but I can't blame her. Right now, all she has is my word that what I'm telling her is true. I can tell her she's safe and that I won't hurt her until I'm blue in the face, but until I show her—or prove it—I expect her to be wary. I saw the shuttered looks behind her eyes. She's hiding something. I'm not sure what it is yet, but I hope in time she'll tell me what caused the shadows in her eyes.

A long time ago, a man told me that not all demons were bad. Willow wears her fear openly, so if there is one thing I am sure of; whatever demons she has, they're bad. When I hear the shower running, a stupid smile steals across my face. I need to get a grip on reality and focus on something other than Willow's timid smile and flushed pink cheeks.

As soon as I breach the opening of the living area, each of my guys start firing off questions. Demon gets his out first. "She awake?"

"Yeah. She's in the shower right now. I came to get her somethin' to drink."

Angel leans back on the sofa. "You gonna tell us what you learned?"

I take a deep breath and rub my hand down my face. "Name's Willow, she's twenty. She's never seen *Sons of Anarchy,* and she's scared to death. I don't know if it's of me, or men in general, but that's about all I've gotten from her."

"We did just find her in a rotten tree in the middle of the forest. Could have nothing to do with you at all, so don't go jumping to conclusions," Bullet reasons.

Demon shoves a hand into his pocket as he leans against the wall. "Patch called while you were sleeping, said he's on his way. Got her blood tests back I guess, wanted to come check on her. Should be here any minute."

Speak of the devil. The door to the club house opens and Patch comes in, go-bag in his hand. "I take it since you're in here and not in there, she's awake."

I raise my brow and nod. "Yeah. She's in the shower, so don't walk in until she says it's okay. Her name's Willow."

Patch gives me a chin lift and continues down to my bedroom.

Bullet clears his throat. "Heard her screamin'."

My brothers' faces show varying degrees of discomfort. Reaching up, I shove my fingers through my hair before gripping the back of my neck. "When I woke, she uh—she was trying to rip the IV out of her hand. I grabbed her wrist to stop her, it was like her body was on autopilot. She struggled to get out of my hold, but I was able to get her calmed down."

Each of my men have their own pasts full of demons they still carry. I'm not concerned about them hurting her. They're great men, scarred by experiences of their pasts. They're hotheads to an extreme when it comes to women or children who've been wronged.

"You know we'd never hurt her," Demon says vehemently.

I raise my hand in a placating gesture. "*I* know that. But *she* doesn't. Try to see this from her point of view. Until we know what her past entails, we need to give her the space and time she needs to adjust."

"How you doin' with all this, Prez?" Angel asks, trying to diffuse the building tension.

I give him my attention, but pause before answering. With his blue eyes and light blonde hair that he keeps styled a lot like mine, Angel looks every bit of his namesake. He's also the only one of us that doesn't have any tattoos, adding to his innocent look. But underneath the pretty boy facade, are scars that mark a man and change the very core of who he is.

"I don't know to be honest. This whole thing is bringing up a lot of shit for me. I wish he'd give me a sign because right now, I have no clue what I'm supposed to do next."

My brothers don't call me Priest for nothing. I know there's a god. I know there's a reason for everything that happens in my life, and I know he has plans for me. I know these things because the Angel of Death told me.

When I was sixteen, my foster father shot me. I flatlined for 8 minutes and 57 seconds. By the time they were able to get my heart beating again, everything had changed. The girl I loved and was willing to die for, was lost to me forever. I was a willing sacrifice, but it didn't matter. It wasn't my name on Death's list that night. And I would know, I met Azrael—the Angel of Death. He told me to wait, and I would be rewarded. He didn't tell me the hell I would have to live through the years following Doe's death. The struggle with guilt, anger and resentment.

Is Willow my reward?

Throughout the years I've had relationships and several one-night stands. A couple times I thought I'd found *the one.* But no matter the amount of time or work I put into it, something was always missing. I've never had an issue with waiting, I've mastered the art of patience. But fuck, I'm thirty-six years old. I'm ready to settle down.

It's times like these I want to strangle that shit Azrael. His metaphorical bullshit was hard enough to decipher when I was sixteen. I saved Demon, then Bullet, Angel, and Patch. Together we started Heaven's Guardians. We spend our days doing God's bidding, searching out the filth that stains this world. Murderers, rapists, abusers, sex traffickers. If they have a level in *Dante's Inferno,* they answer to us before we deliver them to the pits of hell. I've had twenty years of darkness in my world, and I'm ready for some light to shine through.

Giving up on my thoughts, I head to the kitchen to search for something for Willow to eat. After rummaging through boxes of cereal and crackers, I find a can of chicken noodle soup. Figuring she needs to start small, I decide to fix her a bowl to take with her water. I'm just pouring it in a bowl to warm when Demon walks in.

Propping a hip against the counter, he crosses his arms over his chest. "We gonna talk about what's going on in your head?"

I start the soup in the microwave before I grab some crackers from the pantry. "Not sure what you're talkin' about," I deflect.

He arches an expectant brow and I roll my eyes heavenward, knowing I won't be avoiding this conversation. He chuckles at my expense. "Did you expect me to not notice the way you about ripped my dick off the other day when I went to touch her? Hell, Priest, you've practically been her fucking guard dog taking up vigil at her side for the past three days."

"What do you want me to say, huh? You want me to admit this woman I know nothing about, who only just woke up hours ago, has somehow calmed a storm inside of me that's been raging for twenty years?"

The microwave beeps. I rip the door open and take out the soup before slamming it closed again.

He grunts. "She's barely legal, Priest."

"She's twenty."

Demon smirks. "I bet a sweet piece like that would calm several things I got raging inside me."

Willow's bowl of soup clatters against the counter. "The fuck did you just say to me?"

Demon holds his hands up. "Listen bro, no judgement here. I'd be all up in that hot sna–"

I slam him against the counter. "Shut your fuckin' mouth."

A small smirk plays on his lips and he tips his chin down at the soup. "Run along now, *Daddy*." He shoves me back before he casually strolls out of the kitchen.

I stare at his retreating back, all the while fighting the twitch in my fist that's begging to be pummeled into his face. *Fucking Demon.* I don't know what the fuck is going on with him lately, but I've had about enough of his dramatic bullshit.

When I reach my bedroom door, it's shut. Patch must be in there examining her. I knock, eager to get inside so I can see how she's doing, but when Patch comes to the door, the look on his face says I'm not going to like what he's about to tell me. He clears his throat before he looks down to his boots. "Priest, man, she asked if you could stay outside until I'm finished."

Hot jealousy rises inside me. "Say again?" *Why doesn't she want me in there?* "What the fuck is happening that's too private it can't happen in front of me?"

He looks like he'd rather be anywhere than here answering my questions right now. "Look, brother, there's only so much I can tell you. We may not be in a hospital, but I'm still bound by patient confidentiality." He raises his hands in defense. "My hands are tied."

"That's a fucking load of shit," I growl, stepping into his space. "I'm your fuckin' President. If I ask you what's going on, you'd better goddamn tell me."

He nods his head resigned. "You're right, you could order me to tell you, and I would. But honestly, that girl in there needs someone to trust right now. If you want that to happen sooner rather than later, let her tell you when she's ready. If you take that chance from

her, you'll never know when she fully trusts you."
Hand still on the door, he doesn't budge.

I hate that what he's saying makes sense right
now. Just makes me even more pissed off at him. I
shove the soup and water at his chest. "Take her this.
I'll be in the gym when you get finished."

The relief in his eyes is evident. I know he'll
tell me what's going on if I demand it. But the truth is,
what he's saying has merit. It'll mean that much more
when she finally opens up and talks to me. I have to be
patient. Good thing I've had twenty years of practice.

WASHED IN BLOOD

CHAPTER 6

WILLOW

After forcing myself to leave the heat of the most luxurious shower I've had in years, I wrap the thick towel around my breasts and scan the bathroom. *Shit! I have no clothes.* The thought of wearing the filthy underwear and dirty clothes I'd been wearing for the past three weeks causes bile to rise in my throat. I bring my hands up to my face to study my fingernails; not a trace of dirt or grime remains. I'm finally clean and never have I been more thankful for the things I used to take for granted. Hot water and shampoo are a godsend. With my head raised to the ceiling and my eyes closed, I whisper a silent thank you to a god I was sure had forgotten me.

"Hello," a voice calls from the bedroom tearing me from my thoughts and reminding me I'm in a stranger's bathroom, naked.

"Um... hello?"

Footsteps approach, so I lean against the door in a futile effort to protect myself from the mystery man on the other side.

"It's Patch, ah, Doctor Cruz. Can I come in?"

Shit. I drop my head back against the door in frustration. "Um, I just got out of the shower, did ah, Priest leave me some clothes?"

Silence hangs in the air. *Did he leave?* A full minute passes before I call out, "Are you still there?"

"Yeah, I'm here." A heavy sigh follows his footsteps. "Just stay put, I'll find you something."

I tap my foot on the floor and wonder if Priest planned for me to be left here naked in his bathroom so I can't escape. *Ugh, stop overthinking everything, Willow.*

The sound of Patch—Doctor Cruz—rifling through Priest's drawers causes a smirk to dance across my lips. I'm positive bikers aren't the type to go rummaging through one another's underwear drawers.

A knock on the bathroom door startles me and I jump a mile, knocking my elbow on the counter. "Oww..." I whimper.

"Willow? What's goin' on? Do I need to get Priest?"

He's the doctor. Why would he need to get Priest?

"No, no. I'm okay, just knocked my funny bone against the counter." I shake the feeling back into my fingers before I open the door a crack to reach through and grab the clothes.

As if he can sense my fear through the door, he places the clothes in my outstretched hand without making contact. "I swear on my life, no one will hurt you here. I know you need time to trust us, but in the meantime, rest assured you have our protection." His voice is kind, and although Priest has already told me something along the same lines, hearing it from another one of his men, and hearing the truth in his voice, puts me at ease.

Without a reply, I pull the clothes in and close the door. After piling the clothes on the counter, I drop my towel and catch a fleeting glimpse of myself in the mirror. *I look like shit.* My reflection appears as a waif thin ghost of a girl who's no longer living. My face is nothing more than a mask that hides the broken girl beneath the flawed pale skin. For so long, I was dying on the inside, it seems only natural that the outside now matches.

Patch taps lightly on the door. "You okay in there?"

"Yeah, I'll be out in a minute."

He doesn't reply, so I pick up the top item from the stack. A solid charcoal grey t-shirt. The front has the same design as Priest's hoodie. I lay the shirt on the counter and examine the design. A black and white skull with detailed wings behind it that appear to be on fire, stares back at me. Coming from the jaw of the skull are the ends of two skeleton keys, and in the middle, it reads *Heaven's Guardians MC*. This must be their club logo. I slip the shirt over my head and reach for the next item in the stack.

I blush when I realize it's his underwear. I tug on the black boxer briefs then grab the sweatpants that are a few sizes too big. Anything is better than having to walk out of this bathroom half naked in a stranger's underwear—no matter how hot that stranger is.

Finding a new toothbrush still in its packaging is a godsend. I haven't brushed my teeth since I left home, and the minty fresh scent of the toothpaste has me feeling almost human again. *God, I hope I didn't breathe on those guys while I was out of it.*

After drying and smoothing out my matted hair, I wipe down the bathroom counter and with a heavy sigh, I scoop up my dirty belongings and step into the bedroom.

Patch clears his throat as I stand in the doorway, clutching my dirty underwear with an iron grasp. "I um… is there a laundry basket? Or—I can throw them in the trash…"

He shakes his head. "I don't think he cares about that right now, girl. Just drop them on the bathroom floor and come have a seat so I can give you a look over."

After dumping the pile of clothes on the bathroom floor, I walk back into the room and sit on the edge of the bed. Keeping my eyes on the floor, I run through all the ways I can ask him the question that's burning a hole inside my heart.

Patch clears his throat and I look up. Apart from the black scrubs, nothing about this guy screams doctor. His neck and arms are covered in intricately detailed tattoos. And the slight greying around his temples adds to the hot dad bod thing he has going on. *The hell, Willow? Since when have you noticed hot dad bods?*

When he reaches out to shake my hand, I glance at the silver wedding band around his thick, tattooed finger. "You're married?" *Great, real smooth, Willow.* Ugh, I didn't mean to blurt it out, but that alone puts my racing mind at ease. If this guy has a wife, he's certainly not going to hurt me. *Right?*

His face falls into a mask of indifference, and I regret questioning him. He drops his gaze, rubbing his thumb over the silver band. "No. I'm not." His voice is completely void of emotion. "At least not anymore."

Taking a step forward, I extend my hand to touch his shoulder, but I hesitate. I don't know this guy. I don't know these people who found me in the middle of the woods. I need to be wary. I drop my hand by my side. "I—I'm sorry."

He shakes his head and waves his hand in the air, brushing off my reply. "It's okay, happened a long time ago. Now, let's talk about you. Do you mind telling me how you ended up in the woods?"

My palms turn sweaty and my breathing accelerates at the thought of having to tell him what I witnessed. Patch gives me a reassuring smile. "It's okay, you don't have to talk if you're not ready. Let's talk about something else. How are you feeling today? Any soreness in your abdomen or head? Nausea or vomiting?"

I tuck a strand of hair behind my ear. "No, I feel good. My head is fine, and I haven't thrown up at all. I do feel nauseous, but I think it's because I'm hungry."

Concern shows on his face when I mention feeling nauseous. "Willow, when Priest first brought you in, I took a blood sample to ensure you didn't have any serious infections that needed to be treated." He runs his hand through his hair. "Your blood test showed elevated levels of hCG. It's a hormone that's made during pregnancy."

My heart races wildly at the possibility that my baby is safe and has survived the fall down the ravine. "I—" I close my mouth, too afraid to ask.

"Darlin', did you know you're pregnant?" His eyes are fixed on mine, gauging my reaction. Surely he's not missing the way my emotions war against my calm facade. Finding out my baby is alive and still growing inside me, fills me with happiness, but it's laden with fear. If those men from the alley find me, I'm certain they'll shoot first and ask questions later. Right now, my only options are to stay here, or run, but without a job and no home, I don't have the means, nor the ability to care for my baby. As all these realizations start pouring in, my body shakes uncontrollably, and my breathing becomes labored.

Patch reaches out and gives my shoulder a gentle squeeze. "Take some deep breaths for me, Willow. I'm sorry if you didn't know, but I had to tell you. You need prenatal care now more than ever. Especially due to your severe dehydration and near starvation."

I shake my head and the tears welling in my eyes finally break free. My voice comes out thick and scratchy when I reply, "I knew I was pregnant, but I honestly thought the baby wouldn't survive. The last thing I remember before I passed out was praying that God would save my baby." I choke on a sob before bursting into another round of tears.

Patch places his hand over mine and gives it a squeeze. It's silent, but much needed support and I give him a thankful smile. He pulls his hand away and stands by the bed. "I brought a heart rate doppler with me so we can try to listen to the heartbeat. Would you like that?"

"Y—yes, I would love that."

He reaches into his bag and removes a few items which he places on the nightstand. "The rest of your blood work looked good. The antibiotics cleared up the infection and were safe for the baby, so don't worry about that."

Nerves have taken over and all I can manage is a mumbled, "Thank you" as I adjust the pillows behind me. When I lift my shirt, there's a knock at the door, so I tug it back down.

Patch stands. "That'll be Priest."

"Wait," I say urgently. He raises a questioning brow. "I, um—" I stumble over my words. "It's just that, I don't want him to know yet."

"He won't be mad."

"I know," I blurt out the lie. I really *don't* know what his reaction will be, and right now I'm not ready to find out. "I'll tell him soon, I—I just need some time to… ah, come to terms with it all," I admit.

He studies my face and gives a heavy sigh. "Alright. But you have to know if he asks me to tell him what's going on, I have to. He's my president, Willow, that's how things work here."

I chew on my lip, maybe I should let Patch tell him and get it over with. At least then it wouldn't be me having to tell him. *No. This is my baby, it's my choice.* "I understand. I still want to wait, if that's ok with you."

He paces back toward the bed, lowering his voice, "You don't need my approval. There's nothing to be afraid of here, you're protected by Heaven's Guardians now."

With that cryptic statement, he heads back to the door and cracks it open. It doesn't escape my notice how he places his body in front of the crack so Priest can't see in. He murmurs something to Priest before the conversation turns heated.

Priest's voice is like a rumble of thunder, "Say again?" His tone has me shrinking down into the bed.

Their voices become hushed as they talk for several minutes before Patch heads back in. In his hands, he holds a tray with a glass of water and a steaming bowl of what must be soup. "Priest said to eat and get some rest. He'll be in the gym if you need him." He sets the tray down and returns to the bed.

"Go ahead and lift your shirt and we'll check on the little peanut."

I lift my shirt while Patch pulls on a pair of gloves then grabs a tube off the bedside table. "At the hospital, we have a warmer we keep this in. Since I couldn't bring it with me, this'll be a little cold."

I don't care if it feels like being submerged under glaciers in Alaska. I just want to hear proof of my baby's heart beating inside me.

He flips the lid and pours the cool gel onto my stomach. Chills break out along my skin and my muscles tense from the sudden burst of cold. I let out a giggle of nervous excitement.

Patch gives me a smile as he picks up a device with a small wand attached. He presses a couple of buttons before pressing the wand against my stomach and moving it around. I watch him for long, drawn out minutes, hoping to find something in his eyes that tells me my baby is fine, but his eyes are fixed on the wall as he continues to move the wand across my belly. The longer he moves the wand searching for proof of life that's no longer there, my heart sinks and tears fill my eyes.

It seems yet another prayer has gone unanswered. If there is a god, he's already forgotten me. "Patch…" My lip quivers. "It's okay… I—It doesn't matter." The weight on my chest grows heavier with each bated breath. I wish he'd just leave me alone so I can come to terms with the fact that my body is ruined. I am ruined. My baby was never going to survive. I was a fool to believe I could carry something so precious inside this empty, broken shell.

"A waste of fucking space…" Vince's words cut me to the core. A lasting reminder of what I truly am. *Nothing.*

"Damn it, no. Give me a fuckin' minute." I reach out and grab his wrist, halting his frantic movements. He moves his eyes up to meet mine, a haunted expression steals across his face.

"Patch, it's okay."

He shakes his head vehemently. "No. Your levels are too high, let me try again. Please."

Something tells me he needs to do this, so instead of arguing, I release his hand with a resigned sigh.

He tugs the top of my pants down a little as he moves the wand across my lower abdomen. My mind is already shutting down. Does God hate me so much that he'd take my baby from me? This was supposed to be my chance to prove I was capable of bringing something beautiful into this horrible world.

Patch is still furiously moving the wand around my stomach when all of a sudden, a soft *whoosh, whoosh* fills the room. My head jerks to look at him as he lets out a strangled whoop of excitement. "See, I told you I just needed another minute. I don't do this every day and it looks like peanut wanted us to work a little harder."

Shock courses through my veins. My brain finally comes back online and I let out a strangled sob. "Oh God." I bring my hands up to cover my face as tears and snot seep together, giving a new meaning to the term ugly cry. But I don't care. My baby is alive. Somehow, after years of prayers on thousands of stars, God finally heard me.

Patch leaves the doppler placed on my stomach for several minutes, allowing me to savor the sweet sound. The overwhelming love I already feel for him, threatens to drown me; it fills all the empty places inside my broken soul.

"Hey there baby boy." I trace my fingers along my flat tummy.

Patch looks up at me with a raised brow. "Boy?"

I nod. "Just a gut feeling I have. I've always wanted a man that would love me no matter what. Seems fitting I would have a mama's boy."

Patch mumbles under his breath, "Pretty sure you've already got you one of those."

What does that mean?

Patch goes into the bathroom and comes back with a warm washcloth to wipe the goo off my belly. "I brought you some prenatal vitamins. You need to get started on those today. You also need to stay hydrated. Your baby relies on you for nutrients and it's been severely deprived, eat as often as you can. You need to replenish the calories you've lost."

Eyes wide, I nod in agreement. I'll do anything humanly possible to give my baby everything it needs. "I can do that."

"Good." He looks down at his lap as if he wants to say something else. Finally, he looks back up at me with a wary look on his face. "Willow, did anything happen to you that you haven't told us about? Anything that I may need to know about as a doctor?"

I narrow my eyes, confused.

"Was the pregnancy the result of…" he trails off as he tries to find the right words, but he doesn't have to. I know what he's trying to ask me, so I ease his worries.

"I wasn't raped, Patch," I say softly.

He releases a huge breath and the built up tension seems to drain out of him. "Good. That's good."

"The relationship was a situation I would do anything to have never been in, in the first place. Had I known then what I know now, I would have walked the other way the first time I met him. When I found out I was pregnant, I knew I had to leave, so I did." There's more to the story, but that's all he's going to get out of me. Some things are better left unsaid.

Patch packs his things then brings over the soup and water Priest brought in earlier. "Go ahead and eat this and get some more rest. When you're ready, come out and meet the rest of the guys. I'll leave the prenatal vitamins in the bathroom. There's no label on the bottle so you don't have to worry about anyone finding out what they are. You can just tell Priest it's an antibiotic for now, but he's smart. He'll start to suspect something if you take them for too long."

Luckily, I'm eating my soup, so I don't have to come up with a lie. I'm not worried about Priest questioning me. I don't plan on being here long enough for him to notice that I'm taking antibiotics longer than normal. These men may have saved me, but if life has taught me anything, it's never to rely on anyone other than myself.

They may be acting nice now, but as soon as they realize what a waste I really am, they won't keep me around. They'll throw me away like the trash I am, and it's about time I start saving myself from heartache.

WASHED IN BLOOD

CHAPTER 7

PRIEST

I've been in the gym for over thirty minutes. My arms are burning and my shirt is drenched in sweat. I thought working out my frustrations would help calm me. But apparently, all it did was the fucking opposite because it gave me time to get lost inside my head. The thoughts that are plaguing me, plus the adrenaline running through my system are not a good combination.

By the time Patch comes to find me, I've gotten myself pretty worked up.

"What the fuck took so goddamn long?"

He doesn't react to the vehemence in my voice. He rolls his eyes at me as he takes a seat on the bench press across from where I'm doing pull-ups. "I had to do a workup. You know, check her stats, listen to her heart and breathing. Make sure nothing was hurting on the inside that we couldn't see."

"And?"

"And what?"

I growl. "Stop fucking around and tell me what I want to know."

He sighs. "Listen, like I said before, there's only so much I can tell you before I'm breaching patient confidentiality, which she mentioned, so I'm going to assume it's important to her for her private things to stay that way."

Releasing the bar, I stalk over to the area where our punching bags hang. I grab a pair of gloves and roughly shove my hands inside before tightening the Velcro. I start on the bag, all the while imagining Patch's face. The rational side of me knows that none of this is his fault, but the irrational side of me needs someone to blame. And since he's here and already pissing me off with the fact that he won't give me even a shred of information, it's easy to put all the blame on him.

Patch stands from the bench press and comes to lean against the wall next to the punching bags. He puts his hands in his pockets and looks down at his boots for a few minutes before he finally speaks. "I know you Priest. You have a classic hero complex, hell we all do to some extent. But do not fix this woman just to throw her away once she's not broken anymore."

"I *do not* have a hero complex—"

He cuts me off, "Bullshit. What about Taylor? Then there was Paige, and Halie… every one of those women were broken or in a dire situation, you either fixed them or you fixed the situation. As soon as they didn't need a hero anymore, you were gone."

I stop raining hell on the punching bag and seriously consider raining hell on Patch's face. Throwing him a glare, I cross my arms over my chest. "First of all, Taylor fucking cheated on me. And Paige, that was nothin'. We were just friends…"

"And Halie?" He casts me a questioning stare. "Stop making excuses. It's time you found someone to settle down with. Find an old lady, make some fuckin' babies and shit. You gotta stop waitin' around for something that may never happen."

Resting my arms over the punching bag, I drop my head against the cool vinyl. *Well, shit.* Seems I have a fuckin' hero complex.

All my brothers know my story. They know I was murdered, declared dead, brought back to life, and met the Angel of Death in the in-between. They say I'm superstitious, and maybe I am. But so far everything in Azrael's premonition for me has come true. Yes, there are still some vague comments that I haven't figured out yet, but I have no doubt that in time, I will.

I'm not sure if it was an actual divine plan coming into place, or pure luck that none of them thought I was fucking crazy and bolted as soon as I told them. Regardless, they all believe in what happened as much as I do. And they've all had experiences in their lives that led them here. For most of them, I was their only hope. Their last option before they either landed in prison, died on the streets, or died by their own hands. Together, we formed Heaven's Guardians Motorcycle Club, and for the past ten years we've dedicated our lives to making our mark.

On the outside, we seem like an average Motorcycle Club. We have our day businesses, Wicked Wrench Auto, and our bar slash strip club, Corrupt. While both businesses are legitimate, they each serve a different purpose. The auto shop helps us keep current with the town's people and shines a positive light on us. We're also the only auto shop for 60 miles, so if people have a problem with anything that has a motor, they come to us.

The strip club is an entirely different story. And while it may seem cliché for a motorcycle club to own a strip club bar, we have ulterior motives and a damn good reason behind it. Corrupt is our way of helping the women in our area have a safe way to make a legitimate income when they would otherwise have to use alternate methods. Most of the women who currently work for us, we saved from the streets. Whether it be prostitution, drugs, or theft, we've taken them in, helped them find a place to live if they were on the streets. The women who had drug problems were put through rehab. The women who choose to, can go to the local community college on our dime. As long as they keep up passing grades and pass both scheduled and random drug tests, we foot the bill for both their classes and their books.

Surprisingly, the original idea came from Demon. He wasn't always so callous and cold. It wasn't until after his sister, Sara died that he became the man he is today.

No one imagined Sara would die the way she did, but certain choices and circumstances in her life turned her to the streets. It started off rather harmless. Her boyfriend, a small-time dealer named Tony, convinced her to go to parties around town and hand out drugs to buyers. What she didn't realize was, these little favors for her boyfriend put her on the police radar. She had inadvertently become his right-hand man, and a distributor herself.

After a close call with the police, Sara was ready to get away from Tony and the street scene and start over somewhere new. But Tony convinced her to stay. He told her they'd make a life together. He played it straight for a few weeks, but when buyers started asking where their supply had gone, he cracked under the pressure and got back to work. When the guise was up, Sara tried to leave, but Tony had been prepared for that. Instead of letting her go, he slowly got her addicted to the same drugs they had been pushing.

What started as selling dime bags at parties, morphed into an addiction which fueled her decision to turn to prostitution. Once she became reliant on the drugs, she would agree to do anything as long as it resulted in her next fix.

Apparently, Tony was even more of a dumbass than we thought. What none of us knew at the time, was that Tony had gotten caught up with some dangerous people. People whom he had naively fucked over, thinking he could outsmart them. People who just so happened to belong to a cartel. *Demonio de hielo*— The Ice Devils, led by its ruthless leader, Santos. Tony, being the dumb fuck that he was, thought he could weasel them out of the drugs they supplied him with, as well as their cut of the money, by telling them that he'd been mugged.

Him being a fucking idiot was what ultimately led to Sara's death. He had no fucking clue drugs weren't the main part of the cartel's business. No, the drugs were just for fun. Their real money came from the innocent lives of those they personally had a hand in selling for sex trafficking. That said—You still don't mess with *Demonio de hielo,* and that's where Tony made his mistake.

Demon, who was deployed at the time, was none the wiser. While he was off fighting one evil, his sister was home being destroyed by another. By the time word reached Demon about how bad things had become for his sister, and how far down the rabbit hole she had journeyed, Sara had already been kidnapped and sold to the highest bidder.

Sex trafficking is nothing like it can be portrayed to be in the movies. Big wigs in Hollywood like to put a spin on the evil things in the world, making them seem desirable. They show girls being bid on by rich men in expensive suits with forbidden tastes. Lies of them being sold into lives of luxury where they'll be lavished with the world's finest things. Real life isn't so fucking peachy. These girls aren't being rescued from their drab lives, and they sure as hell aren't being sold to their very own prince charming.

Most of the women who are sold are specifically targeted. And the cartel that took Sara are marksmen at choosing. They're patient and observant. They take their time, watching those they can extort into getting addicted to drugs. By the time the women turn to prostitution, most of them have been disowned by their families. They've burned bridges and destroyed relationships with their friends. The Ice Devils watch them obliterate their lives piece by piece until no one cares to notice they're missing. That's when they make their move.

Problem was, with Sara they didn't dig deep enough. They fucked up. Too focused on the boyfriend that was trying to fuck them over, they strayed from their routine. They didn't follow their standard procedures and, in their attempt to get retaliation on him—not realizing that Sara no longer meant dick to him—they kidnapped her on a whim when they passed by her usual spot where she picked up Johns.

Demon's search for Sara left a trail of bodies in its wake. The weeks spent searching for her, chasing tip after tip, was a literal bloodbath. When we finally tracked down who she was sold to, and found where she was being held, we were devastated to find we were too late.

I will never, for as long as I live, forget the gruesome scene we walked into when we broke into that warehouse, guns blazing. Along with the other two girls she was chained next to, Sara was unrecognizable. Her face so badly beaten that not only were her eyes swollen shut, but she was also missing several teeth. She had wounds on her body that had become infested with maggots, hinting at just how long she had been there. All three women were lying in a mess of their own urine and feces which along with their rotting corpses, had caused a vile odor to permeate the surrounding air.

It changed all of us, but none more so than Demon. Any good that was left inside of him, died that day. It's been so long now that sometimes it's hard to remember the man he was before. There's no doubt he's still a good man somewhere in the depths of his heart and soul, but outwardly, he's cold and callous to anyone he encounters. The brothers are all used to it, but most of the townspeople steer clear of him for fear of being faced with his cold-hearted demeanor.

One night, Demon and I were in my truck on the way to the clubhouse after delivering a custom-made bike to an exclusive customer. When we passed a corner in town that was popular for whores and junkies, I attempted to drive by the area quickly not knowing how Demon would react. It was several miles before he finally spoke and pitched me his idea for the club. I'd never wanted to buy a property and transform it as quickly as I did in that moment. He presented the idea to all the brothers. A unanimous vote was made and Corrupt was born.

That was seven years ago. We've helped over twenty-three women get off the streets and make a life for themselves. I wouldn't change anything about those years. But sometimes, I wonder if we've allowed ourselves to become too immersed in the MC life. None of the brothers have an old lady. Hell, not a single one of us has a steady lay. I can't remember the last time I got off to anything other than my own fist.

Hanging my head, I sigh and press my heated skin against the cool concrete wall. Closing my eyes, I picture Willow, and for the first time in my life, I wonder if the MC is enough for me on its own. I want more. Marriage, babies, I want it all. And I want it with her.

WASHED IN BLOOD

CHAPTER 8

WILLOW

When you're a ward of the state and live with a foster family, nine times out of ten, you're a meal ticket. See each child in the system comes with a price tag attached. The money goes to our foster parents, and the funds are supposed to go toward things we need. Food, clothes, the sort of things you would expect to provide for a child you care for. That's not how it worked in my home. While our foster parents were living it up with the finer things in life, and by finer, I mean a deluxe meal from McDonald's complete with an apple pie; we lived off ramen noodles and 10 for $10 soups. Years of eating soup and bread for almost every meal, caused a profound distaste for any form of soup. But sitting here scarfing down the bowl of steaming chicken noodle soup, I'm certain nothing as delicious has ever graced my tongue.

Placing the empty bowl aside, I discreetly wipe away any droplets that escaped my spoon. I lay back against the covers and relish the shiver that dances up my spine when I get a whiff of Priest's cologne. Burying my nose in his pillow, I try to go back to sleep knowing my body needs rest, but the longer I lie here, the more alive my body becomes.

Quietly opening the door to Priest's room, I look left and realize Priest has the last room on the hall. There's a wall with a dead end, so I turn right and tiptoe my socked feet down the hall. As I near the end, the sounds of sports and newscasters fill the air. I creep to the opening of the hall and peek my head out.

The first thing I notice is that the living area is huge. Vaulted ceilings with solid wooden beams run across the wide expanse. A large rustic light fixture made from steel pipes hangs across from the A-frame window that seems to be the main source of light in the room. Continuing down the walls, I realize they too are solid wood and stained a deep mahogany with all the natural knots and inlays. The room is stunning. When Priest first explained to me that this was his motorcycle club's clubhouse, I didn't really know what to expect. A rundown house with holes in the walls, littered with women and beer bottles, yes. This astounding work of art? Heck no.

Three brown leather U shaped sectionals are strategically placed to form a large semi-circle around the massive flat screen that hangs on the wall. The worn, cracked leather is littered with oversized pillows in hues of beige, cream, and fawn.

Moving my attention to the men on the couch, I take a moment to study each of them. Patch, who is nursing a beer is sitting next to a blonde headed man who looks almost childlike compared to the rest of the men. His face is clean shaven, and his hair is pulled into a high, messy man bun at the back of his head. His arms are completely free of ink, and the carefree way he laughs at the man yelling at the TV, instantly puts me at ease about him.

The man he's laughing at, clearly doesn't find anything amusing. Turning to his side, he grips a large throw pillow in his fist before chucking it at *Barbie Ken.*

"Shut the fuck up," he growls at Ken, causing him to laugh harder.

The grouch crosses his muscular tattooed arms over his chest before turning his glare back to the TV. "My team never fuckin' wins," he mutters.

The smooth skin of his head is shiny and reflects the sunbeams breaking through the windows. Tattooed on the back of his head is a bullseye. I wince, imagining the needle piercing his tender scalp. His unruly beard is clipped close to his face, wiry sprigs jutting out every which way.

The last man in the room is seated farthest away from the other men. His shoulders and body are stiff as he stares straight ahead at the TV. While the other men appear relaxed, the tension lining this man's face is unmistakable. His jet-black hair is cropped close to his scalp and his equally thick black beard is cut close to his face showing off his angular jaw. His hands, which are resting in his lap, clench into tight fists, veins bulging underneath his skin.

My heart stutters in my chest when my gaze clashes with his cold stare. I shrink back into myself as his emotionless eyes peruse my body. The cold indifference lets me know he already sees me for what I truly am. Worthless. A misuse and wasted effort of God's power for even lifting a finger to create me.

"The fuck you lookin' at, Demon?" Ken asks before following his gaze.

Blondie spots me hiding in the mouth of the hall and a bright smile crosses his face. "Morning, sleeping beauty." He stands and rounds the couch before approaching me with his hand outstretched. "Name's Angel."

For a moment, I stare at his enormous hand and can't help but imagine the pain it could inflict. Angel senses my hesitance. "I promise, I only bite if you ask."

I cover a giggle as I take his offered hand.

"Something funny?" His lip quirks in amusement.

I quickly shake my head and duck my chin to my chest. Just because his name is Angel, and it looks like his picture could very well be somewhere in the Bible, I have no clue who these men really are. I don't know his nature or temperament, and I'm not risking opening my mouth and getting backhanded by a man who towers over my five-foot frame.

A large hand comes into view. He gently uses his thumb and finger to tip my chin up so my eyes are on his. The gentle look on his face helps put some of my apprehension at ease. "No one is going to hurt you here, princess," he whispers quietly.

Several long seconds pass before I glance up at his smiling face and answer his original question. "I, um… I laughed because the whole time I've been over here watching you guys, I've been calling you Ken in my head."

Angel's face scrunches in confusion. "Who the fuck is Ken?"

"You know, like Barbie, the doll. You look just like her husband, Ken, except blonde."

The sudden boisterous laughing catches me off guard. Years of self-preservation kicks in, and I drop to a hunched position with my hands covering my head. After several seconds of deep breathing to calm my racing heart, the room goes completely silent. Peeking up, my face pales as I realize what I've done. I stand quickly, stumbling into the wall at my back. "I'm sorry. I—I didn't mean to do that." My voice breaks but I raise my head and do my best to meet each of their eyes.

Angel looks heartbroken, and the pity he's casting my way causes my heart to crack. The man who was earlier yelling at the game has gone completely white and looks a little sick. My guess is he's the one who started the round of laughter and is now feeling responsible. I can't see Patch's face because he's staring at the ground with his hands clasped together in front of him. But it's the man farthest away who causes me to flinch. The fury on his face is palpable. His body, which already seemed tense before, is now radiating unmasked rage.

The man who now resembles *Casper* with his white complexion, clears his throat and steps forward. "I'm Bullet. I was with Priest when he found you."

I smile at him trying to ease his obvious discomfort at my reaction. "Thank you, for um... helping him save me, I guess."

Bullet waves his hand in the air brushing away my thanks. "It was nothin'. Sorry about scaring you. It's about time someone put pretty boy over there in his place."

His comment brings Angel out of his trance. He turns and folds his arms over his chest, a smirk crossing his face. "Hey now asshole, you're just mad because all the MILFs you try to pick up, want me instead. They like to feel naughty thinking they're fulfilling a forbidden, barely legal fantasy." He wags his eyebrows suggestively.

I chuckle under my breath, relieved my little moment seems all but forgotten.

The back of my neck prickles in discomfort and I barely suppress a shiver.

Glancing to my left, I tense when I meet the dark stare of the loner man. I try to pretend I don't notice, but my discomfort is radiating off me in waves. I'm not sure what it is about this man, but he sets off every alarm bell ingrained in me. He makes my palms sweat and my skin crawl. When I glance up again, his gaze is trained on the floor, but his brows are furrowed and his fists are still clenched.

With a frustrated growl, he storms from the room and out the front door. I hear a motorcycle start and speed away, slinging gravel in its haste.

"That's Demon." I look to Patch when he speaks, but his gaze is on the door that Demon just stormed through, and his eyes are sad. "We all have scars. Some of them we bare on the outside for the world to see, some we carry on the inside, close to our hearts." Patch turns and looks at me before he finishes. "Demon's scars left him without a heart. He can't help how he is now. Just know it's not the person he used to be." He stands and grabs his beer before he leaves the room.

I study Angel and Bullet trying to read their expressions, but Bullet is already watching the game, and Angel is watching me with a smile on his face. I guess Demon's behavior is nothing new to them.

Just as Angel begins to reach his hand out to me, the front door opens. I tense, thinking it's Demon coming back to confront me after all, but when Priest comes into view, the tension that filled my body drains away.

His eyes scan the room, widening when they land on me, a surprised smile forming on his face. But the surprise quickly morphs to anger as he notices Angel, and his hand that's still reaching out to me.

Before I can blink, Priest wraps his left arm around my middle and pulls me into his side, his right arm shoves Angel away. "Back off," he growls. Pulling me closer, his grip tightens and he turns his attention from Angel to Bullet. "Mine."

Mine? What's that supposed to mean?

Bullet gives him a chin lift and Angel has his hands raised toward Priest in a placating manner. "I was just gonna show her around, that's all."

"Yeah? Well, I'm here now so she won't be needing your tour services."

"Think I got that, Prez. See you later, princess." Angel smirks, sending Priest a wink before walking away.

Priest shakes his head and grumbles to himself, "Smartass." Turning so his back is to the room, he raises his hand to cradle my face. "You okay, baby?"

For a moment, I'm lost in the rhythmical sensation of his thumb as it rubs across my cheek. My eyes drop closed as my body clings to the unfamiliar feeling, savoring every brush of his skin against mine. Forcing my eyes open, I start to apologize, but when my eyes meet Priest's, the words die on my lips.

The array of emotions that play across his face completely disarm me. But it's his eyes that hold me captive. Seeming to feel my hesitation, Priest takes a deep breath before releasing it and lowering his hands from my face and waist. Taking a step back he holds his hand out to me. "Come on, I'll show you around?"

Darting my eyes between his outstretched hand and face, I try to judge the sincerity in his question. Life circumstances have taught me to guard myself heavily. Now that I have someone else to protect, I know I can't lose sight of my goal. I need to get well and get gone. Taking his hand, I decide the quicker I can do that the better. I don't need to form relationships with these bikers, no matter how kind or unbelievably good looking they are.

WASHED IN BLOOD

CHAPTER 9

PRIEST

As I lead Willow toward the other side of the clubhouse, she stops as we pass my office. She takes a hesitant step forward, her eyes scanning the room before she steps back. I give her a small smile before tipping my head and encouraging her inside the room.

The smile that takes over her face is so beautiful, my breath stalls in my chest as an iron fist squeezes my heart. I take a minute to myself hoping to rationalize my reaction toward her.

My mind is screaming at me to slow the fuck down. This woman is twenty years younger than me. She probably has no interest in starting something with an old man like me. But something about her calls to me on a primal level. And I don't give a fuck what

Patch says, it's not some damn hero complex. It's almost like I'm a compass that's been spinning on an endless search for north. As soon as I held her in my arms, everything else ceased to exist. Like a puzzle piece clicking into place, I found my north.

While allowing her to explore my office, I cross my arms and lean against the doorframe. She stands in front of one of the walls looking over the pictures hanging in wooden frames. She takes her time examining each one before she walks the length of my office, pausing on a picture at the very end. Her eyebrows dip and her nose scrunches before she takes a tentative step forward to examine the picture behind the glass.

I take a step forward. "That's my mom."

"Your *mom*?"

I laugh at her reaction. "Yeah, can't you see the resemblance?"

It's always been a conversation starter when my mom or I would introduce each other. Her dark brown skin is a stark contrast to my light olive. "She adopted me when I was almost seventeen years old. Still don't know what possessed her to do it. She's the best woman I know. We lived in a rough part of town, but she wouldn't leave. Said that was where she was needed. Our house was a safe haven for the neighborhood kids. They'd come over after school and my mom would always have warm cookies waiting. The kids would snack and do their homework, some would stay for dinner. In those hours, she gave them all the things they may not get at home."

She doesn't acknowledge me, instead she reaches a hesitant hand toward the picture before running a finger over my mom's face, as her eyes fill with tears. I move toward her, closing the gap between us before I place a hand on her shoulder. "Talk to me." The desperation in my voice is evident.

"I just... you look so happy."

Looking back at the picture of me and my mom, I smile. "Yeah, that was the day we broke ground on the clubhouse. We'd been a club for a while, but that day made us feel official, real, you know? Mom showed up with two six packs acting like I was graduating with a bachelor's degree or something." I chuckle to myself remembering the look on the guys' faces when she wanted a picture.

"She sounds great," Willow replies, but something in her voice catches my attention and I turn to face her. Once again, she's focused on the picture, but this time there's longing in her gaze. She faces me and flashes a small smile before turning to survey the rest of my office.

Walking over to my desk, she takes in the array of papers and files scattered. Half torn receipts stick out from under random scribbled notes that I can't even read.

"Your desk is a pigsty." She giggles.

I grab the back of my neck, unused to the feeling of embarrassment that grips me. I clear my throat. "Yeah, keeping my room clean is one thing because it's something Mama always required, but my desk…" I look at the mass of papers and grimace. "When we started the club and our businesses, I never realized the amount of official stuff that would need to be handled. Never realized it would be so… papery."

She barely contains her laughter. "Papery? Is that even a word?"

I bark out a laugh. "Fuck if I know, but I'm pretty sure if it is, there's a picture of my desk next to it in the dictionary."

She grins before looking back to the desk and fingering some of the papers. "I'll organize it for you. Get everything in order, alphabetized files with clear labels. You also need some trays on your desktop. I can—" She stops mid-sentence and looks at me with a sheepish smile on her face. "Sorry. I didn't mean to get carried away. I'm great at organizing. Making things easy to find and giving everything its own place. I've found that life feels a lot less hectic when the space around you is clean."

I stare at her, awestruck by the carefree smile and giggle coming from her mouth. She reaches forward still talking about different types of organizational systems, but my mind is caught on the sight of her pink tongue coming out to wet her lips.

Still holding a stack of papers, she turns to me with a blinding smile that sears my black heart.

"So... is that a yes?"

"I ah—" *Fuck! Say something dumbass!*

Dropping the papers like they burned her, Willow steps back, her face closing down. "If you don't want me in here or going through your papers, I understand. You don't know me, and you probably don't want a virtual stranger looking at your private things." A look crosses her face that hurts me to see. I'm almost positive there was some extra dialogue that just went on in there that I wasn't privy to.

Right now, I'd do anything to get that look off her face, replaced with the one of excitement from before.

"Actually, that would be great. I've noticed some of the books have been off because I've copies of invoices that should have been logged before getting thrown out. It's also annoying as fuck to need something and not know where the hell it is. Usually by the time I find it, it's weeks later and I don't need it anymore."

The happiness in her eyes is almost too much to bear. She looks like I just gave her the world, all because I told her she could clean my fucking desk. If it puts that kind of smile on her face, I'll make sure the bastard is just as dirty, if not worse every week so she'll always have something new to organize.

"We can pick up supplies next time we go into town. Get anything you need, my tax guy will find a way to write it all off."

She stands, nodding with a goofy—but fucking gorgeous—smile. "That sounds great,"—she hesitates—"Bikers have tax guys?"

I bark out a laugh. "Yeah, babe. Bikers have tax guys."

She grins, a slight blush coloring her cheeks. Before I get carried away thinking of all the other places I could make that pretty pink appear, I clear my throat. "You ready to keep going? There's another room I want you to see."

"Yeah, I'm ready."

Back in the hall, I stop at the last door before turning to look at her. But she's not looking at me, instead she's staring at the door. Giving her a minute, I let her take in the iron design hanging eye level. The skull is ordinary. It looks like any other skull on any other MC logo. But the additions are what makes ours unique. Protruding from either side of the skull's head are black angel wings with intricate rose designs placed closely next to the skull. Toward the bottom, two skeleton keys face each other with our MC name in the middle, *Heaven's Guardians MC.* Those keys, our name, they all have meanings. We hold the keys to those pearly gates. You want in? You have to go through us first.

"I know that all of this is new to you, there's a lot to learn and I'm going to tell you, every last thing. I don't want you to be scared, but before we go in here, there are a couple things you need to know." I hate the way she tries, and fails, to cover the fear she's feeling. I hate even more that I put it there, but she needs to know everything about us if she's going to stay, and there's no better place to do that than here. "This room is sacred to us. Not just us, this room is sacred to any MC. It's a sign of salvation and brotherhood. Inside this room, there is no judgment. There's no right and wrong or black and white. Inside this room is who we are at the barest level."

Wide eyes stare back at me, but with her subtle nod, I reach out and take her trembling hand in mine before pulling her inside. After giving her hand a squeeze, I drop it before walking to the other side of the room, hoping the space eases some of the tension that's radiating from her body. Crossing her arms over her chest, she surveys the room with wide eyes.

In the middle of the room, is a solid wood table my brothers and I built with our own hands. Six chairs line the sides, mine denoted by the gavel lying in front of it.

The rest of the room is barren. There are no windows. No pictures hanging from the wall or any other decor or furniture, so it doesn't take her long to look around before her eyes find mine with questions floating.

"This is Church."

Her nose scrunches. "Um, I don't see a cross, or any bibles." She gives the room another glance.

"Yeah, you definitely won't find either of those in this room."

"So why is it called Church?"

"Because this place is sacred. It's our holy ground, Willow. Our confessional. When we walk through those doors, everything else is stripped away."

She stares at me with wide eyes hanging onto every word.

"The men you've met are my brothers. We're bound together by blood and experience. Our club is different because we don't have prospects. We don't take on new recruits. Our club was born with us and it will die with us."

"What's a prospect?"

Looking into her deep blue eyes, I revel in the innocence I see there. Softening my voice, I explain. "Prospects are future potential club members. All other MC's have members that hold office, regular members that are just patched in members, and they have prospects. Sometimes they approach you, other times it's a family member that wants to be in the life one day, or maybe you just see someone with the potential. They start as a prospect and have to work to prove their worth and gain trust."

Her brow raises with a questioning stare. "How do they do that?"

I chuckle trying to think of the nicest way to explain it without painting bikers in a bad light. "To put it bluntly, they're basically our bitch for however long it takes for them to earn their place. They're gophers, errand boys, maids, cooks, whatever we need them to be. They get the shit jobs, but they do them without complaint because they know the reward will be greater than the sacrifice."

"So, you haze them?"

I grin. "No baby, we don't haze them. Sometimes they're assigned a task and they have to complete it to our satisfaction. Other times, they prove themselves in an extreme situation. They have to choose the club over everything else. Prove they'd be willing to lay down their life for their club."

Her nose scrunches. "Well that seems dumb. If they die, they'll never get to be a member."

I nod in agreement, it's a complicated thing to understand. "In some ways, you're right, but laying down your life for the club, making that ultimate sacrifice—it's akin to dying in war. If they die before they're patched in, they still get a member's burial. A vest is made for them and they're buried in it. If they have a family, they're taken care of indefinitely, monetarily."

Her brows hit her hairline, wonder showing on her face.

"Bikers take care of our own, sweetheart. Once you're one of us, you're in for life. You become a part of the family and families look after each other, always."

"Wow. I guess even though I don't really know much about bikers, I kind of assumed they were all criminals. Cold and mean." Her face flushes deep red with embarrassment.

"There are those who live by their own set of rules. They have little honor and look out for themselves before their brothers. Those clubs are also the most dangerous, most of them are involved in high gun trade, drugs, and human trafficking."

Her sharp inhale of breath is small, but I still catch it. I reach out to cup her face and brush my thumb against her cheek. *Christ she's beautiful.*

Lowering my voice, I rush to reassure her. "This is one of the ways we're different. Even the good clubs can deal in guns and drugs, but draw the line at trafficking of any kind. Other clubs refer to us as an anomaly. We don't deal in drugs. A few of the brothers smoke to relax and have fun, but we don't distribute. You'll also come to see that each brother is never without a weapon, but we don't trade or sell them."

Fuck, I hate the way her face pales and her muscles tense when I mention guns. I wish she would tell me who she's running from. What led her to hiding in a rotten tree in the middle of a Colorado winter? I want to pepper her with questions until I know every facet of her life. But I can't do that yet. While I've had almost a week to adjust to the fact that Willow is mine, something I've yet to make known to her, she has only been awake for a day.

She doesn't know that for three days and nights I held her when nightmares plagued her sleep. She doesn't know the hours I spent at her bedside, bargaining with God and making deals with the devil so that she might survive. For the past three days I've been living my own fucked up version of *Sleeping Beauty*, now my princess is finally awake. But I don't want to be her prince. No—I want to be her King.

WASHED IN BLOOD

CHAPTER 10

WILLOW

After showing me the rest of the clubhouse, a wave of exhaustion hits me out of nowhere. I sway on my feet as my vision swims.

Priest reaches out to place a steadying hand on my arm. "Hey, you okay?"

I nod. "Yeah, a little tired. I think I'm gonna go lie down if that's okay?"

Eyes soft, Priest raises his hand and grips the side of my face before pulling me toward him. I try to hide it, but I know he hears the small gasp when he places his mouth to my forehead. Lips still touching my skin, he murmurs, "Yeah, baby. Let's get you settled."

When we reach his door, Priest places his hand on the small of my back before ushering me inside. Following behind me, he leaves the door open before going to his dresser. While he rifles through the drawers, I watch as he pulls out another shirt and a pair of pants. Placing them on the bed, he looks to me. "I thought you might like some fresh clothes. Use anything you need. Tomorrow we'll go into town and get you stocked up on supplies and clothes."

He walks to where I'm standing inside the door. My body is on full alert when he reaches out and wraps his arm around my waist pulling me into him. For several seconds, my body is frozen in fear. I stand, waiting for the other shoe to drop. The fist in my hair, or the bruising grip on my hips, but it never comes. Letting go of the fear that holds me captive, I lean into his embrace and lift my arms to fist the back of his shirt. With my eyes closed, I soak up his warmth and allow it to settle deep in my bones.

He presses his lips to the top of my head. "I'll be right outside if you need me."

"I'll be fi—"

"I just want you to know I'm not far. You're safe here, Willow." His eyes show the depth of his promise and I find myself grasping onto its truth.

"Thank you."

He nods and gives my waist a final squeeze. "Good. Now get some rest. I'll see you in the morning." Without another word, he releases me and leaves the room, closing the door softly behind him.

After cleaning up and changing clothes, I finally climb into bed, whimpering when my tender knees hit the edge of the mattress. Pulling the covers around me I can't remember the last time I felt as safe as I do right now. I know it's a feeling I can't take for granted, so I settle deeper into the blankets and fall asleep to the smell of Priest.

The nightmare flashes before my eyes, reminding me of the danger I still face.

"No... please! I swear to God, I'll get the money!"

POP.

POP.

POP.

Oh God. Oh God. They just killed him. For several moments, my body is frozen in fear. Footsteps get closer to where I'm crouched in hiding, and my adrenaline kicks in. Run, now! Taking off, I pump my legs as hard as I can. I push them to take me away from this place, this life.

"What the fuck? Get her!"

Running to the safety of nearby trees, I let out a shrill cry when the ground beneath my feet disappears. I barely have time to comprehend what's happening before I'm tumbling down a ravine. My entire body feels like it's on fire as branches and vines tear into my skin.

Finally, I come to rest at the bottom of the ravine. I manage to roll to my hands and knees before I lose the contents of my stomach. Behind me, branches snap and heaving grunts fill the air.

They're coming.

Oh God please, no. No.

Ahead of me the remnants of a fallen tree prove to be my only salvation. The hollowed trunk looks big enough for me to wedge my way in. Scrambling forward, I pull the top half of my body inside. My feet slip and scrape against the wet ground as I try to make purchase on the soil. Before I can push the rest of the way inside, a fist clamps around my ankle.

Soulless black eyes stare back at me, putrid breaths escape through his rotten teeth.

"Gotcha."

"NO!"

"Willow! Goddamnit, Willow, wake up!"

Priest's voice rips me from my nightmare. Gasping for each small breath, my chest heaves as I struggle to give it the oxygen it demands.

Cradling my face, Priest murmurs to me while stroking my hair. "Breathe baby. In… out. In… out."

Mimicking his breaths, my lungs cry in relief as they're filled to capacity. My body shakes violently, the after-effect of the adrenaline rush from my dream.

"Priest," I choke out.

Later I'm sure I'll focus on the fact that my cheek is pressed against his bare chest, but for now I cling to him as if he's a buoy and I've been lost at sea. *Save me.*

"Christ," he bites off before crushing me into his chest and rocking me side to side. "Baby, please. Talk to me."

Whimpering, I shake my head and burrow closer into his neck. He wraps his arms around me, pulling me flush against his solid chest. God, how has this happened? I've known this man for less than twenty-four hours and yet here I am holding onto him as if he's the only thing tethering me to this world. I'm not sure how much time passes before my tears dry and the shaking abates, but not once does Priest let me go.

"The night I got lost in the woods—"

Priest's hand, that had been gliding up and down my spine pauses at the sound of my voice before resuming its journey.

I clear my throat, my voice scratchy from crying out in my dream. "I... I wasn't lost, I was hiding."

"What were you hiding from, baby?"

"Not what... *who.*"

Priest's body goes rigid. I'm not stupid. I'm sure he has questions about how and why I was in the woods. I mean, who wouldn't want answers from the person they rescued from a rotten tree trunk. He's vowing to protect me, but he has no idea what he's up against.

"Someone was after you?"

I nod. "I—I saw something I wasn't supposed to."

My head lifts with his chest as it expands with his breath. Cupping my face, he turns my head to face his. "What did you see?"

My nose burns as tears build behind my lids. I shake my head, not wanting to relive the experience recounting the story will provoke.

"They… they just killed him," I whisper.

Priest's eyes turn murderous. His grip on my face tightens and I flinch away from his hold.

"Fuck, baby." He presses his lips to my forehead. "I'm sorry, I… that's just not what I was expecting you to say."

I nod and rub his hand hoping to soothe his guilt. I know he wouldn't hurt me. I don't know how, but it's something in the way he watches me. All day, his eyes tracked my every move. It's almost as if he's worried I will disappear if he looks away.

Priest grips me underneath my armpits and effortlessly positions my body so my legs are straddling his. I focus on his hardening length underneath me when he speaks.

"Willow, I need you to tell me everything you remember."

I'm already shaking my head before he's even finished his sentence. "I can't, please."

"Baby, look at me. I will not let anything happen to you, do you hear me? Swear on my life."

And something tells me, this is it. Years down the road, I'll look back on this moment and know whichever direction I choose, it's what changed everything. For so long I've lived in a constant state of fear. And what good has it done for me? If my life has taught me anything, it's that fear does not protect us. Fear doesn't save us from heartache or death. Fear holds us prisoner. And I'm ready to start living. So I tell him.

I tell him about Mr. Guidelli. About how he begged and pleaded for his life. About how the men taunted him with the horrors they had inflicted on his wife. And for the first time, I cry for a stranger I didn't know. A stranger whose last thoughts in this world were filled with the knowledge that his wife could have died at the hands of those monsters.

In his arms, I fall apart trusting him to keep my pieces safe until he can put me back together. When the last of the story pours from me, I sag against his chest. Priest wraps his arms around my body; I love how small I feel in his embrace. Because of my past, I would have assumed the size difference would be an instant cause of anxiety. But sitting here in his arms, cocooned by his protective embrace, I find myself savoring it.

"My strong girl," he whispers. "Thank you for telling me."

"What are you going to do?"

It's scary how fast my feelings for him are forming and I wonder if it's some type of situational thing. Am I only attaching myself to him because he saved me? *No.* No, it's more than that, but either way I can't deny that something is there. And no matter how or why, I don't want him to get hurt, or in trouble because of me. I'm not worth it. I hope he realizes the same before it's too late.

"You don't need to worry about that, just know I'm gonna take care of it. Okay?"

He doesn't give me a chance to respond, instead he leans forward and presses his lips against mine. My body catches fire, and to my complete horror, I moan loudly at the barest touch of his lips.

Priest leans back, a satisfied smirk on his face. "You ready to go back to bed?"

Bed? Is he crazy? I want to tell him yes as long as he comes with me, but my newfound confidence from earlier has all but disappeared. Instead I pull my body away from his so that I can climb off his lap. Only when I lean back, my pussy grinds against his thickening cock and I can't stop the moan. Hunger flashes in his eyes.

"Babe. Tryin' my best to give you the space I know you need, but honest to Christ it's killin' me. Goes against everything inside me not to pull you to me and explore that mouth until I know it better than my own."

Oh God. Warmth floods my belly and tingles race up my legs before meeting at the juncture of my thighs. A rush of wetness drenches my panties. I want that. Everything he just described and more, I want it all.

Priest's narrowed eyes roam my face, not missing my reaction.

"Christ." Flipping my body beneath his, Priest settles between my legs, the weight of his cock teasing me through his sweats. I lift my hips and whimper helplessly, searching for anything to soothe the ache inside of me.

Oh my god, what is happening to me? This man is practically a stranger, and already my body craves him like an addict lusts their drug.

"Hold on baby, I'm gonna give you what you need."

Teeth clashing, Priest possesses my mouth and I'm lost to him. Finding the hem of my shirt, he pushes it up, baring my chest to him. My nipples pebble at the chilled air and he growls low in his chest before dropping his head and sucking my breast into his mouth.

His tongue flicks over the peak and my pussy clenches.

"Please…" I beg, needing more.

He gives my breast one last bite before showing the other breast the same attention. My mind can hardly focus. Between my legs, his hips have started to move, grinding against me. The tip of his cock hits my swollen clit at the perfect angle, and I arch into him, moaning.

"That's it, baby. Take it… take what's yours."

His hands glide along my rib cage before he slips them inside the waistband of my pants. He growls low in his throat when he realizes I'm not wearing any panties, his hands instead meet the warmth of my pussy. He strokes my mound, tugging slightly on the delicate curls.

"Naughty girl, leaving your pussy bare. Is this what you wanted, Willow? Did you hope I'd come back and touch your sweet, young pussy?"

Oh my God, who am I right now? His filthy words should have me pushing him away but a depraved part of me craves them, and my body shudders.

"Look at me, Willow."

Eyes locked, Priest's fingers part my folds gliding through the wetness. He teases my opening as the rough pad of this thumb rubs slow deliberate circles against my clit.

A choked sound escapes me as my body becomes possessed by his touch. My hips move of their own accord, desperate for more.

Oh my God. I'm going to come.

"Yeah… I can feel that pussy getting tighter. You going to cum on my fingers, baby?"

The same time he curls his fingers inside of me, Priest leans down and bites my nipple. The combination is more than my body can handle and I succumb to the sweet relief that my orgasm brings.

I cry out as he milks every ounce of pleasure my body has to offer. As I come down, his nimble fingers continue to tease my folds. My face heats as the reality of what I just did hits me with full force.

I just let a virtual stranger touch me. And I didn't just *let him*. I opened my legs and invited him, willingly. Oh my god! *Way to go Willow. What a perfect way to show him you're not a two-timing hoe.* Ugh.

"Get those thoughts out of your head." Priest leans down and rubs his nose along the length of mine. "I don't like the look on your face baby. What just happened, what we did—it was not wrong, do you hear me?" He brings his hands to hold my face, his thumb caressing my jaw.

"I'm not going to lie to you, Willow. Not ever. So believe me when I say that I feel something here. I know it's fast, but after three days of watching you sleep in my bed, and wear my clothes—you've already rooted yourself here in my life baby. And you did that just by sleepin'. I did not expect what happened here tonight, but no way do I regret it."

What is this world that I've woken up in? I feel as if I'm Alice, waking up in Wonderland for the first time. A world so similar to my own, but the differences here make me long to stay. So many times in my life, I've dared to hope for something better, something more. Only for it to be so viciously yanked away just as it's within my grasp. I don't want Priest to be another thing on the already long list. But still, there's no denying that his words have taken root. And I want them to grow. *Please, grow strong.*

His kiss is deep and I open for him, taking everything he has to give and more. Finally slowing, Priest pulls back and presses his lips to my forehead.

"Sleep baby. I'll keep the monsters away."

There'll be no escaping the monsters tonight... I'm already here.

WASHED IN BLOOD

CHAPTER 11

PRIEST

The next morning, my eyelids feel like lead weights from the previous night's lack of sleep. Wanting to soak up her warmth, I reach my arm out for Willow only to be met with cold sheets.

Alarmed, I sit up in bed searching the room for any sign of her. I'm already pulling the covers back when her sweet laugh, intermingled with my brothers' voices float through the cracked door. The invisible grip inside my chest loosens. Knowing she's safe with my brothers, I collapse against the bed.

I don't know if I've ever felt the level of fear I did last night when I woke to hear her screaming. In the days following her rescue, I held her body countless times when her dreams made her body restless. But last night was like nothing I had seen or heard before. I ran into my room, gun drawn, fully prepared to send someone straight to the pits of hell for daring to lay a hand on her. At first, relief coursed through my system to see she was dreaming. But when I realized that whatever she was experiencing was much more than a dream, the relief turned sour as her horror-stricken screams pierced the night.

For the first time in my life, I was helpless. I tried to wake her, but she was a prisoner to her dreams. But the dream is the least of my worries now.

Willow witnessed a murder, and according to her, they leave no witnesses. When I questioned her about names, she said none were mentioned. They didn't address each other by name, only mentioning someone they referred to as "the boss". My gut tells me this isn't good. We'd heard about the murder of Mr. Guidelli and his wife, Frances. Mr. Guidelli was found behind his deli with bullet wounds to the torso and a final execution shot between his eyes. Remnants of Frances Guidelli's mutilated body was spread throughout the couple's home, requiring DNA tests to confirm her identity.

As she recounted the horrid tale, I listened to every word, careful not to let my face give away just how scared I was. Fear isn't an emotion I experience often, but as my brain pieced together her story, terror settled in my bones. Willow didn't just witness a murder. She witnessed an execution.

From the nightstand, my phone screen lights up with a text. I wince at the bright screen while opening the message. A picture from Angel shows Willow standing at the stove pouring pancake batter into a pan.

Angel: Hope you haven't already laid claim, this one's all mine.

After getting dressed, I head into the kitchen to find Willow sitting at the bar top, hands wrapped around a steaming mug. Ignoring the looks from my brothers, I stop next to Willow, appreciating how the bar stool makes it easier to look into her eyes.

"Mornin', baby."

The blush that pinks her cheeks doesn't go unnoticed by me or my men. From the corner of my eye, Angel, who had been standing in front of her, turns to rummage through the fridge. Patch and Bullet, who are at the table, start talking about a bike we have to get finished today.

Happy with the privacy they've given us, I take my time looking over every inch of her face. All traces of her nightmare are gone, the only visible signs of her long night are her slightly swollen lips and her mussed blonde hair piled on top of her head. Seeming to have a mind of their own, my arms raise and my fingers sift through the silky strands.

"Hey," I say again, but this time it's quieter, and the husky tone is undeniable.

"Hi," she replies with a shy grin.

The obnoxious clearing of a throat has her flaming bright red before she jerks away. Lowering my hand, I turn a glare on Angel who grins, unaffected.

"Willow said something about going into town today to get office supplies," Angel mentions before shoving another bite of pancakes in his mouth.

I smirk. "Is that right?"

Turning back to Willow, I laugh at the glare she has aimed at Angel.

Looking at me, she explains, "I was just thinking I could go ahead and get started on your office. If you don't wan—"

I cut her off before she can second guess herself. Leaning forward, I grip her chin in my fingers before lowering my lips softly to hers. Backing up so I can see her eyes, I whisper, "Go get ready, baby. I'll meet you out front."

Eyes glazed, she nods and hops off her stool. She drops her plate in the sink before going to get changed.

Behind me, Angel clears his throat. "So, it looks like things are going good."

Turning from watching Willow's ass as she leaves the room, I send Angel a menacing glare. It clearly misses its mark as laughter spills from him and the other men at my expense.

Fuckers. I nab a pancake from the plate and fold it in half before dipping it in the syrup on Angel's plate. Shooting a quick glance at the door to make sure Willow isn't in earshot, I turn my attention to Bullet. "What've you got?"

Bullet lets out a frustrated breath before shoving his hands through his hair. "A whole lotta nothing. Ran her name through every database I have access to. She's not listed, Priest. No DMV records. I also searched hospital databases, cross referencing her name and age with birth and death certificates. Started in Colorado, and expanded from there when nothing pinged. So far, any person with the name Willow Jane, is either deceased, the wrong age, or the wrong ethnicity."

"Did you run a missing persons?"

He slaps a palm to his forehead. "Well fuck me sideways. Why didn't I think of that?" His heavy sarcasm is impossible to miss. "Jesus Christ, Priest. I'm not some fucking amateur here. Of course I checked missing persons." He narrows his brows pissed that I would insult his intelligence by asking.

Growling in frustration, I stalk to the window and take stock of the snow covered ground outside. It looks like we got at least six inches last night. A shiver runs down my spine imagining Willow curled in on herself inside that rotten tree. Christ, what if Bullet had ignored the tripped wire?

As if he knows the exact thoughts going through my mind, Bullet walks over and grips my shoulder. "Don't let your mind go there, brother. We found her. She's safe. Right now, that's all that fuckin' matters."

"Is it though?" Turning, I face the other men in the room. "Last night Willow had a nightmare. But this was different. Her screams were so real, I busted inside, gun drawn. Thought someone was in there hurting her. After I managed to wake her, she was so terrified she was damn near catatonic."

"She tell you what it was about?" Demon asks from the corner of the room.

Fuck. Of all the men, he's most wary of Willow. I don't know what his fuckin' issue is with her, but I'm sure this isn't going to help matters.

"You remember a few weeks ago, the deli owner and his wife, he was—"

"Murdered behind his deli, wife found dismembered at their home. No witnesses, case still open," Demon cuts me off, and I nod.

"Except there was a witness," I finish.

It doesn't take a genius to put two and two together.

"Fuck." Angel snarls. "She get a look at who did it?"

"Yeah. And they got a look at their only living witness."

Demon steps away from the wall. "Your sweet little piece sure comes with a lot of baggage Priest. And that is exactly the kind of shit we do not need right now."

119

I glare at him. "And what would you have me do, D? Send her on her way in the snow?"

Putting my back to him, I address the rest of my brothers. "She goes nowhere by herself. I want at least one man on her at all times. Take constant stock of your surroundings, anything or anyone that seems out of place, I wanna know."

Meeting each man's gaze, I drive the point home. "Hear me now, that woman is mine. You view her as an extension of me, and you protect her to the same extent."

The solemn look they each possess tells me they understand what I'm saying. If it comes down to it, they die before her.

Their life for hers.

We take my truck into town. Fresh snow means black ice, and there's no way I'm taking my bike without Willow having the proper gear or experience.

"It's so beautiful here," Willow whispers, captivated by the scenery passing her window.

Glancing to my left, I take in the view I've seen countless times. The clubhouse sits in the middle of a ten acre plot, surrounded by nothing but Aspen pines and forest. We were methodical when choosing land, and the forest and natural terrain give us optimal protection. Couple that with the measures Bullet has in place for us, and we're practically impenetrable.

"Yeah, it's definitely a scene. Been here twelve years now, and sometimes it's still shocking."

When we reach the edge of town, the club's automotive shop comes into view. Slowing the truck as we approach the red light, I point it out to Willow. "See that building right there? That's Wicked Wrench, one of the businesses the club owns and runs."

She looks, taking stock of the full bays and the line of cars outside waiting.

"Should you be there? Looks pretty busy."

"Nah. It's fully staffed. The brothers alternate their time between the shop and club."

"Club?" Confusion mars her brow.

Shit. I didn't mean to mention the club this early. "Corrupt."

"And is that—"

I cut her off. "It's a bar... and a strip club."

She doesn't say anything else. Just sits there staring out her window. I don't know what she's thinking, but I want her to know the truth. I clear my throat and hope she can hear the honesty in my voice. "We started the club ten years ago. It was never in our original plan to have one, but circumstances brought us to Colorado, and we started the garage. We were happy with that. Wicked Wrench brought us good money, *still* brings us good money, but one night Demon saw a hooker getting worked over by her John."

Willow gasps and I turn to her, the sadness on her face gives me hope. At least she hasn't shut me out yet.

"After he stepped in and took care of the John, he brought her back to the clubhouse. While Patch, patched her up, she opened up. Told him this wasn't the life she pictured for herself. She had no family, no education, but what she did have was a kid at home she needed to provide for. So she did what she had to do to make sure he didn't go without." I pause, trying to decide how much to tell her.

Demon's story isn't mine to tell, but she needs to hear it to understand the bigger picture. "While Demon was stationed overseas, his sister, Sara, was murdered by a local cartel notorious for human trafficking. When word reached him that she was missing, we used every resource at our disposal to find her. Through our search, we found out Sara was addicted to drugs. She'd taken to hooking in order to pay for her next fix. One night she hooked a John who was actually a trafficker—he kidnapped her." I take a deep breath trying to calm the rage that always resurfaces when I think of the night we finally found Sara.

"When we found her, she'd been dead a while; left there to rot like trash. After that, Demon was never the same. Any trace of the man he was before, died with his sister."

Willow sniffs, using the backs of her hands to wipe the tears from her eyes. "That's awful. I can't imagine what that was like for him. I feel so bad for judging him the way I did."

I reach over and grip her hand, giving it a reassuring squeeze. "The club is more than the sign says it is. It's a refuge, a second chance. We give them every opportunity that Demon's sister didn't have. If they have a drug problem, we pay for rehab. If they want to, we pay for them to go to school. They get to work in a safe environment and are never expected to perform outside their comfort zone. All we require in return are clean drug tests and passing grades for those in school," I finish explaining as we pull into the parking lot of Aspen General.

I switch the truck off before turning hoping to catch her eyes; her gaze is already trained on me. Her pale blue eyes dart across every inch of my face. It's almost as if she's trying to find the secrets I hold inside. I can only hope when she discovers the true secrets I keep buried, she still looks at me as she does right now. As if I'm the answer to every question she's ever asked.

CHAPTER 12

WILLOW

It's after three when we arrive at Aspen General. People are bustling in and out of the store, carts filled with groceries, arms laden with bags. Any other time, a crowded place like this would cause panic to take hold, but today, my mind is stuck in a cloud of fog.

Priest's words replay on a loop through my mind. A refuge. A second chance. Is that what this is? I thought ending up in Colorado was a coincidence, but as I stand beside Priest, I can't help but wonder if this is all part of something bigger.

Lost in my thoughts, I flip through the rack of sweaters. It's been so long since I've chosen my own clothes. My fingers stop on a grey sweater, the soft fabric reminds me of a hoodie I wore years ago, way back before I ever met Vince and became a slave to his vile needs. *He's gone. I'm safe.* I repeat the words to myself over and over in my head, but the truth lingers—he could still find me.

"See anything you like?" Priest's voice startles me and I jump a mile, knocking my elbow into a rack of leggings. I watch helplessly as the entire rack tumbles to the ground. With a gasp, I step back, years of muscle memory take over as I drop to my knees and smother my face with my hands.

"I'm sorry. I'm sorry." Dread fills the pit of my stomach. "I'll clean it up, I swear, just give me a min—" Logic tells me I'm safe, but the years of abuse I suffered at the hands of Vince are a deadly reminder; I need to be on guard twenty-four-seven. Black spots blur my vision and my heart races wildly as I choke on each breath.

"Willow?" Priest's voice is firm, questioning.

When he extends his hand, I scramble back, raising my own hands in defense. "No, no please don't—" Flickers of memories flash before my eyes. Fists coming toward me, blood splattering, voices shouting.

> *"You stupid whore!"*
> *"Worthless piece of shit."*
> *"Get on the floor."*

His words, his voice, his footsteps. A shadow towers over me, forcing me to cower down, my arms over my head and my knees pulled up to my chest.

"Willow," his voice is barely a whisper, and when gentle hands take mine, the panic crushing my chest subsides. "Baby, focus on me."

Blinking, I stare into his deep blue eyes searching for any shred of rage. It's not there. All I find are brows knitted in confusion. As he kneels in front of me, he squeezes my hands.

"Priest?" I blink back tears. "What hap—" *Oh God. Another flashback.* "I'm so sorry."

His broad shoulders rise and fall, but he remains silent. One hand tucks under my legs, the other around my back, and with one swift movement he stands, effortlessly lifting me off the floor with him. Burying my nose against his chest, his cologne invades my senses, a wave of calm washing over me.

As he walks, he calls out to someone named Phyllis, saying something about using her office. I don't hear her reply against the calming rumble of Priest's chest. "One minute, baby, just hold onto me."

I peek up as he enters a small office and kicks the door closed behind him. He sits with me still in his arms. "Fuck, Willow, talk to me…" His voice strains as though he's trying to hold himself together. "Does this have to do with what you told me last night?"

God, I'm a mess. For the second time in as many days, he's holding me in his arms as I fall apart.

"My ex—he was abusive. In the beginning he treated me so well, better than I could have ever dreamed." I force a smile, but it dies on my lips with a heavy sigh. "I uh, didn't have a great childhood." *That's putting it lightly.* "It's a long story, one for another day." No way am I about to try to explain that clusterfuck of confusion. "Anyway, I guess it caused a nasty habit of latching onto people. I was desperate to feel loved. Just to have someone."

Priest nods. "I understand that better than most. It's how almost every child in the system feels."

"The first time he beat me was because I spilled a glass of water."

Priest's body goes rigid. "Fucking bastard," he growls. He presses his lips to my hairline; his voice lowers to an ominous whisper. "I'll find that fucking bastard and I'll kill him."

I shake my head hard. "No, no you can't. He's dangerous, please don't."

His strong hand slides up my back and he twists his fingers through my hair. "Tell me his name."

Another shake of my head. "No. I ca—I can't."

Pulling me into him, he releases a heavy sigh. "I'll find out, whether you tell me or not, I'm gonna find that fucking bastard and end him." The determination in his tone leaves me with no doubt he'll try.

Taking my face in his hands, he tilts my head and our eyes meet. My breathing turns shallow as nerves dance around my belly. Priest's eyes burn with hunger and ever so slowly he lowers his head to mine. "Cut my fuckin' arm off before I ever hurt you, baby."

I inch closer, my tongue darts out and wets my waiting lips in anticipation. Stopping the barest breath away, Priest pulls back and looks into my eyes. Eye's ablaze with passion, he breathes against my lips.

"Please," I beg. Like a rubber band, my whispered plea snaps his restraint and the second his lips touch mine, something inside me shifts. I've been searching for meaning my whole life. A puzzle piece lost to the void of emptiness and despair, and finally, the puzzle is complete. The missing piece back in place. With Priest, I am finally whole.

Priest takes his time kissing me, like it's the only chance we'll ever have. His grip on the side of my face is a reassuring anchor, keeping me tethered to reality when the blissfulness of the moment threatens to take me away. Slowly, methodically, his tongue strokes mine before exploring the rest of my mouth. Like a miner leaving no stone unturned, Priest savors every inch of my mouth. I am hopelessly at his mercy as he enters my mouth, searing himself onto my soul.

He gives my swollen lips the barest of nibbles before finally pulling away. "Come on. Let's go get you some clothes."

Back out in the store, Phyllis has already cleaned up the leggings and put them back on the display. I grab a few pairs of sweater tunics that will pair easily with the leggings. Sneaking over to the undergarments and pajamas, I rifle through stacks of panties quickly stuffing several pairs between the layers of clothing in my arms. I'm just reaching out to finger a midnight blue satin nightie when Priest's deep voice comes at me across the store.

"What size?" Priest is rifling through a rack of cream colored fur-lined coats.

"Pardon?"

"What size? You need a jacket. It's already in the low forties outside, and it drops even more once the sun goes down."

"Oh, I don't thi—"

My words die when Priest walks toward me, stopping when the toe of his black boots meet my ragged salvation army find.

"Baby," his voice is quiet. "You haven't fully gotten this yet, and you're probably not ready for it all, but you're mine. I'm gonna take care of you, that means making sure you have what you need. Now, please tell me what fuckin' size. I do not wanna have to come back tomorrow and exchange it."

Even though I'm planning on paying him back when I have it, I hate the thought of how much money he's spending on me. But I can't deny how it makes me feel knowing he wants me to be taken care of.

"Small."

Giving me a relieved smile, he leans forward and pecks my lips. "Thank you."

My cheeks heat as I give him a small smile in return. I'm definitely not used to the public display of affection, but I'm not going to protest. Priest's eyes dart away from mine and widen slightly before turning heated. I follow his gaze to the midnight blue nighty I was eyeing moments ago. Before I have a chance to explain, Priest reaches around me and grabs the nightie before draping it over the pile of clothes in his arms. After bickering back and forth, Priest puts his foot down and demands I get at least three pairs of new shoes.

We finally make our way to the register to pay when I remember. "Crap, the office supplies."

Priest turns to Phyllis who's peeking over the enormous pile of clothes and shoe boxes.

"Phyllis, darlin' where are the office supplies? Willow is gonna take on the task of organizing my office."

Phyllis laughs. "My Herb was a right slob. I swear that man would have lost his head if the good Lord didn't attach it for him. You start on him now, honey, they can be trained," she says with a wink.

My eyes dart to Priest's face and I burst into laughter seeing just what he thinks about being 'trained'. But as soon as he hears my laugh, the glare he had aimed at Phyllis melts away and his soft gaze finds mine.

"Go get me some office shit, baby."

"Kay." I sigh.

Heading off in the direction Phyllis said, I'm horrified to see the smallest supply section known to man. I grab the few essentials they have and head back to the checkout wondering if Priest wants his office cleaned bad enough to order some supplies. Surely Amazon will deliver to the clubhouse.

When Phyllis gets close to the bottom of the pile, Priest hands me the items already in bags and sends me to the truck.

"Here, baby. Why don't you go ahead and load these up? I'll unlock the door, just toss 'em in the back."

Rather than calling him out on his master plan to divert my attention from the total of our shopping spree, I take the bags and head outside after saying a quick thank you to Phyllis. Attempting to juggle the bags while trying not to slip on the icy sidewalk, proves near impossible, but I manage to make it to the truck without landing flat on my ass.

As I'm about to grab the door handle, a commotion across the street catches my attention. Voices float through the air, followed by someone shouting in Spanish. When my eyes lock onto the scene, fear paralyzes me. In slow motion, the bags fall from my hands and clothing spills around me like confetti.

The clatter causes the two men in black suits to look directly at me. In that moment, the world stops. *Oh god. It's them.*

The bigger of the two men—the same man who chased me into the woods—starts in my direction, but as he lifts his foot to step off the curb, the man behind him grabs his arm, yanking him to a halt.

Strong arms wrap around me from behind. "Hey, you okay? Did you slip?" Priest runs his hands along my shoulders and arms. Misreading my fear, he lowers his voice, "Willow, baby. It's not a big deal, alright?" He leans down and scoops up the clothes saturated with melted snow before he stuffs them into the bags.

With his full attention focused on me, Priest is oblivious to my world imploding around me. He continues reassuring me as I watch the two men take stock of Priest then step back.

The shorter man turns and walks in the direction of the same black Escalade from the alley. The other man stays, malice and hatred roll off him in waves. With a sinister smirk, he raises his arm and delivers a promise. Using his thumb and pointer finger, he trains his 'gun' on me before slowly pulling the 'trigger'. I swallow down the bile rising in my throat as he mouths one single, terrifying word.

"Boom."

WASHED IN BLOOD

CHAPTER 13

WILLOW

Four weeks later

It's been almost four weeks since Priest rescued me from the woods. My days are spent at the clubhouse organizing his office, or at Wicked Wrench where I've taken over the role of office manager. I have no idea how that place is still running. While I was working in his office one day, Priest made an offhand comment that his office here was nothing compared to the one at the shop. The smirk on his face told me he knew what he was doing. He dangled that bread crumb in front of me and I took it, hook, line, and sinker.

Thanks to Angel, I have also become the unofficial laundry fairy.

He stormed through the door one day pissed that he'd gotten a stain on his favorite shirt. He begged me to get it out. All it took was a little stain remover and soaking, and it was good as new. When word got out that his shirt was *"softer than it had ever been"* the other men followed suit. Clearly bikers have never heard of fabric softener.

Priest has been on them daily, demanding they stop bothering me, but I wouldn't have it any other way. It's nice to finally be appreciated. To be asked to do things instead of having them demanded of me.

With the laundry basket on my hip, I head to Priest's room, smiling at the scent of his cologne in the air. He must have come to take a shower while I was putting dinner in the oven. The bathroom door is open and I peek inside, condensation still fresh on the mirror.

Hefting the basket off my hip and onto the bed, I grab a handful of my panties and socks. Turning toward the corner of the room, I notice the chair I've been using as my temporary dresser, sits empty. My things are gone. Frantically, I search the room. I freeze when I see a duffle bag sitting on the bed, hidden by the laundry basket. My heart clenches as a wave of nausea hits me. *This is it. It's time to go.*

After taking a moment to steady myself, I raise my head high and start toward the bag. Pulling it to me,

I drop the clothes that are still in my arms inside. After they're in, I grab the rest of my things from the basket and toss them with the others. I take extra care to count the items as I add them. I can't risk leaving anything behind. The last time I was forced to pack a bag like this, I spent the next six months on the streets. This time, that's not an option. Because it's not just me anymore, now I have someone else to think of. *What am I going to do?*

Lost to the darkness of my thoughts, I don't notice Priest walk into the room. Shoulders hunched, I turn toward the bathroom to get the few basic hygiene items that I've accumulated, but stop when a pair of scuffed black motorcycle boots come into my line of sight.

Keeping my eyes downcast, I try to step around him. I can't do this. Can't hear his apologies or the reasons he wants me to leave. But when I move to pass him, his arm darts out and his hand presses flat against my tummy. My heart pounds for an entirely different reason. He must know about the baby. Maybe that's why he's ready for me to leave.

Did I really think these bikers would want anything to do with me once they found out I was pregnant? *God, I'm such an idiot.*

Eyes still trained on the floor, I clear my throat. "I won't be much longer, I just need to grab my jacket and a few things from the bathroom." I pause a moment to steady my breathing, the tears harder to keep at bay than I anticipated. "Thank you so much for everything you've done for me. It means more to me than you'll ever know."

"What happened?" he growls.

My brows scrunch in confusion. "Sorry?"

Priest drops his hand and my hackles rise as he lets out a sarcastic laugh. "Sorry? That's all you have to say?"

Finding the courage to look up, I'm dumbfounded at the betrayal I see. "I don't understand why you're so mad. This is what you wanted. I mean you left the bag on the bed, and my things are gone..."

His eyes narrow before sliding to the bed. Understanding seeps into his gaze, and his eyes close. He was probably trying to avoid running into me before I left, and now he's faced with an awkward situation. I don't know why since I'm the one being kicked out, but the need to ease the tension flowing through him, prompts me to speak. "Priest, it's okay. I never expected this to be a permanent situation. There's no need to feel—" I stop talking when he stalks over to the bed and grabs the duffle in a clenched fist.

Snatching the top open, he reaches in, grabbing handfuls of my things. Once his arms are full, he stalks over to his dresser and pulls open the top drawer. He shoves the contents of the drawer to one side before going through the items in his arms. His fingers pick out what he's looking for before he drops them inside.

Taking a hesitant step forward, my face burns when I realize it's my panties. "Priest, what—" He slams the drawer with such force that the mirror above it shakes.

Ignoring me, he goes back to the bed, gathering more of my clothes from the bag before adding them to his drawers. Heavy boots thud against the floor as he marches to his walk-in closet.

Peeking inside, I see Priest with his arms raised, braced against the floor-length mirror hanging on the wall. His black t-shirt is stretched across the broad expanse of his back and his muscles are bunched tight, shoulders heaving with each breath.

Looking away, I focus my gaze on the floor, trying to make sense of what just happened. Why is he acting like this? He's the one who wants me to leave. Why is he making this so hard? Steeling myself, I take a deep breath through my nose before I lift my head to confront him. The words die on my lips at the intensity of his slate blue eyes locked on mine.

His face may be a mask of blank indifference, but his eyes give away every emotion he's trying to keep hidden.

Priest walks toward me, confidence pouring off him with each determined step. The look in his eyes is predatory, and for once in my life, I don't mind being the prey.

His tattooed arm reaches out, fingers grasping the back of my neck to pull me toward him. His tongue

137

plunges into my mouth as he tightens his grip, and God, all I want to do is lose myself in his embrace.

A moan slips free when the thick column of his cock rubs against my thigh. I'm confused and turned on all at once. *Holy shit.* Minutes ago, he was kicking me out, now he's humping me against the wall. *What is happening?*

I lift my leg, desperate for more. The growl he gives in response ends on a tortured moan when I press harder, spurred by his reaction. *Oh my god.* That sound. I want to hear it a thousand more times.

Ripping his mouth from mine, Priest pulls back, chest heaving as he brings his other hand up to cradle my face.

"You know what this means?" His voice is thick with lust, his control wearing thin. Too stunned to answer, my nipples harden when he growls low in his chest and tightens his grip on my face.

"Willow, look at me, baby. This is your last fuckin' chance, because once we go there, there's no goin' back. I need you to look at me and tell me you understand what I'm sayin'."

The world stills and tears sting my eyes at the intensity of his voice. This man... despite the fact I don't deserve him, he's everything I need and more, and I'm not turning him away. Not when I need him more than my next breath. My throat tightens and the words come out in a hushed whisper. "I'm yours."

"Thank fuck," he mutters before he reaches back and pulls his shirt over his head, giving me my first glimpse of the muscles I've felt beneath. He throws it to the floor and bends over to pick me up. My legs wrap around his waist, and my pussy clenches in anticipation. Rough hands cradle my ass, and I nearly come when his fingers trace the seam of my leggings. A rush of wetness saturates my panties.

"*Christ,*" he groans, grinding into me until we reach the bed. His muscles flex and strain as he releases one arm from my body and throws the laundry basket to the ground. He sets us down and my hips buck against him, still lost in the feel of his body against mine. I never expected this. To want a man after everything I've been through. From the moment I woke up in his bed, I knew this was different, *he* was different. He lifts his hands and I look down at him with hooded eyes.

"Baby, I fuckin' need this. But, you gotta let me know it's what you want, too."

I fuckin' need this. Unable to speak, I trail my lips down his neck.

His body trembles beneath my touch and *God*, I love the power I have over him. He lets out a deep groan, spurring me to continue on my path. With newly gained confidence, I flick out my tongue, teasing his nipple. His body spasms as I grasp it lightly between my teeth and give it a tug.

139

"Fuck," he growls as he fists my hair, holding me to his nipple. I flick my tongue over the stiff peak again and he moans. He thrusts his hips up, just as desperate for me as I am for him. But I'm not nearly finished with him. Not now that I know I'm in control.

"God," he chokes out.

I grin at him, my mouth still around his nipple. Growing bolder, I drag the tip of my tongue lower. Lust surges through me when Priest flips me over with a growl.

"My turn," he says with a sexy smirk. His hands bunch in the bottom of my t-shirt and my breathing stalls.

The baby… what if he figures it out… he isn't going to want me...

Sobered, a tear falls, escaping the corner of my eye before I have a chance to swipe it away.

Priest's worried gaze finds mine, his body going stiff. "Willow. Look at me baby, give me those eyes." I shake my head and let out a small whimper.

"Princess," he whispers as a broken sob escapes my chest.

I need to tell him. The thought of taking this last step and not telling him, chills me to my core, but how can I? "I'm scared." Not for the reasons he's probably thinking.

"I know." The rough pad of his thumb gently traces the path of my tears. Leaning down, he presses his lips against mine. There's a truth in his eyes, an understanding that silences my worry and possesses my soul.

"But I'm not him, Willow." *Kiss.*

"Fear has no place in this room." *Nibble.*

"In our bed." *Grind.*

I moan at the sensation of his tongue stroking my own as he grinds his cock into my center. "I'm gonna show you what that pussy was meant to feel."

"Wait, there's something I need to te—Priest!" I cry out as his hot mouth closes around my nipple. My back arches off the bed. *Oh my god.*

"Fuck," he growls before switching to the other breast.

I thread my fingers through the ends of his hair and his chest rumbles against mine in appreciation. Giving it one last flick, he trails his tongue down my torso. Holding my gaze, he hooks his fingers in the band of my leggings and drags them down. He licks his lips and rests back on his heels. Lowering his gaze to my pussy, he eyes it like a man starved. With deliberate movements, he pushes up my legs and slides one finger inside me before pulling it out to taste the wetness.

"Fuckin' perfection."

My nerve endings explode when he flicks his tongue out and licks from my clit to my ass. My puckered hole squeezes in response to the foreign feeling. He chuckles darkly against my pussy; the vibration causes another bolt of pleasure to travel to my clit.

"Don't worry baby, we'll save that for next time."

God, yes. I want there to be a next time. I whimper, lifting my hips to grind my pussy deeper into his mouth. *Oh, shit. I'm gonna come.* The pressure inside builds, but Priest lifts his face right before it explodes.

"No," I mewl.

"Shh. I'm gonna make it better baby," he soothes.

Using his thumb, he parts my swollen lips and presses the firm pad of his thumb against my clit before circling.

"Priest," I beg, needing more. He raises up to kiss me, and I ache for what strains against his jeans. I want to grab him, pull out his cock and push it inside me, but I don't. I can't. Not yet.

"Christ, you're so fuckin' sexy, you know that?" His lips move against the base of my neck as he frees himself. Dipping his fingers inside me one last time, he swipes the wetness around the tip of his cock. My eyes close when presses it to my entrance. He stills with just the head of his cock inside. "Eyes on me baby. I want you to know who's fuckin' this pussy. There's no one here but us, you and me?"

"No one but us," I repeat.

The walls of my pussy stretch as Priest slides his cock into me, filling me to the brim. His lips hover over mine as he thrusts into me over and over. His hands grip my ass, pulling my cheeks apart to get deeper, possessing me even more.

I scream at the intensity of my orgasm. My pussy clenches as he continues to pump inside me. Any control he had snaps the second he feels the first ripple of my pussy around his cock.

"Fuck yeah, babe, come all over my cock." He sinks into me with a punishing rhythm until he stills, body tensing as he roars my name. He keeps his body on top of mine, his hips slowly moving his cock in and out as he kisses me slowly.

Hours later, we're still in bed wrapped around each other and tangled in the sheets. My cheek is pillowed against him, and my fingers dance across his chest. I brush against another puckered patch of skin. I wonder when I'll be able to work up the courage to ask him what happened. My fingers seem to be drawn to them because seconds later they land on another one. I startle when Priest's voice cuts through the content silence we've been lying in.

"They're bullet wounds."

My hands freeze. *Bullet wounds*. My nose burns as I mentally count the scars that are spread across his chest. I sniffle, hugging him closer to me as I realize how different my life would be right now if he weren't here.

Priest grips my chin and tilts my face up to his. "It was a long time ago, baby. There's nothing to worry about now. Okay?"

I nod and try to hold back a full on ugly sob. Who the heck wants that for post coital pillow talk?

"I just... I can't help thinking about how different things would be right now if you hadn't lived. I would... I mean, I'd be de—"

"Don't," he cuts me off. "Don't let those fuckin' thoughts invade your head. It wasn't my time to go, and it's not gonna be for a long time. You hear me?"

I nod and press my lips against a scar. And I cling to him while he's here and pray he's right.

WASHED IN BLOOD

CHAPTER 14

PRIEST

I walk into Church to see that everyone is already here. *Good.* We've got too much shit going on without me having to track someone's ass down. Taking a seat at the head of the table, my eyes catch on the sly smirk Angel is sending my way.

"What?"

"I didn't say nothin', Prez."

I cross my arms over my chest waiting on him to explain why he looks like the cat that just ate the fuckin' canary, except the canary was actually a tasty pussy.

"You look a little tired today boss. You uh, get enough sleep or did that noise last night keep you up too?"

I look to Bullet knowing he would have come and gotten me if there were any issues surrounding the clubhouse. Raising my brows, I wait for him to explain Angel's fucking riddles.

Bullet clears his throat before throwing a glare of his own at Angel. "Not sure what he's talking about, boss. Everything looked good from my end," he replies.

"Angel boy, maybe you need to explain a little further to our Prez just what it was that you were listenin' in on—I mean what you heard." Bullet smirks over at Angel.

"I wasn't fucking listenin' in! It was hard to ignore since we share a wall," Angel rushes out.

I growl as the realization of what Angel heard sets in.

"Priest, man I swear, the second I realized what was going on I left," Angel says.

Raising my eyes to the ceiling, I count to ten in an attempt to calm myself from ripping pretty boy a new one. "Say one word to her about this, I swear to Christ they'll never find your body." I glower at him.

In typical Angel fashion, he raises his hand and zips his lips before throwing away the key. I sigh and shake my head before addressing the other men at the table.

"Now. If we're done talking about my fuckin' sex life, I think we have more pressing matters at hand."

146

The mood in the room changes at the mention of the issues that have been plaguing not only the garage, but the club as well. At first, the problems that popped up were sporadic and written off as a coincidence. But things started to get out of hand. After a lift at Wicked Wrench almost crushed one of our employees, we knew it was time to reassess. Taking the lift apart was tedious and a bitch of a job, but what we found was evidence to know that we hadn't just been having a rough go at things.

The men start talking amongst themselves, throwing out ideas of who would be stupid enough to come after us. Leaning back in my chair, I listen while going over possibilities myself. We're the only MC in our immediate area. The Sons of Pandem used to have turf here but after we disposed of their President and VP for raping our previous Mayor's daughter, the rest of the members split town.

"Bullet, what do we know?"

Bullet sighs and runs a hand over his tattooed head. "Honestly, not fuckin' much. No one has seen or heard anything around town, all of our usual contacts say far as they know, it's all kosher."

"So what, we're just supposed to believe that all the stuff happening is what? Some freak coincidence? An act of fuckin' God?" Angel objects.

Bullet glares at him. "That's not what I'm sayin' and you fuckin' know it. I want to say all of our contacts are sound, but money talks. If someone has deep enough pockets, they'd turn on us faster than we could blink."

Bullet glances at Demon before he continues, "It's not their usual MO. They're more direct and don't deal in petty bullshit…" He takes a deep breath before finishing, "But I found Breva cigar clippings behind Corrupt earlier tonight," he says low, like it will somehow lessen the impact on all of us, but one in particular.

Demon's chest expands on a breath at the mention of the chosen tobacco smoked by the Demonio de Hielo Cartel. The same cartel responsible for the death of Demon's sister, Sara.

"It's not something we'd expect from them, but I don't think we should rule them out," Bullet adds. "I heard Manuel's been letting Diego step up. Run a few things on his own before he hands over the reins permanently."

"What do you think?" At the sound of my voice all other conversation stops. The men all turn to look at me, but my attention is on Demon.

He gives me a droll look, but I don't miss the flex of his knuckles or his increased breathing since the cartel was mentioned. "Your guess is as good as mine, boss."

My eyes narrow at his nonchalant answer. "You got somethin' you need to get off your chest?"

He snorts. "You gonna get your head outta Willow's pussy long enough to listen?"

My voice is menacing. "The fuck did you just say?"

Seemingly unconcerned with the threat to his life, he leans back in his chair, a picture of calm. "You heard me. You 'bout ready to remember just what the fuck your role is here, or you going to play house some more with Miss. Barely Legal?"

"What the fuck is your problem?" When the hell did this become about me and Willow, and not about the war that's brewing on our doorstep?

Demon relaxes back into his seat. "No problem here, Prez. Just wondering if we all get a club whore or if that's a perk exclusive to you?"

"Brother," Patch growls a warning.

My brothers each have varying degrees of rage on their faces and I wonder which one will snap first.

"Suck my dick, Patch, you're as bad as him— all of you are. Always at her beck and fuckin' call. Shit, maybe she's spreading for all of you and I'm the odd man out," he muses before addressing me again. "That what it is, Priest? You gonna let me have a go at her sweet little cunt too, or do I have to suck your dick first? Tell me, man cause I gotta know. That mouth feel as good as it loo—" That's as far as he gets before my chair slams against the wall with the force of my lunge.

Before the other men can comprehend what's happening, I'm raining down blow after blow to his face. Patch and Bullet stay seated but Angel hovers close as we grapple on the floor.

When Demon manages to flip me so that our positions are reversed and I'm pinned to the ground, he's finally able to get a few connecting punches in. The brothers seem content to let us work this out on our own, but when Demon lands a hard punch to my temple, causing my head to bounce off the floor, all hell breaks loose.

The room spins and my ears ring as I roll to my stomach and pull my hands and knees underneath me. I close my eyes and wait for the spinning to stop before opening them again. When I do, Bullet and Patch struggle to hold back an enraged Angel.

Standing, I rush into the fray to help Bullet and Patch restrain Angel from beating Demon to a bloody pulp.

"Fuck you, mother fucker. He's done fuckin' everything for us," Angel rages.

Wiping the blood from his mouth, Demon looks to where Angel stands struggling against the hold Bullet and Patch have on him, an ugly sneer covers Demon's face.

"Give it a fucking rest, Angel. You've been panting after Priest's dick for years," Demon sneers.

My head rears back as my brows reach my hairline. *The fuck?* My gaze darts quickly to Angel whose face is mottled with rage.

"Asshole. *You fucking asshole!*" Angel thrashes wildly against Patch and Bullet, their arms struggling to contain him.

Glancing at their faces I see the same shock I know is mirrored on my own. *Angel is gay?*

"Enough." The rough timbre of my voice resonates through the air.

Angel thrashes once more, catching Bullet and Patch off guard as he charges at Demon. I intercept him and plant my hand in his chest as I fist his shirt and cut. As I shove him against the wall, I drop my mouth beside his ear. "I said enough," I growl and give him another shake.

Angel's eyes are still focused where Demon sits hunched on the floor. His body trembles beneath my hands and I pull back to catch his eyes. "Maddox." I use his real name hoping it will pull him back from the depths of whatever hell he's lost in right now. It works, but my own anger boils when his eyes finally meet mine. Betrayal and shame flood the normally playful depths.

"Prez—" he chokes out. "I—I'm sorry. I tried. I tried so hard, I swear, *I fuckin' swear*. You have to believe me. H—he always told me to be good and I wouldn't get punished."

I release his shirt and lift both hands to grip the back of his neck before dropping my forehead to his. "Brother. He's not here anymore. We took care of him, remember? He's not here, you're safe."

With a choked sound, Angel shoves me away. Looking to Demon, he ignores the other men in the room and stares at his brother with a lost and desperate

151

look in his eyes before he turns and walks out of Church.

Demon watches him leave, a sliver of regret flickers in his black eyes before he masks it.

"You," I growl, pointing at Demon. "The fuck is wrong with you?"

"You seriously going to stand there and act like none of you knew?" Demon stands from where he was splayed out on the ground.

"We're not acting, dumbass," Patch growls going back to his seat at the table.

Still glaring at Demon, I ask, "Was that fucking necessary?"

"I gave him plenty of time to come clean. He wasn't going to tell you, so I did." He shrugs and heads to the bathroom at the back of the room.

"That's not your decision to make," Bullet says heatedly.

Demon ignores him and washes his bloodied face in the sink. He dries it off and takes his seat again. "He's been panting after Priest for years. He needed to realize it was never going to happen."

"Even *if* that's the case, it wasn't your fuckin' place, Demon, and you know it," Bullet returns.

"Enough," I cut in. "Find him. Apologize, and fucking fix this shit storm that you've caused," I say to Demon who lifts his chin in acknowledgement.

Bullet clears his throat. "Not to bring it up again, but we're behind on slaying. I know things are

152

hot right now, but we have a couple that can't wait any longer."

Christ. Maybe this is why everyone is so fucking tense. I can't remember the last time we were able to purge.

"What have we got?"

Bullet grabs a stack of files from the table and passes two to each of us. He hands me two extra which I know he means for me to give to Angel when I find him later to talk things out.

"Let's start with the top file. Myles Davis, twenty-six. Troubled kid. What was small time drugs and dealing took a turn when he attended a campus college party last weekend."

I scan the information and pictures inside. Myles was raised by his grandma after his mom died of an OD. Unfortunately, granny was already getting up there in age and wasn't able to tend to him the way he needed. He eventually spiraled and became more than she could handle until she kicked him out when he was 16. Granny mysteriously died two weeks later from what seems to be natural causes, but I'm thinking otherwise.

The boy in these pictures seems to be just that. A gangly young man who at first glance seems harmless. It's his eyes that give him away. The cold, unfeeling eyes staring back from the paper cause a chill of anticipation and excitement to race along my spine.

Yes. This is what we all need.

153

The excitement vanishes when I flip to the next page and see evidence of the evil that resides inside Myles. A teenage girl, head lolled to the side, oblivious to the heinous acts inflicted upon her body. Bruises along her wrists and legs show the exact places of Myles's harsh, unforgiving grip. Her lip is swollen and red, and streaks of mascara stain her face.

The pictures cause a fire deep within my soul, but the next ones enrage the beast. They look to have been taken at a hospital, so I've no doubt who helped procure them for our files. I glance at Patch and my suspicions are confirmed when I see the closed file sitting in front of him. He already knows the contents within.

Reluctantly, I drop my gaze back to the picture and fight the bile rising in my throat. She received 20 stitches as a result of the rape and sodomy he inflicted. *Christ.*

"…suicide," Bullet says jerking me out of my internal thoughts.

"What?" Dread fills the pit of my stomach. She's a fucking kid.

"Brielle Cossgrove, eighteen. Freshman at Aspen Community. Committed suicide thirty-four hours after being raped by an unknown male at a party."

"*Fuck,*" I rumble at the same time a growl tears from Demon's chest.

"Alcohol and marijuana both present in the bloodstream along with traces of GHB," Bullet finishes.

And with that comment, the final nail is hammered, sealing the fate of Myles Davis. "Bullet, find out where he's going to be Saturday night. That gives us two days to do a pre-clean and prepare for his arrival."

Bullet nods, closing the top file before grabbing the second and opening it. "File number two. Andrew Hemminger, thirty-seven."

"I know that name," Demon interrupts, scanning the papers in his file.

"He's the principal at the high school," I answer.

Patch lets out a low whistle. "This is gonna be a tricky one. Extremely well thought out." He glances at Bullet before flipping through the papers in his own file. "You sure he's deserving? Police won't let this go as easily as some of the others."

Bullet glares at Patch. "Have I ever delivered anyone that wasn't deserving?"

Patch holds up his hands and gives him a wave to continue.

"Like I was saying. Principal Hemminger recently found himself immersed deep in the world wide web; he appears to have a newfound fascination."

Like with the last file, I study the details of our latest sinner. Andrew Hemminger is an overweight

155

middle-aged man with premature balding. Sweat mars his brow and his smile is wide and friendly in the school faculty picture that Bullet included with our files. Unlike Myles, it's people like Hemminger who are most dangerous. They live amongst us completely undetected. They're friends, people in our church, people we trust with our kids.

"And where exactly did he find himself when he got lost?" I ask, wondering just how sick and twisted this man is.

"You want the long story or the short?" Bullet asks.

"Short," Patch grunts.

"What started as a harmless video in a live chat room on a popular porn site quickly spiraled. After certain comments were made by Hemminger, he was contacted privately by another viewer to converse about their similar kinks." Bullet pulls out a picture of a different man from his file; he holds it up for all of us to see. Olive skin and dark hair denotes his Italian roots, but even without those we know who the man is.

"What Hemminger didn't know was, he was speaking with a lower level spy for the Russo Crime Family."

"Fuck," I say.

Bullet lets out an unamused laugh. "That about sums it up."

"What the hell would the Russo family want with a high school principal?" Demon finally adds to the discussion.

"They're looking to branch out. Guns and drugs must not be enough anymore, now they're looking into trafficking of the human variety."

"Again, what is Hemminger's part in all of this?" I ask.

"He was tasked with delivering girls. Told him they want girls that no one will miss, ones from broken homes, no friends, troublemakers."

"And when was this assignment given to him?" Patch mumbles searching the file.

Bullet grimaces. "Three weeks ago. This was brought to our attention after an eleventh grader went missing a week ago. A boy who had a crush on her started asking around. Word got back to us and I looked into it."

We sit in silence for several minutes studying each of the files.

"And the girl?" Demon asks staring at the table, his file remains untouched.

Bullet's eyes dart to me, a helpless look in his eyes before landing on Demon.

"By the time I was able to locate her, she'd already been sold. An executive in Japan. She's gone, brother, there's nothing we can do."

Demon stares into my eyes, the tremble of his body reveals the rage that simmers beneath the surface.

"Hemminger is mine."

I take a deep breath and nod. There's not an ounce of remorse for the poor bastard who will come to regret the day he wanted to stroke one out to some porn. You sin, you face the consequences. "Done," I agree.

Without another word, Demon pushes his chair back from the table and leaves the room.

"Any idea what's gotten into him?" Patch asks.

"You noticed the date?" I eye him, waiting for it to sink in.

His brows dip only seconds before his eyes squeeze closed. "Fuck."

Standing from my chair I rap my knuckles on the table. "Just give him a couple days. It's like this every year, I'm sure Hemminger will help too."

Bullet barks out a laugh. "Poor bastard," he chuckles.

Yeah. Poor bastard doesn't know a Demon is after him.

WASHED IN BLOOD

CHAPTER 15

PRIEST

I find Angel in his room, and I can't say I'm shocked to find Willow there too. Curled up on the bed next to him sound asleep, my sweet girl is giving him what she doesn't even know he needs.

"How long she been in here?" I lean against the wall next to the door.

"Thirty minutes or so…" He looks down at my woman currently using his arm as a pillow; a line of drool coming out of the corner of her mouth. His face has a warm look and his mouth tilts up in an affectionate grin. "Walked right in like this was y'alls room. Climbed up on the bed and asked what I was watching."

Grabbing the remote, Angel turns the volume down several clicks and my eyes leave the perusal of my woman. "Priest—What Demon said, it's never been like that with you."

His eyes are already on me but they quickly dart away, color heating his cheeks. "I just wanted to let you know. That said, I understand if you and the guys want me to leave."

My stare goes hard at the mention of him leaving and the implication that we wouldn't accept him. "So it's true then?"

His eyes close as if the answer pains him. "Yes."

Studying him for long moments I wonder what signs there were that we all missed. "So the girls?" I leave the question hanging.

Angel lets out a short laugh and shakes his head. "We really gonna do this?"

"Yes." My tone leaves no room for negotiation.

He stares blankly at the TV. "To an extent, it's all been real. For a long time, I thought if I ignored it, it would go away. Don't get me wrong, I love everything I do when I'm with a woman, so I buried myself in as much pussy as I could." He shrugs.

"Did it work?"

"Not even close. If anything, it cemented the fact that I could never be fully satisfied with just a woman… I'm—Even after everything, I turned into exactly what that fucking sicko wanted me to."

"So you like little boys?" I ask.

Angel jerks so sharply I'm surprised Willow doesn't wake.

"How could you even fucking say that to me?" he snarls. "Kill myself before I ever touched a kid."

I nod. "That's what I'm trying to make you see. You being gay, or bi is not a product of what he did to you, brother."

Angel's chin drops. "I feel so fucking weak," he says in a broken whisper.

"Why? You're gonna have to help me here because I don't fuckin' see it. You were a *child*."

"By being gay, it means he won," he admits.

I shake my head, slashing my hand through the air. "No. *Fuck no.* The moment you decided to step off the bridge that day, he lost. Him winning would have been you jumping and giving in to the dark and you fucking know it."

Angel's eyes get a faraway look, most likely remembering the night I found him on the ledge of the bridge I pulled him from. Looking at him now, I barely see the broken boy he used to be.

My eyes move to Willow. I'm caught off guard at the steady stream of tears trailing from the corner of her eye. Sneaky girl. My heart warms seeing how strongly she feels for Angel. If he wasn't into dudes, there's no way in hell I'd let her be cozied up next to him.

"So how did Demon find out? Cause I gotta admit, man, the rest of us had no idea." I smirk, picturing Demon walking in on Angel jerking it to dudes.

Angel cracks his first smile since I walked into the room and it eases some of the tightness in my chest. "He walked in on me and Jax at the shop one night." He laughs. "Fucking tripped over one of the creepers left out. If I wasn't so fucking terrified of him finding out, I would have laughed."

I smile, picturing Demon's face walking in on such a moment. "So Jax, huh?" I smirk. Clearly I have a shit gaydar because I never would have pegged our tatted gym rat employee at Wicked Wrench to be gay either.

"Nah." Angel tries to play it off. "He's not my type."

We sit in comfortable silence for several minutes both of our attention on the TV. "She's good for you."

I glance back to Angel when he speaks but his eyes are on Willow.

"Yeah. I know." And I do. I know with every fiber of my being this woman was made for me. She calms the beast that lives within my soul. Gives him peace like he's never known.

"Don't fuck it up, Priest."

"You think I'm gonna fuck it up?" I question him.

"I think you're not gonna mean to."

I shake my head. "Die before I ever hurt her man." And even though I know Willow is awake and hearing every word of this, the words aren't a show. They're not a ploy to fool her into believing I'm something I'm not. They're the truth.

"You good now?" I check one last time.

"That depends—they hate me?" he asks, vulnerability seeping in.

"Damn, man. I never realized you thought so highly of us," I droll.

Angel laughs but there's still doubt clouding his eyes. "You really don't see it do you?" I ask stunned. "We may all be brothers bound together by life, or circumstance or whatever you want to call that shit. But we wouldn't be half of what we are today without you. Me, Demon, Patch... even Bullet, we're all the same, then there's you."

Angel's chest expands on an aggravated breath. "Wow you really know how to make a man feel special, you gonna try to give me dating advice next?"

My own aggravation goes up a notch, but I need him to understand exactly what his place is here.

"Angel, have you ever noticed how you don't have a title within the MC?"

He shrugs. "I mean yeah I noticed it. Never really thought anything of it though, just figured there were no more to hand out. Though I 'spect now, I'll be the resident gay or bi guy." I hate the self-depreciating way he refers to himself, as if he has a disease, and we've all been subjected to the plague.

"We couldn't give you a title because there wasn't one for what you do for us. You fit seamlessly into every role we have within the MC. I may be your President but you're the best of us, brother. Don't ever doubt that." Straightening from the wall, I stretch my neck. "Now, I'm about to head to the gym. Grab your bag—we can spar while I catch you up on the latest sinners.

"What you want me to do with her?" he asks, looking down at Willow.

"I got her." I slip my arms around her back and under her knees to cradle her to my chest. Once I have her situated, I look to Angel. "You head on over, I'll lay her in our bed."

"You going to quit playing opossum anytime soon?" I murmur into Willow's hair once we're in the hallway.

She peeks up at me from the corner of her eye. "Me?" she asks innocently.

My chest rumbles with my chuckle and Willow bounces slightly from the movement. "Yeah, baby. I'm talkin' about you." I watch her closely. "You okay?"

"Is he going to be okay?" she questions, eyes filled with worry.

I drop my forehead against hers before gently kissing her lips. "Yeah, sweetheart, he's going to be fine."

I'll make sure of it. I vow silently.

"Priest, can I ask you a question?" Willow whispers.

"Always." I look down at where she lays against my chest, her delicate fingers playing with the hair and brushing over my scars.

She doesn't respond immediately so I squeeze her bare shoulder where my arm is cradling her to me. "Willow?"

"I was just wondering… *What are sinners?*" she rushes out, blurring the words into one big one. But I don't need her to repeat herself.

I've thought about how to explain this to her a hundred times, but I couldn't figure out how to do it without her seeing us as anything other than monsters. Even though I've touched on it slightly when I told her about being shot, she has no idea the full extent of how these scars changed my life. I battle daily with how much of my past I'm willing to give her and when. It's not that I don't trust her, I just don't want to weigh her down any more than she already is. She's come out of her shell so much since the day I found her in the woods, and I don't want any of my dark tainting her light.

Her fingers run along my tense brow, "Why so serious?"

My mouth quirks but it does nothing to help my inner turmoil. Willow sits up and straddles my lap, wrapping her arms around my neck. Her center is pressed firmly against my cock and it hardens beneath her. "Really?" she says amused.

I shrug and smirk at her. "What do you expect?" I lean down and flick her nipple with my tongue. She laughs, but the distraction is short lived.

"When I took you, that made you mine." Even though we've fucked several times since the first, Willow's cheeks turn pink at the mention of it. "But when I tell you this, it will make you the club's, you understand?"

She nods immediately. "Yes," she says with zero hesitation.

Her trust in me makes me dart forward to capture her lips. Breaking the kiss, I stroke my fingers along the smooth skin of her thighs. "The long explanation is just that… long, dark, and sordid. I'm going to do my best to break it down. Some parts are going to seem unbelievable, impossible even. But I need you to trust me."

Again, she nods, but this time she leans in toward me. "I trust you," she whispers against my lips.

"When I was sixteen, my foster father shot me. I'll spare you all the gruesome details, because in the end, they don't matter. I stood up for what I knew was right, and I paid the price. He shot me point blank. My heart stopped before paramedics could even make it onto the scene." I wince at the pain that lances my heart, reminding me that wasn't the true price I paid. *Doe.*

Her wide eyes drag along the expanse of my chest as she puts my story together.

"But I was saved... given a second chance."

"By a doctor?"

"No." I shake my head. "By the Angel of Death."

Willow's eyes go wide. "The Angel of Death?" Her question is full of skepticism, and I don't blame her. My brothers had the exact same look on their faces the first time I told them.

"His name is Azrael."

I wait while she whispers the name, testing it on her lips. "What happened next?" she asks, excitement lighting her features.

"He told me it wasn't my time to die. Told me God had bigger plans for me, and he needed me."

"So, are you like, immortal now?" she whispers in awe.

I laugh. "I wish, baby, that'd be really fuckin' cool. But only if I could bite you and make you immortal too." I lean forward to nibble where her pulse thrums steady in her neck. "This next part is where things get tricky and some lines get blurred," I warn her.

"This *next part* is where things get tricky?" she says. As if being saved by the Angel of Death wasn't crazy enough. "So what was the plan God needed you for?"

I take a breath and lock my arms around her waist. This is what I've been most afraid of telling her. It's too late to turn back now. "Azrael spoke mostly in riddles—riddles that took me years to figure out, some I still haven't. But one thing he told me was to guard heaven."

Her nose scrunches. "Guard heaven? What does that even mean?"

"Let me ask you a question. If someone had known about what your ex was doing to you, would you have wanted them to step in? Save you?" I ask gently.

"Of course," she whispers. "I always felt so alone. And I was—it's why I wasn't able to get out sooner."

"That's what we do," I say, but I'm not explaining it enough because she's still confused.

"So you rescue women from abusive relationships?" she asks.

I rub my hand over my face and look her dead in the eye. "We're executioners, baby." I wait for her reaction.

The moment understanding sinks in, her body jerks back, eyes wide, face pale. "You... you kill people?" Both horrified and scared, her eyes dart around the room as if looking for a way to escape.

Cradling her face, I keep her gaze on me while I explain. "Yes," I say simply. "But they're never innocent, and leaving them alive would do more harm than good. We dispose of people who taint the earth just by breathing our air."

Her body relaxes marginally, but she still seems hesitant. "What do they do?"

If I don't explain the kind of filth these people are, she'll never fully understand. I don't sugarcoat my answer, instead, I give her what she needs to hear. "They're monsters. Rapists, murderers, pedophiles."

Willow sucks in a harsh breath. "They're filth, Willow. They do sick and terrible things, and they have to pay the price."

"But why does it have to happen that way? Why not let them die whichever way, and they can face God on judgement day?"

I rub my hands over my face knowing that her question is warranted. Fuck, I've asked myself the same question. The answer doesn't change. "Dying by any means other than our hands, it's too easy. Less than what they deserve. I've no doubt that one day, when it's my time, I won't be pardoned for what I've done here on earth. I fully expect to answer to each and every death that was dealt by my hands, and I'll make sure that when it's time, the evidence against each one will be nothing short of damning. But while I'm still here, I'm the judge, the jury, and the executioner."

The look on her face tells me she has questions she's too afraid to ask.

"Ask me," I say

"How… how do you find them?"

"Bullet," I answer simply. "Well, mainly Bullet. We have informants within the city limits. But outside that, Bullet has a system set up that pings when certain criteria are met."

"Are you the only one who kills them?" she whispers.

My face softens and I hope like hell I don't regret telling her the truth.

"No baby, I'm not."

She's silent for several moments before she speaks again.

"So do you all like, take turns?"

I laugh. "Not quite. We all have things that are important to us. Things that led us to each other, circumstances we no longer have any tolerance for. When a new case is brought up, we know which one of us will be responsible for that particular sinner."

"And which sinners are yours?"

Fuck. Just the question I didn't want to answer.

WASHED IN BLOOD

CHAPTER 16

WILLOW

I regret the question as soon as I ask it. Do I really want to know what kind of people he kills? *Yes.* I have to know… I think.

Priest stares at me for several seconds before speaking, but when he does, it's not to answer. "Willow, I don't—"

"Tell me, Priest," I cut him off, surprising both of us with my backbone. I shrink away out of instinct, but Priest doesn't react to that. Instead, he waits patiently while I come back to myself and relax my body back into his.

Leaning forward, he presses his lips against my forehead. "That was better," he murmurs. "Didn't take you as long to correct your body," he says with a pleased smile.

I give him a pointed stare. I'm not letting him out of answering my question.

His chest expands on a deep sigh. "Like I said, each of us are products of our upbringing. Different circumstances and events led us to each other. While some are worse than others, they all changed us in some way."

I raise my brows, waiting for him to continue.

"Relentless." He laughs under his breath. "For Demon, it's sex traffickers, or kidnappers with the intent to violate or rape."

I suck in a breath, hating the way my heart softens toward Demon with the knowledge that his life has been touched by something so horrific.

"You know his story, so it makes sense that any type of transgression to do with the selling of another human for sex or otherwise, that person goes to him."

"And Angel?" I ask.

"You probably have a good idea about Angel. From twelve to fourteen, he was raped by his stepdad."

Tears run down my face as my heart breaks for the little boy who lost his innocence at the hands of a monster.

"Pedophiles die by his hands. Not even God can help them once they've made it to his reach," he says ominously.

I shake my head. "It's hard to imagine him being anything other than who he is with me," I say.

Priest grips my chin forcing me to meet his gaze. The look on his face makes my breath stall in my chest. "We're all different men when that time comes. It's the only time the demons inside are allowed to come out and play. But it doesn't change who we are. Who you see, who we are around you and others, that's who we are at our core. We do very bad things for a very good reason, but it doesn't make us monsters, Willow."

"So does that mean Demon's sunshine personality is here to stay?" I joke, trying to lighten the mood.

Priest lets out a sharp laugh, his chest bouncing with the force. "Unfortunately, sunshine is here to stay. That's his everyday cheery self."

"Damn," I mutter. "What about Patch?" I ask getting back to our conversation.

Sadness clouds Priest's eyes. "Patch was the last to join us. Unlike the rest of us, Patch had a normal childhood. Came from a good family, had a wife and daughter—"

I wince, remembering the way I questioned him about his wedding ring.

"Yeah. Listen babe, Patch's story really isn't mine to tell. He's not as open about his past as the rest of us are. But I can tell you that Patch takes care of addiction fueled crimes. Anything resulting from the

173

overuse of drugs or alcohol, they go to him." Priest nods.

My stomach clenches as I put the pieces together in my mind. *Had a wife and daughter… Addiction fueled crimes… drugs and alcohol. Oh God.*

"Patch," I croak out, my heart breaking for the extent of loss that's touched his life.

I sit there a moment thinking about who's left. Priest is obviously leaving himself for last so that leaves Bullet.

"And Bullet? What's his story?"

"Bullet's entire family was killed during a home invasion when he was fifteen. Bullet was at a friend's house at the time of the shooting."

"Oh god."

Priest wraps his arms around my body, covering me in his warmth. "It wasn't planned. They had no clue whose house they were breaking into. Just a couple kids doing a gang initiation challenge. They took four lives that day."

"Four?"

Priest nods. "Four. His mom and dad and his two little brothers. They were three and five."

Sobs wrack my body at everything these men have been through. Their pain envelopes me, invading my senses. If my pain is even a fraction of theirs, I understand why they do what they do. How could I not? In another world, I like to think I'd have avenged all the little girls out there wronged by the system. The forgotten children. I'd avenge them all.

"So Bullet gets the gang members. Demon gets the sex traffickers. Angel gets the pedophiles and Patch gets the addicts," I say and Priest nods.

"Who does that leave you?" I ask.

Priest looks to me and I shiver at the wild look lighting his eyes.

"Everyone else," he admits. "Murderers default to me for obvious reasons, but I also get rapists." He watches me intently trying to gauge my reaction.

Is this something I can be okay with? The man I'm falling in love with kills people. Those hands that caress my body and bring it so much pleasure also bring death and destruction to others. How is he able to slip in and out of it so effortlessly?

"Don't hate them." I look at Priest sharply when he speaks.

"Hate them?" I ask. "Hate who?"

"The others. I know from the outside this can be hard to understand but we're not like the monsters who die by our hands."

My chest aches at the vulnerability pouring off my strong man. *God. Does he really think so little of me?* "Baby," I whisper leaning forward and touching my lips to his. "Don't you see? If you're the king of the underworld, I'll be your queen. Whatever happened to you in your past made you into the man you are today. I hate that bad things have happened to you, but I'm thankful for them, because they led you to me. Priest, I would have died out there in the woods. Cold and alone, those would have been my last memories of this world. But you saved me. Gave me a second chance. How could I hate the man who breathed life into me, just because he takes it from others who don't deserve to have it?" I question softly.

Priest growls and attacks my mouth. "I need you," he rasps against my lips.

"I'm yours."

PRIEST

Her words hit me hard. Her fucking ex abused her, tortured her to the point that a life on the streets was a better option than living another day with him. Terrified for her life, she was forced to hide in a rotted out tree encased in snow, or face her death at the hands of two murderers. Despite all that, she managed to hold onto life, and just as she was on the brink of death, I saved her. She's so fucking strong.

"I need you." The words creep out before I can stop them. I don't care that I may sound like a pussy, it's the truth, I do need her. She's mine, and I'm going to make damn sure she knows it.

Like putty in my hands, she sinks back into the pillow, the long strands of her hair fanned out behind her like a fucking halo. *Goddamn, she's beautiful.*

"I'm yours." Her voice is steady, and there's no fear in her eyes.

"Damn right, you are. Come here."

Sucking her plump little lip into my mouth, I savor the way she tastes. Like peaches and fucking sunshine. Willow moans and arches her back, her nails raking across my skin. My restraint is slim knowing her tight little pussy is just millimeters away, but my woman deserves to be praised. To have every single inch of her glorified to the fullest extent.

I pull her panties to the side and run a finger up her slit. So damn wet. Fuckin' ready for me. I grab the waistband of her panties and she moans, arching her hips.

"*King.*" She runs a hand up her thigh, before cupping her pert little tits as I rip her panties down her legs.

Goddamn she's fuckin' sexy. She has no idea how hard it makes me seeing her come alive at my touch.

With a teasing grin, she leans back, her eyes on me. In one quick move, she snaps the last of my restraint in two. She spreads her legs, and like the good Priest I am, I kneel at her altar, and pray.

Diving between her thighs, I lick one long stroke from her ass to her clit, scoring my teeth on the tiny nub. She moans, reaching for my head, but I grab her wrists and push them back up.

Her eyes open and she leans up to look at me. "I want—" She pauses and bites her lip.

"You wanna watch me eat you, baby?" She nods, a slight blush warming her cheeks. "Fuck yeah, keep your eyes on me." Her ass jumps off the bed as I lightly pop her clit with my hand before soothing it with my tongue. She moans, her head thrashing as she's consumed by lust.

Her hips lift off the bed when I suck her clit into my mouth, so I anchor my arm over her waist to hold her down. She grinds into my mouth, desperate for more. I take advantage of her lust fueled actions and press my thumb against her puckered hole. She gasps and stiffens slightly.

I chuckle against her pussy. "Don't worry, baby, your ass is safe... *tonight,*" I taunt before plunging my fingers into her sweet pussy. *Fuck.* She's dripping for me. The urge to drive my cock deep inside her almost overwhelms me, but Willow seems to have other plans for her sinful body tonight.

Grabbing my cock, she uses the distraction to her advantage and rolls me over onto my back. I lift a brow. "There something you want, sweetheart?"

Her cheeks are on fire, but my girl holds strong and bites her lip, eyes darting to where her hand is jacking my dick. Well I'll be damned. "You wanna ride this cock, baby?" Her resounding moan is all the answer I need. Gripping her hips, I lift her off the bed and lower her down my cock, inch by inch.

The urge to cum hits me hard as she tilts her hips, adjusting to the feel of sitting on my cock for the first time. *Fuck, she's killing me.* She finally starts to move up and down, drenching my shaft with each stroke. Her nails dig into my chest, leaving tiny half moons in their wake, but I relish the pain, and crave her marks.

As Willow rides my cock, lost in her own pleasure, I lick the pad of my thumb before dropping it to her where her tiny clit peeks at me. I make it one full circle before she cries out, her body trembling with the force of her orgasm.

My balls are heavy with the need to fill her with my cum, but I manage to hold off until the last ripple of her pussy around my cock. Depleted, her body falls to my chest and I grip her ass, pushing her down against me with each thrust of my dick.

"You gonna come inside me, baby?" She licks my jaw and grabs my earlobe in her teeth. "Fill me up, Priest, fill up my pussy with your cum."

My dick tunnels through her slick heat chasing its own release, but all it takes are her words, and I'm spilling inside her with a roar.

WASHED IN BLOOD

CHAPTER 17

PRIEST

My skin tingles with anticipation. The men have been on edge lately and I'm hoping after tonight some of the tension will subside. My phone rings from where it sits on my desk and I reach out to accept the call. "Yeah."

"Everything's in place," Angel tells me.

A rush of adrenaline courses through me. *It's time.*

"Take him." Standing, I pocket my phone before closing my laptop. I slip on my worn leather jacket that fits like a second skin, and I leave my office.

When I reach the living room, I smile at Willow lying on the couch curled up and surrounded by blankets, sipping a cup of hot chocolate. She smiles when she spots me. "Hey."

"Hey," I murmur against her forehead before kissing her.

"You going somewhere?" she asks eyeing my jacket.

I pause before answering. Hearing that I've killed people, that *each* of us have killed is different from knowing that's what I'm leaving to do. But if Willow is going to be my old lady, she has to accept each of us. That includes the blood staining our hands.

"Got some sinners coming tonight." I gauge her reaction.

She seems stunned at first, but quickly recovers. "And do they deserve it?"

"Yes," I say.

"Okay." She nods before snuggling back in facing the TV again. "Don't be gone too long."

I stand staring at her, shocked at how well she handled that. I shouldn't be surprised. Willow has taught me an entirely new level of strength that I'm constantly in awe of. I cup her face and press a kiss to her lips, only pulling back once we're both panting and struggling to keep up with our breaths. "Made for me," I murmur against her lips.

"Yeah," she agrees softly.

"You got your phone?" I check.

"Yes, Master," she mocks, and I feel my dick harden.

"Careful, princess," I warn. "I don't know if you're ready for those type of games yet."

Willow flushes bright red and I chuckle darkly.

"Not funny," she gripes, causing me to laugh harder.

"Text me if you need me. All the guys are gone so don't turn the alarm off." My sassy girl lifts her hand in a mock salute, and I smile.

"Night babe." I walk out the door and transform into a Priest she doesn't recognize. I start up my bike and head in the direction of the lodge. It's time for confession.

Angel and Patch's bikes are already parked when I pull up at the lodge which means Demon and Bullet aren't back with Hemminger and Myles. I walk through the door and I'm met with silence, but that's nothing new. Silence is always the first and last sound heard here. But the in between? The in between is filled with tortured screams, the likes of which haunt the darkest of nightmares.

The heavy metal door slams behind me and Patch looks up. The excitement in his eyes quickly dims when he sees it's only me.

I chuckle at his obvious disappointment. "Careful, Doc, I can feel your excitement from here," I joke.

Patch flips me the bird, mumbling something under his breath before turning his attention back to his laptop.

I glance at Angel to try to read his mood. Even though he may seem fine on the outside, if I learned anything this week, it's that he's a better actor than we've all given him credit for.

"You okay?" I ask quietly so Patch doesn't hear.

Angel doesn't look up from where he's prepping his weapons of choice for the night. "I'm good." He grunts and reaches into his bag to pull out his favorite instruments. I can't hold back the wince at seeing the cheese grater and corkscrew that he places on the table.

Christ, we're going to have a mess to clean up.

The crunch of gravel alerts us to an approaching vehicle. A glance to Patch shows he's already checking the security cameras we have set up around the property. Clicking on the screen detecting movement, he zooms in to check the vehicle before giving me a chin lift.

They're here. The door to the converted garage swings open and Demon walks in dragging a screaming and thrashing Principal Hemminger behind him. Of the two men, Hemminger was the more difficult to plan. Not only did we have to make sure we covered each and every possible scenario that could result from him leaving town, we needed to ensure that in the days leading up, he didn't hand over any other girls to the Russos.

"Piece of shit! I'll kill you, you fucking bastard!" his screams echo off the empty walls.

Hemminger groans when Demon jerks his victim's legs at just the right moment, causing his head to crack against the solid cinder blocks that are stacked haphazardly around the room. I shake my head and glance at Demon who smirks back. With a grunt, Demon leans down and grips the rope that binds Hemminger's hands and legs before he hefts the fat piece of shit onto the table. As soon as he's in place, Angel and Patch fasten him to the table using leather belts.

Hemminger screams and fights against his bonds. His crazed eyes make him appear as though he's a mental patient those exact belts were once used on. The struggle finally takes its toll on his body as exhaustion seeps in and he collapses against the cold metal. Tears run down his face as pathetic begs replace the vile threats he'd been using only moments ago.

"Please, you—you've got the wrong guy. This is all some kind of mistake."

It's time to make my presence known. I stand from the chair disguised by the darkness of the room and stroll to the table. The other men have already shed their cuts in preparation for the night's festivities, but mine is still on. When I step into his line of sight and our MC patch is finally visible, Hemminger's face pales so fast he may pass out before we can start, which defeats the purpose of *torture.*

"Are you Andrew Duane Hemminger of two-ninety-four Westbooke Lane? Forty-seven years old, Principal of Aspen Mountain High?" I ask the slimy piece of shit in front of me.

"Yes." The pathetic piece of shit shakes as he replies.

"Then we've got the right guy."

Angel slides a chair to me, the metal legs screech against the concrete. I take a seat, eye level with the good principal, and lay out exactly why he's here. What kind of Priest would I be if I didn't give him a chance to confess? "You know who I am?" I ask as I scrub a spot of motor oil from my hand. When he doesn't answer I lift my head and raise my brow, waiting. You don't live in our town and not know who I am, who the MC is. "Now, now." I tsk. "You should always answer when spoken to, Andrew. As a principal, I'm sure you understand the importance of manners."

"Yes." He nods vigorously. "I know who you are."

I grin wide and slap my hand roughly against his shoulder. "Atta boy," I praise him. "That wasn't so hard now was it? I just wanna ask you some questions, that's all." Relief floods his features as the men around me chuckle. *Happens every time.*

"Now, Andrew," I say, my tone drips with sarcasm. "I'm sure this is all just one big mistake on our part, but we have to check into things when they're brought to our attention. You understand, right?"

Hemminger nods. "Oh yeah—I mean, yes. I absolutely understand. It's the same being a principal. Have to uphold the rules and all," he babbles.

I nod in fake excitement and snap my fingers, "Exactly! So you see, when we got intel that you sold a girl from your own school to the Russo Mob, that's a claim we have to investigate."

"Of course." He nods like a good little school boy. But it's not long before my words sink through his terrified exterior and cause his eyes to go wide as his breathing stalls.

"Now I'm going to tell you, Andrew, when I first heard about this, I knew there had to be some kind of mistake. Who would believe an upstanding citizen such as yourself, could commit such a vile, heinous act?"

"Heinous…" Hemminger whispers under his breath, terror drips from every syllable.

I stand from the chair and his body jolts against the leather belts as he whimpers. I walk to where Bullet is standing, arm extended and holding the same file he gave each of us earlier this week.

Inside the file, I find the picture of the shy, doe-eyed teen this monster sent to the lion's den. I toss the file onto a nearby table before I walk back to where the piss-ant lies and shove the picture in his face. Like the little bitch he is, Hemminger closes his eyes and attempts to turn his face away.

"Look at it," I demand. He whimpers and shakes his head, eyes squeezed shut. "FUCKING LOOK AT IT!" I roar.

Demon's boots pound against the floor as he stomps to the head of the table and grabs Hemminger's head between his hands. Demon turns his hands until the man's face is pointing toward me and the picture, still grasped between my fingertips.

Using his thumbs, Demon pries his clenched lids open, forcing him to look at the face that should haunt his nightmares.

An agonized wail escapes his chest. "Oh, God—I'm sorry. I'm so fucking sorry." His body shakes with the force of his cries. "Please, God. Please, forgive me."

I have no sympathy for the man. In our world, you pay for your sins in blood. And it's time to make him bleed.

I lean down, my mouth next to his ear. "Unfortunately for you, I'm your God tonight," I say as he begs for his life to be spared.

I shake my head in disgust. "And Andrew?" I have his eyes before delivering my final part. "Thank you for your confession." I walk away, leaving him in the hands of a Demon.

Hemminger's tortured wails fill the silence of the abandoned lodge, quickly followed by the metallic scent of blood.

One down, one to go.

An hour and a half later, we're creeping up on 1 a.m., and for the first time since I started the MC, I'm considering skipping Myles Davis's penance so I can get back to Willow.

I don't like that she's been alone so long. And even though she texted me an hour ago saying all was well and she was going to bed, I can't ignore the prickling sensation on the back of my neck telling me something isn't right. Luckily, Myles will be a quicker case. Angel doesn't have the same patience Demon does.

I walk back into the converted garage from taking a break outside to check my phone. Myles is already in place. Angel has him tied to a chair, preferring his victims to be seated rather than lying down. Angel hovers by, anxious to get started, but it's customary for me to make sure they know why they're here before we go any further.

It doesn't change the outcome if they have no idea or refuse to admit it, but it's a ritual I've always made sure to include and this time is no different. I take a seat on the chair directly across from Myles before crossing my arms.

"Priest," he greets me.

"Myles," I return meeting his cool stare.

"You know why you're here?"

He shrugs. "Eh. Figured you'd come for me eventually," he says. "It was only a matter of time."

"Cut the shit. It's late, I'm tired and I'm fuckin' ready to go home." I glare. "He's all yours, Angel." I stand from the chair having had enough of his games, but his next words stop me in my tracks.

"Yeah," he murmurs appreciatively. "I'd be hurrying home too if I had that sweet little piece of ass waiting in my bed."

I charge him so fast the others don't stand a chance of stopping me. I fist his shirt as my right fist connects with his face. Myles's head snaps back with a chilling crunch. If it weren't for his muffled groan, I would have thought I killed him.

The chair he's tied to teeters on its legs before it crashes back onto the unforgiving concrete.

I crouch over him and jerk his body up until he's facing me.

"The fuck did you just say?" I seethe.

Myles grins, his teeth stained with the blood that pours from the gash in his lip. "Heard you've been having a little trouble at the club *and* the garage. Such a shame."

I try to mask my surprise, but his cocky chuckle tells me I didn't succeed and I growl low in my throat.

"What do you know?"

"I know a lot of things," the shit twerp mocks.

I release another punch this time to his kidney causing him to hunch into himself. Looking to my right, I catch sight of Patch. "Pliers."

Seconds pass before a pair of pliers are tossed to me. Knowing my next move, Bullet helps grip Myles's head before prying his mouth open and fitting a wooden block inside. Securing my grip on the pliers, I reach in for a rear molar, but before I can grip it, Myles squeals like a little bitch. His body thrashes wildly in an attempt to dislodge the pliers' grip. Saliva pours from his mouth, trailing down his jaw and soaking his shirt. He blubbers unintelligibly, so I remove the block.

"I—I know who's behind it. I'll tell you, I swear," he pleads pathetically.

"Name," I snarl.

Myles shakes his head. "Man, it ain't that simple. You rat once, you're a rat for life."

"Good thing yours won't be lasting much longer anyway." I shrug. "No skin off your nose."

The men around me laugh and Myles's gaze darts to the door at my back. Turning to look at the closed door, I chuckle before turning back to Myles.

"You expecting someone, Myles? Cause if you are, they're late." I smirk.

He shakes his head in denial. "No, no, no! This—this isn't how it was supposed to go down. They just told me to do something to distract you, get you all in the same place."

"Who?" I growl, shaking him by his shirt. "I need a fucking name."

"They'll kill me," he chokes out.

"You're dying tonight either way." I chuckle but it holds no humor. "I'll let you decide if you take them down with you."

The filthy weasel doesn't take the out. "Don't think I'm gonna be able to do that."

"Fine by me." I shrug before looking to Bullet. "Tell me, Bullet. Myles got a mama?" I ask, though I already know the answer.

"Nah. Bitch got rid of him while she could," he says.

His answer causes Myles to snarl. "Fuck you, man. Fuck. You." He spits at me, but I ignore him.

"Yeah, I didn't think he had a mama." I sit a second pretending to think. "He got a daddy?"

"Nah, he ain't got one of those either." Bullet chuckles.

"Well fuck," I mutter in fake disappointment before sitting silent several more seconds.

I snap my fingers. "Oh! I remember now."

"Tell me, Myles, just how is your brother doing these days?"

191

Myles's face drains of color. "No," he begs. "He's a good kid. He ain't got nothing to do with me."

"Then tell me their goddamn names."

Myles drops his head in defeat. "Give me your word you won't touch him, and I'll tell you what you want to know."

"You give me the *names,* then we'll talk."

"I don't know their names. Just what they wanted me to do," he says

"You gotta give me more than that, Myles. It's not enough and you fucking know it."

I wonder if I'm doing the right thing. The kid sitting in front of me is exactly what I imagined he would be. Or, at least he was... right up until I mentioned his brother. Looking at him now, I see the product of shit circumstances that life threw his way.

Fuck. Am I getting soft?

"Three weeks ago, I was contacted by a couple men. They never said their names, just that they were ready for war and were looking for a few men to gather soldiers. Said they'd heard about me around town and thought I was a good fit. Said I knew a lot of people and would be able to recruit good numbers."

The tension in the room is almost suffocating. Being in the life, there are words we all know. War, soldiers, recruits. Words that become as common to us as teen girls and Starbucks, but they don't bring the same warm and fuzzies. War is something we've managed to avoid since we started our MC. Other than a close call six years ago, we've managed to stay under the radar. Knowing someone has us in their sights has my gut tightening with unease.

"Did they say why?"

Myles shakes his head. "They're tired of you ruling the streets. Said it was time for someone new to be in charge."

My eyes dart to Bullet. That is not something we want to hear.

"And you expect me to believe you didn't ask who they were?" I ask.

"Believe it if you want to or not, boss. I don't give a fuck who they are. They offered cash and pussy, and I took it."

And just like that, all thoughts of Myles having something real underneath that bad boy hood exterior, evaporate.

"I told you what you wanted to know, now I want your word," Myles says, his tough guy face back in place.

"Lucky for your brother, innocent people are safe from us. Sinners are our only concern."

From the corner of my eye, I see Angel closing in, ready to finish what I started. I stand and drag the chair across the floor to move it from Angel's path when I remember something.

"Did it bother you even a little?" I ask him.

"What?" he says, brows drawn together.

"You were paid to beat and rape a teenage girl to get our attention. Now you're going to pay the ultimate price."

Myles laughs manically to the point of tears escaping his eyes. "Oh man. You have no idea, do you?"

I wait for him to finish. I'm done fishing for answers. This is all a game to him, and I'm no longer playing.

"They didn't pay me to rape her. That was all me." He grins proudly.

Wait, what? "Then what was your job?"

"Tell me, Priest, how long's it been since you checked in with the Mrs.?"

WASHED IN BLOOD

CHAPTER 18

WILLOW

The sound of the lock turning echoes throughout the room when Priest closes the door. I sit, staring at the TV, seeing but no longer processing what's playing on the screen. My chest loosens with the breath I was holding through the entire conversation that just took place.

Laying my head against the back of the couch, I close my eyes and think about what Priest and the others are on their way to do. I also wonder when I became the type of person to sit and watch *Project Runway* instead of calling the police. *Is that even a real question?* Inner me says cattily. *Shut up,* I sass back.

Ugh. I honestly don't know if I've ever been that person. Growing up the way I did, the environments I was subjected to, meant I never had the pleasure of wearing those rose-colored glasses kids are so often accused of having. I was not spared from the horrors of the world solely because I was a child. If anything, I saw them more. I'm not sure if the people around me assumed that since I was *just a kid*, I had no idea what I was seeing, or if they just didn't care. I'm no stranger to the darkness that lurks in this world. It's already touched my life in more ways than I care to count.

So far, I've managed to steer clear from any conversations that may lead to questions about my childhood. How do you explain to the man you're falling in love with that you're a murderer? *God, do you have to be so dramatic?* Okay, fine. So calling myself a murderer is a bit of a stretch, but it only takes hearing something so many times before you start to believe it yourself. It was no secret that my mom died during childbirth, and the knowledge cost me greatly in my childhood years. I was known as *Weeping Willow*. The other foster kids claimed that everywhere I went, death followed in my wake. I snort to myself. I sound like the punch line to a horror movie.

Shaking the thoughts from my head, I return my focus to the TV. A sudden rush of nausea forces my hand over my mouth. *Ugh.* Lately, the nausea has been getting worse. It's almost like the baby is reminding me I have more than one secret I need to come clean about.

I need to do it soon. History has shown that karma seems to have an extra speciality for making me her bitch.

Placing a hand on my lower abdomen, I cradle the small baby bump. My heart almost hurts with how much I love this baby. I only hope Priest comes to feel the same way.

You really believe he's going to stick around and raise someone else's baby? You'll be back on the streets in no time. Right where trash like you belongs.

Tears flood my eyes at the thought. *Don't think like that. He's going to understand. He has to.*

I get up from the couch and switch the TV off before I head to the kitchen to fix a glass of milk and warm some chocolate chip cookies before I head into Priest's room. I wonder if I'll ever get used to seeing my things mixed with his. The few small pieces of jewelry I've acquired since I've been here are laying on top of the dresser, mingled with various leather bracelets and chains of Priest's.

The freshly mounted TV is the newest addition to our room. I grab the remote and climb into bed to finish the last episode of *Project Runway*. Once I'm settled, I giggle as I remember the scene Priest caused when he found me in Angel's bed yet again. His macho appearance was all for show though, he knows I'm safe with Angel. Still, it feels good to know he wants me here in *our* bed.

The episode finishes and I watch the previews for next week while I pop the last bite of gooey chocolate goodness into my mouth. After brushing my teeth and washing my face, I climb back into bed and turn the lamp off.

I settle down into the covers and scoot to Priest's side, relishing in the scent of his cologne on the pillow. For the first time since I was a girl, I'm one hundred percent content with my life. If I want to stay that way, I have to tell Priest about the baby. I can only pray he cares about me enough to stay when he finds out, instead of becoming yet another man to leave me behind.

I wake with a jolt, my eyes heavy with sleep as I wince at the blaring red numbers on the bedside table. I blink several times attempting to clear the sleep from my eyes and focus. 1:27 a.m. Ugh. I stretch my arm out toward Priest, but instead of his warm body, my skin meets the cool sheets. *Where is he?* Does it normally take this long to kill someone? Scolding myself for not asking more questions, I reach for my phone sitting on the nightstand, but I freeze when I hear glass shatter somewhere in the house.

It's been nearly two months since the nightmare that led me to tell Priest of how I ended up in the forest. Two months of retraining years of ingrained reactions to fit my new life. No longer do I need to cower in fear for talking without permission, or hide at the sound of slamming doors. I'm learning how to subdue those reactions. But this… this is not one of those times.

I hold my breath, frozen with fear. This time, it's not glass shattering but the unmistakable crunch of shoes splintering the shattered pieces. Oh god. *Run.* Adrenaline floods my system and causes my hands to shake uncontrollably. Years of experience with this very feeling has my body trained and I move from under the covers, grab my phone from the dresser, and immediately mute the ringer.

Keeping my ears trained on the door, I make it to the closet where I grab the first pair of shoes I can find. I clutch them to my chest, fitting my back against the wall in an attempt to steady my breathing. Hopefully the intruder will make another sound and alert me to their location in the house.

After several seconds of silence, I know my time is running out. I have to move. Eventually, they'll make it to this room and no matter my size, they'll find me. My body remains frozen, warring with the demands of my mind. Mentally, I map out the quickest way to an exit.

The closest door is at the other end of the hallway. To get there, I'll have to pass through the living room, which from the sound of the glass breaking earlier, is where they entered. Bile rises in my throat. I may not make it out of this alive. I've come so far and after everything, I'm going to die in a place where I've never felt safer.

My tummy flutters and tears roll silently down my face as I barely manage to choke back my sobs. I have to try. This isn't just about me anymore. I count to five before I make my move.

When I open the bedroom door, pitch darkness greets me. My eyes are open wide as if it will help me see in the dark. As I move down the hall, I try my best to place my location based on my steps. My ears perk, and I still as the sound of wind and sleet pierce the silence.

Taking a risk, I dart toward the sound of the elements, but I let out a harsh cry as my body is jerked back by an unforgiving fist in my hair.

"Well lookie what we have here." The stench of his breath makes me gag, but it's his hardness pressing against my leg that makes me lose my stomach. With a grunt, the man pushes me to the ground, disgusted by the action.

I hit the ground hard and take advantage of my momentary freedom. I scramble forward and make it to the door, but before I get it open, I find myself in the man's clutches again.

No. I'm too close. Too fucking close to go out like this. Bucking wildly, I flail and hit, making purchase anywhere my hands and feet can reach. Finally, I get the money shot and my captor hits the ground with a groan, cupping his groin. "Fucking bitch!" he hisses.

"What the fuck, man," another voice shouts from somewhere in the house.

"In here!" the man on the floor yells. The sound of shoes thundering against the floor has me darting through the door and into the storm.

Yells pierce the night as the men shout at me.

I yelp as branches and limbs cut the tender skin of my legs. My feet scream in agony as the chill of the snow invades. My feet sink several inches in the layers of snow before they reach solid ground as I pump my legs. I run as hard and fast as I can; my mind screaming at me to find safety—shelter. *Priest!* He's not here. It's up to me to save myself, an action which has become all too familiar.

I don't know how far I've run or for how long, but when pain tears through my stomach, my legs give way and I fall to my hands and knees with a groan. The moon gives me enough light to make out my immediate surroundings, so I crawl to the nearest tree and prop my body against its base.

Another cramp tears through my abdomen and I cover my mouth as tiny whimpers escape. After my body has settled and my breathing has returned to normal, I fight to keep my eyes open. It's not long before exhaustion consumes me, and I concede to the darkness.

"Princess." Fingertips gently caress my face. "Come on, baby. You gotta wake up for me." I try to open my eyes, but they're so heavy. I need to sleep a little while longer. "Hang on for me, sweetheart. I'm almost there." I lift my arm to swat him away, but it drops heavily at my side. His persistent voice continues, teasing me. "You do like your sleep."

"Willow!" he shouts before I'm pulled back under.

Cracking my eyes, I glare at the man who holds my heart. "And yet you woke me anyway."

There's a chuckle of laughter. "I know I did, but you have to stay awake. I'm almost here, princess, I'm so close—just a little longer, okay?"

"Willow!" He's closer now, but the darkness won't release me from its grasp.

I reach out to him, my fingertips brush past his jaw. "When will I see you again?"

My eyes close as he leans forward and presses his lips to my forehead. "Soon, sweetheart. Real soon."

"Oh fuck. Oh shit. Willow, baby—" Hands frantically search my body, gripping my face and arms.

Voice cracking, he bellows, "Patch!"

"Come on, Willow, open your eyes for me, sweetheart, open those eyes," he begs before shouting Patch's name again.

I fight with all my might to open my eyes, but the darkness calls to me, and this time I'm not strong enough to deny it.

CHAPTER 19

PRIEST

S cooping Willow's body into my arms causes a rush of memories to assault me. Memories of doing the exact same thing months before crash into me and my heart clenches in my chest as rage thunders through my veins.

Clutching her lifeless body to my chest, I run as quickly as I can back to the compound. Dawn is just starting to break, the sky lighting my path through the dense woods. God, we've been searching for her for hours. The guys didn't think there was any way she could have made it this far from the clubhouse, but something was pulling me—leading me this way. Thank fuck I listened.

Breaching the edge of the woods, Angel runs toward us, phone lifted to his ear. "Ambulance is thirty minutes out."

She doesn't have that long. "Grab my keys and get the truck." Angel darts inside the house to get my keys. Bullet opens the door, allowing me to climb inside while still cradling Willow.

"Priest!" Patch emerges from the woods not far from where we exited. Racing to the truck, his face pales when he sees Willow. "We'll meet you at the hospital," he says as Angel climbs into the driver's seat.

"She's gonna be okay, man," he says, confidence in his tone.

Looking down at my broken princess, I cup her cold face in my hands and gently kiss her lips. *She better be. Or I'll storm the gates of whatever afterlife she goes to and join her there for eternity.*

Patch runs out of the doctor's bay as we pull up to the emergency room. The screech of the truck's tires against the pavement alerts several more staff members who come running over to help.

I've never felt as empty and as helpless as I do the moment I lay Willow's frail body against the gurney. Her arms dangle lifelessly, and my breath catches in my throat. *She has to live.* My knees buckle under the weight of the realization—I failed her.

"Clear the room!" A nurse rushes to herd us in the direction of the door. "Get these clothes off her."

A doctor leans over Willow's unconscious body and shines a penlight into her eyes. "She's responsive. I need an IV started, stat. Push one liter of fluids." He continues barking orders as the nurse cuts off Willow's shirt and pants.

My eyes catch on the soft, round swell of her abdomen. My brows furrow, searching for bruising around the area but all I find is smooth creamy skin.

The door slams shut, blocking my view and forcing me to step back to where Patch is waiting. "What's going to happen to her?"

He grips my shoulder, giving it a reassuring squeeze. "They'll do an assessment, take blood. Run scans if they need them. She's in good hands here, Priest." His words should be all the reassurance I need, but they do nothing to calm the storm raging inside.

Bullet steps forward and claps his hand across my back. "I'm gonna head to the cafeteria and grab some coffee. Be right back."

As he walks away, an older nurse with kind eyes approaches me with a clipboard in her hands. "Hi there, my name is Margot. I'm one of the intake nurses here in the ER." She hands me the clipboard. "If you could fill this out as soon as possible, the more information we have the better."

With a quick glance at the paperwork on the clipboard, I sigh.

Patting my arm, Margot gives me a warm smile. "Your wife is going to be okay, she's in good—"

I cut her off. "Girlfriend, Willow's my girlfriend." I flip through the paperwork filled with questions I can't answer.

Margot's brow creases. "Oh, you're not her next of kin?"

"No. But she has no one else." As far as I know, that's the truth, but it's all irrelevant now. No matter her past, that woman's future is mine.

An hour later, I've filled out Willow's name. A name that may very well not even be her real one since our searches of it bared no fruit. The rest of the paperwork is still blank, and no one will answer my questions because I'm not her next of kin.

Bullet sits next to me in a silent show of support.

"I know almost nothing about her."

"Does that really matter?" he questions.

I don't answer. We both know it doesn't.

An hour later, we're all tired and pissed off. No one has updated me and each time I asked her status, I was told I'd have to wait since I wasn't Willow's "next of kin". Fucking Patch wasn't helping my mood either with his refusal to go check on her. When a tiny mouse of a nurse finally approaches me, I glance around the waiting room. As I stand, the other occupants move clear of my warpath.

"Um, ex-excuse me, sir? Doctor Nijaro sent me to get you. The um, young lady you brought in, she's been moved to a room and—"

"Where. Is. She."

She squeaks and jumps back at my harsh tone as Bullet stands, partially blocking her from my sight. Taking in his protective stance pisses me off. Does he really think I'd ever hurt a woman? "Brother," I warn, "you do not want to do that."

"You need to calm the fuck down." He stands his ground, one arm behind him steadying the terrified nurse.

Heaving a deep sigh, I look back to the nurse. "Please, lead the way."

Eyes wide and darting back and forth between Patch and myself, her head nods in jerky movements. "Follow me." She turns, leading us out of the emergency waiting room.

We take the elevator to the fourth floor before stepping off. The soft pastel hues of blue and yellow walls are a stark contrast to the sterile white walls and the strong scent that lingered in the emergency room. Several of the rooms we pass have pink and blue wreaths on the doors and with a quick glance at my men, I see confusion mirrored on their faces. All except Patch whose face has gone deathly pale.

"She's resting now, but the doctor will come speak with you soon... Um, o—only—" The nurse hesitates, drawing a shaky breath before edging closer to Bullet. "Only two of you can go in." Bullet, Angel, and Demon step back, knowing they'll be waiting outside. "I'll just let the doctor know you're here." She scurries away.

The weight on my chest releases when I see Willow's dark lashes resting peacefully against her pinked cheeks. But my heart clenches at how frail and vulnerable she looks lying in the middle of the hospital bed. The steady beep of her heart rate on the monitor puts my racing one at ease as I take a seat beside the bed. I'm vaguely aware of Patch walking up to check the monitors before examining the bags they have dripping steadily into her IV.

"All good?" I ask, not removing my eyes from Willow and the steady rise and fall of her chest.

Patch grunts his approval before sitting in a chair across the room. His coloring has returned to normal, but it doesn't last long, draining as soon as the doctor walks in.

I stand as the doctor, dressed in a white coat and scrubs, enters the room before closing the door behind him. "I apologize for the wait. I had a patient's waters break just as I was notified you were ready for me." Pushing his glasses up his nose, he extends his other arm to me. "Bradley Martin, I've been looking after Willow since she was brought up for observation."

"Priest." I give his hand a firm shake. "She gonna be okay?" Gripping the tablet in his left hand, he swipes his fingers several times before speaking. "Right, so whe—"

"Priest." My body jerks toward the bed at Willow's hoarse croak. I rush back to the bedside and cup her face, softly kissing her lips before resting my forehead against hers. "Never letting you out of my sight again." She nuzzles her face into my hands.

The doctor clears his throat and Willow jumps. She frowns before looking around the room in confusion. "What happ—oh god!" She gasps, eyes darting to mine in fear.

As subtle as I can, I shake my head, hoping she gets the hint. Whatever happened to her, doesn't need to get out. The last thing we need are the police sticking their noses where they don't belong.

The doctor clears his throat. "Would you like me to come back later?"

"No, Doc. Please continue."

"As I was saying, when Willow was first brought in, she was showing signs of severe dehydration and hypothermia. Other than that, all the scans and bloodwork came back normal." Dr. Martin presses several buttons on a machine by the bed before making notes in his chart. "Once you finish this bag of fluids, I see no reason why you can't leave." He aims a polite smile at Willow. "No more exploring the woods, young lady. You might not be so lucky next time."

Willow chuckles.

Fuck. I could have lost her today. Overwhelmed with an intense burst of gratitude and love for this woman, I wrap my arms protectively around her before pulling her closer to my side. "Don't worry, Doc. I'm not letting her out of my sight again."

"That's good to hear." Moving to her bedside he lowers the blankets that have been warming her body. Pressing around her abdomen, he taps a few times while assessing Willow's reaction. "All good? No pain or discomfort?"

Willow's "No," is barely audible.

The doctor nods. "Well, your stats have remained steady since you were brought up for observation. Despite the dehydration, you haven't shown any signs of contractions or preterm labor." The doctor walks to the sink across the room and washes his hands while I stare at the stranger in front of me.

He continues to ask her a few more questions. Words like "fetal development", "gestation" and "prenatal vitamins" are fired off one after the other. *A patient's water broke.* The doctor's earlier words hit me like a punch to the gut.

My mind drifts away as I take in the room surrounding me. Pastel walls, bright, colorful paintings of nursery rhyme characters alongside framed black and white portraits of newborn babies. A rocking chair sits in one corner beside a rolling cart with a bassinet on top. Diapers and wipes fill the lower shelves along with pale yellow blankets. On the bedside table, a booklet reads *Your New Baby*. Fighting to remain calm, I let my eyes close as everything clicks into place.

Willow is pregnant.

A plethora of emotions flood my system, sending it into overdrive. Happiness unlike anything I've ever known is quickly chased out by the realization of what I almost lost today. *Christ. I could have lost them both.*

Coming back into the conversation, I listen closely as the doctor continues, "I'd like to get a sonogram before you go just to be safe. Do you know how far along you are?"

Willow's eyes flicker to me nervously before landing back on the doctor. *Did she already know?* There's no way she can be more than—

"Um… about 17 weeks, I think."

And in one defining moment, my world stops. I clamp my eyes shut as my heart splinters deep inside my chest. *Fuck no. Please tell me this is all some kind of sick fucking joke.* When I finally open my eyes, Patch is there. One look at his remorseful eyes tells me all I need to know. This is real.

Vomit threatens its way up my throat. I may be a man, but I know how babies are made. It takes time. I also know by doing some simple math, that the baby inside my woman—isn't mine.

WASHED IN BLOOD

CHAPTER 20

PRIEST

The click of the door closing behind the doctor echoes through the silent room. My skin itches, feeling ten sizes too small for the hurricane sized emotions currently invading every inch of my body. We haven't been together long, but Willow's already become a permanent fixture in my life and the thought of losing her now, kills me. Fuck… I think I fell in love with her the second I pulled her lifeless body from the hollow log in the woods.

"Priest," she begs, apology in her tone, but it doesn't distract me from my anger.

"Got something you need to tell me, baby?" There's an aggressive edge to my voice I can't hide.

She shrinks down, rubbing her eyes. "I—I was going to tell you."

Scrubbing my hands down my face, I step back, barely able to look at her. Everything I thought I knew about this woman, was wrong.

"When?" I demand. "Next week? Next fucking month?" How long was she going to keep this a secret?

Her head jerks back as if I've slapped her, and her hands shoot up to her mouth. A mumbled "I'm so sorry" leaves her lips, but I've heard enough.

Leaning down to her, I enunciate every syllable as if I'm speaking to a child. "Whatever this was between us, it's over." My words cut me to the core, but I'll be damned if I spend the rest of my life taking care of some other bastard's child.

A sob breaks free from her chest as she chokes back tears. "Prie—"

Patch clears his throat and I turn to him. I narrow my eyes at his sheepish expression and refusal to meet my gaze.

"You knew?" I sneer at the double-edged betrayal that's been shoved into my back tonight.

A pathetic nod is all I get as he shuffles from foot to foot. *Lying bastard.*

Closing the distance between us, I glare at him. "How long?"

He shoves his hands into his pockets and stares down at his boots. There's no way in hell I'm letting him ignore me this time. Doctor patient confidentiality went out the window when *they both* decided to fuck me over.

Both of them! A sudden thought forces its way into my turbulent mind. I fist his shirt in my hands and shove him against the wall. "That your fuckin' baby inside her?" Patch's head whips back so hard it slams against the wall. I tug him forward before slamming him back again. "I said, is that your fucking baby inside her?"

Face red with rage, he shoves me back and raises a fist. "Are you fucking serious?" The smack against my jaw is unexpected, but well deserved. *Damn that bastard throws a mean punch.*

What else am I supposed to think? My thoughts are in disarray. I fucking love this woman... *I love her.* But right now, my love for her is clouding my vision and I'm beginning to question my own sanity. Pacing to the window, I run a frustrated hand through my hair. Willow said her ex was a bastard... Is this why she was running from him? To protect her unborn baby.

Glancing at her, a lump forms in my throat. Part of me wants to storm over there and pull her into my arms, tell her everything will be okay. But a bigger part of me is beyond pissed off, not to mention betrayed, especially by Patch.

"Priest, can we please tal—" Her soft voice tugs at my heart.

Raising my hand, I step back. "I'm done here." I turn to leave the room, and I don't look back.

* * *

Ever since I can remember, my actions, my life, has been dictated by someone else. I was never in control. Growing up in foster care doesn't leave you with many choices to be made for yourself, you're nothing more than a payday to them. It wasn't just foster care that took my voice from me, it was gone long before my biological mom ever was. She was never the *Leave it to Beaver* mom. I knew she loved me, but she fucked up more often than not.

Sometimes she'd forget to pick me up from school, or forget I was in the car and she'd leave me there while she went shopping. I think deep down, she *wanted* to be a good mom, and there were times when things were good, *great* even. She'd be so fucking happy it almost hurt to look at her when she shined so bright. But then something would happen and the scales would tip, that light inside her snuffed out so fast, I half expected her to have frostbite with how cold she was.

It wasn't until I was an adult that I realized how sick she really was. But for a kid who was getting candy for dinner and skipping school to go on adventures to the zoo, who was I to care that she had some bad days?

It's easy to look back now and shake my head at the things I never noticed. Like how she could afford to take me to the zoo when she had no job. Those things don't cross a six-year-old's mind. Not until you're getting picked up by a social worker because a John killed your mom when she refused to let him fuck her ass.

I've never had much control. I was always at the mercy of my mom's moods, scared to whisper a word for fear I would send her spiraling.

The first time I rode my bike, a piece of me clicked into place. It was the only time in my life I had complete control. Riding instantly became a form of therapy. So, on a day like today when the control I crave so desperately is ripped from my grasp, I ride hard.

Chasing the distance, my grip strengthens with every mile I gain. The only thing that could make it better would be having my brothers riding beside me, and my girl behind me. *My girl. Fuck.* Is she still my girl? Was she ever really?

There are so many questions I need answers to, but having to face her, knowing she's been keeping it from me... I can't do it. I need to be in the right frame of mind when I sit her down and lay it all out.

I've been riding the winding roads of the Aspen mountains for hours when the call of the road lessens. After turning around, I head back toward town, not stopping until I pull my bike up outside Corrupt, the club's bar.

Getting off the bike, my muscles scream in protest and I stretch my back before walking to the front doors of the club. Like every Saturday night, there are a line of men waiting for their turn to get a peek at the forbidden fruit held inside. Bruno, our bouncer, spots me walking up while pushing what appears to be an anxious bachelor party back.

He pulls the door open for me and tips his chin. "Boss."

I stop just inside the door, running my gaze along the crowd in front of the stage before glancing at the bar. "Any problems?" Everything looks to be running smoothly right now, but I like to stay informed of any issues I may have missed.

"Nah." He glances at the waiting bachelor party. "Just the usual so far. Had to throw out Dave Morrison earlier when he got a little handsy with Ginger. Nothing I can't handle."

I make a mental note to stop at the drug store and check in with ole Dave. "Sounds good my man. Stay vigilant." I slap him on the back before heading deeper into the club.

After taking a seat at the bar, I lift two fingers to signal the bartender, Malcom. Making his way down the bar, he pulls a rag from his back pocket and wipes the area in front of me before laying down a clean bar napkin. "Usual boss?"

"Whiskey." It's going to take something a hell of a lot stronger than my usual Killian's to erase this clusterfuck of a day.

When he returns with my whiskey, he places it on the napkin before turning to leave, no questions asked.

For the next hour, I attempt to drown my sorrows, searching for answers at the bottom of every glass, but they're not there. No amount of alcohol can erase the moment I realized the woman I'm in love with has been lying to me for months. The pain I felt at hearing the depth of her betrayal—a knife to the heart would have been kinder.

Hours later, the betrayal still burns, searing its way through my insides. How am I supposed to trust her now?

I'm on my third refill when he finally shows up.

The bar stool to my right scrapes against the wooden floor when Patch pulls it away from the bar. Taking a seat, he signals Malcom then points at the amber filled glass tumbler in my hands.

"You ready to talk yet?" Patch eyes me over the rim of his drink.

Throwing back the rest of my drink, I shrug. "Think I said all I have to say."

"So that's it then? You're just gonna throw her away like every other person in her life." His lips curl in disgust.

I shove away from the bar and turn to face him. "What would you have me do? She's carrying another man's baby. I got no right to that."

"And what? The piece of shit she's running from *does*? Have you stopped to think about the fact that she could be running *because* she's pregnant? Or have you only been thinking about yourself?" he sneers.

Sitting back, I stare into my empty glass not willing to give him the satisfaction of seeing my face. *Fuck, he's right.* Not once have I thought about what she's been through or that she could have been running to protect her baby. *Shit.* When my mind first pieced together what the doctor was saying I was hit with an array of emotions. The love I felt in that moment for a baby I didn't know existed, filled up every space of my black heart until it was so full I was sure it would burst. Realizing I could have lost Willow *and* our baby, almost brought me to my knees.

I wouldn't survive losing her. *Then what the fuck are you doing here, dumbass?* "Fuck."

Patch chuckles. "Yep. That's about right."

When I stand from my stool, the alcohol I've been chugging like water for the past three hours hits me and I sway on my feet.

"Just where do you think you're going?" Patch grips my arm to steady me so I don't fall on my ass.

I shrug his arm off, the move causing me to sway again, so I grab the bar. "You know where I'm going," I growl.

"So what, you can get in a wreck and die before you have the chance to grovel and win your girl back? Yeah, I don't fuckin' think so. You can see her tomorrow." He digs into my pocket and snatches the keys to my bike before I can stop him.

Patch raps his knuckles against the bar and Malcom appears. Patch tosses him the keys to my bike. "Give me the keys to your truck. Gonna take Drunken Daisy here home. Come by and get your truck when you get off your shift."

Malcom takes the keys to my bike, exchanging them for his truck's keys.

"Don't wreck it." I glare at him.

He chuckles. "Don't worry, boss. I'll return her in perfect shape." He winks.

"Fuckin kid." I growl as I stalk out to the employee parking lot.

On the way to the clubhouse all I can think about is the last thing I said to Willow. *I'm done here.* Shit. I have some serious fuckin' groveling to do.

WASHED IN BLOOD

CHAPTER 21

WILLOW

I'm not sure how long I stare at the door after he leaves. *What did you think was going to happen, Willow? You're pregnant with another man's baby.* I mean sure, I never thought he would jump up with both hands raised to volunteer for the position, but I never thought he would walk out like that.

I'm done here.

Those words. *His words.* Said with such finality. I never should have stayed. I knew from the moment I woke in his room that I could fall in love with him. And I did. But that's not the whole truth. I didn't just fall. I jumped... I ran full speed ahead and let him consume every part of me until I was no longer sure where I ended and he began.

My eyes burn with tears and my lip trembles as agonizing pain invades my body. I'm no stranger to pain. Emotional, physical, I've felt and dealt with it all my life. But pain like this, the all-consuming ache that destroys you from the inside, it's the same way I felt when I thought Priest was asking me to leave. Unfortunately, experience doesn't make it any easier.

A throat clears and I jump, sucking in a startled breath.

Patch stands awkwardly in the corner, his eyes darting between me and the door. I don't know why we keep staring, we both know the truth. He's not coming back.

"Willow—"

Raising my hand, I cut him off. "Don't."

A knock sounds at the door and a nurse sticks her head in. "Hi, I was just wondering if you could fill out some paperwork for me. Your, ah—boyfriend did the best he could, but we weren't able to find you in our system, so if you could fill out the rest, I'll get it put in for you." Her chipper voice grates on my nerves and I give her a bland smile as I take the clipboard and pen. When she leaves, I set to filling out the papers. My heart clenches at the things Priest didn't know how to answer. *How could he? Almost everything I've told him has been a lie.* I shake my head as I scratch out the name he had written and fill in the one I know will show my files.

"Just give him some time. Let him ride. He'll be back." Patch tries again, giving me a warm smile, but I can hear the lack of confidence in his tone.

Yeah, he's not coming back.

Patch walks over and gives me a kiss on the forehead. "Try to get some sleep. We'll be back tomorrow to check on you."

I smile and nod as he turns to leave. They can come, but I won't be here.

"Hey, Patch?" He stops in the doorway and looks back. "Thank you… for everything."

"Sounds an awful lot like you're saying goodbye, Wil," he teases.

I crack a smile hoping he can't read the truth of his words in my eyes. "Will you tell him I'm sorry?" I whisper.

Patch steps forward, his brows creased. "Willow," his voice is serious, "it's going to be okay. I know Priest. He just needs some time to cool off. Tell him tomorrow yourself, okay?" His eyes beg me to wait it out. *Stay,* they say.

But I can't. It's time for me to do what I should have done from day one.

Three hours later I've had almost every test known to man. Doctors agree that based on the date of my last period I'm 17 weeks pregnant even though my belly is measuring small.

"Some women just carry small. Seems you're one of the lucky ones." The woman doing my sonogram goes on and on, pointing out all the parts of my baby as I lie awestruck, soaking in every minute.

"Would you like to know the gender?"

My eyes grow wide. "You can tell that already?"

I glance back to the screen searching the image, but nothing is clear to me.

"Mm hmm. Baby is in a perfect position, just a quick peek and I could know in a heartbeat."

My own heart beats wildly in my chest. After several minutes, she pats my hand. "You don't have to decide right now. If you'd rather wait on your husband, that's perfectly fine. I'll be here until ten tomorrow morning, just let the nurse know and she'll page me." She wipes the goop off my belly as a whirring noise sounds from the machine. The sonographer reaches over and rips off a long strip of paper. "Here you go, Mom, baby's first picture."

I run my fingertips along the length of my baby's face on the black and white images. *It's going to be okay baby. I promise.*

My vision is blurry when I wake. For a moment I don't know where I am, but the blinking monitor to my right reminds me.

Men chasing me.
Priest saving me.
Priest leaving.

Squeezing my eyes closed, I will myself to fall back to sleep. At least there I don't feel the same crushing pain in my chest. God, will it ever go away? I turn to my side and pull the blankets tighter around me. Settling into the thin mattress and itchy pillow, I'm on the edge of sleep when I hear something in the room.

A creak from the rocking chair in the corner. *Priest?* No, no. Priest would have told me he was here. More than that, he'd be holding me in his arms with his nose buried in my hair.

My heart thunders as I hold my breath, listening to the room around me. Light from the hallway shines in but the rocking chair is behind me. Visiting hours are well and truly over. Turning around would mean letting the person inside the room know I'm aware of their presence.

My hands tremble as I slide them silently under the covers. The remote is hanging on the edge of the bed. If I can reach it, I can press the call button and alert the nurse. The remote is just within my reach when the chair creaks again, louder this time. Slow deliberate footsteps fall heavy against the floor and I can't suppress my whimper. Eyes downcast, I reach for the call button, but another hand grabs it before I'm able.

Crisp black suit.

Gold encrusted diamond cufflinks.

Oh god. *No.*

"Now, now. You know better than to do such a foolish thing, don't you, Willow?" He tsks.

My eyes remain downcast as the tremor travels from my hand to my limbs.

"Yes, sir." My reply is automatic, instilled from the beatings my body endured when I would forget to address him as such.

His pristine suit rustles as his knees bend. Saliva floods my mouth as vomit threatens.

"How did you get in here?" Speaking without permission is mistake number one. His hand strikes like a snake waiting for its next meal. In an instant my pinkie finger breaks, the bone snapping like a twig beneath the force of his hands. My other hand lifts to muffle my scream, knowing that would be mistake number two. My bed rattles as my body shakes with muffled sobs.

"I'm the mother fucking police, Willow, I can do whatever the hell I want, whenever the fuck I want to do it. Or did you forget that in your time away?" Vince's eyes stare at me, cold and calculating. "Did you really think it would be that easy?" He runs his fingers through my hair, caressing the strands between his fingertips. My eyes squeeze in humiliation as evidence of my fear and pain saturates my panties and gown.

His lip curls as the smell of urine permeates the air. "Pathetic cunt."

Standing tall and straightening his jacket, Vince reaches across to press the button only moments ago I thought was my salvation.

A nurse rushes in. "Yes, Mrs. James, how can I help you?" But her gaze doesn't stay on me long.

Vince walks around my bed, fingertips caressing the length of my arm and my skin burns in the wake of his touch. My body knows the devil is near. The nurse's eyes flash with recognition before quickly filling with fear. Her face pales as her hands visibly tremble.

"Seems my luck has yet to run out, I didn't even have to track you down. How are you, Doris?" He walks toward the nurse, reaching past her to close the door. Vince chuckles under his breath when she whimpers at the click of the lock being turned. "Imagine my surprise when I found out my wayward wife had turned up at the very hospital where you are now employed. It's been a while since you fled New Mexico, right?"

My head rears back as my gaze darts between the nurse and Vince. *Wait. Does he know her?* "One of my first cases on the narcotics team led to an investigation at the local hospital, where certain medications were showing a shortage after a specific shift." He paces the length of the room, hands clasped behind his back. "It took a while. The list of people who had access to that supply closet was pages long. After crossing out all but three names, I took my digging a step further." He paces over and pats the nurse on the shoulder, his fingers squeezing her small frame. "Come to find out, Doris's mother has an uncontrolled medical condition which requires a medication that comes with a hefty price tag. When she was dropped by her insurance company after missing several document deadlines, Doris had to take matters into her own hands. Isn't that right, Doris?" he directs his question at the still trembling nurse.

Her eyes dart to me, helplessly begging, but I can't save her. I can't even save myself.

"So I confronted her." He smirks, looking proud of himself. "And what happened next?" he asks Doris.

"You blackmailed me," she spits.

My body tenses in fear for her. *What is she doing? Doesn't she know better?*

"Ah now, that's not quite how I remember it, but either way—*tomato, tahmahto*." He shrugs before addressing her again. "Find her fresh clothing immediately. My wife requires a shower before we checkout." Doris nods and turns to leave the room but freezes with her back to us when he speaks.

"I don't think I need to remind you why you don't want to cross me, do I, Doris?" The shake of her head is jerky, and even though I can see the slight tremble, she still holds her shoulders high as she leaves.

Vince reaches the bend of my arm where the IV rests nestled in the crook. My eyes never leave his as he surveys where the line enters my skin. After fingering the tubes, he jerks them out, ripping them from my arm. I manage to stifle a scream with my other hand. Sobs wrack my body as I curl my right arm into myself.

Ignoring my tears and pain is as easy as breathing for him. "Now, to answer your question. Did you know I'm listed on *all* your medical forms as next-of-kin?" He paces back to the rocking chair in the corner of the room before taking a seat. Crossing one leg over the other he stares at me expectantly.

"No, sir."

A snide chuckle plays across his thin lips. "I expected as much. Lucky for me, you never were very bright. They called me the minute your information popped up. I was all too happy to hear my poor, mentally ill wife had been found."

Oh god. He told them I'm mentally ill. *Of course he did.* I'm sure whatever he has up his sleeve, it'll play right into his plan. No amount of begging or pleading will convince them otherwise.

"And then to find out that bastard baby is alive and well? Well—" He smirks. "That was just the icing on the cake."

I shake my head, frantically begging him with my eyes. "Vince—"

Doris bustles in pushing a wheelchair, a stack of clothes neatly folded on the seat. Vince steps toward the door, glaring at the phone in his hand. "I have something that needs my immediate attention. Have her ready when I return." His *"or else"* goes unspoken, but we both hear it as if he had said it out loud.

Doris walks to my bedside and lowers the rails before pulling back the covers. Her eyes water as she looks to me with trembling lips when she sees the urine I'm lying in.

"Oh, sweetie." She runs to the bathroom to grab a towel and rushes back in to help me wrap it around my waist. "Don't let him take me." I grip her cold hands tightly in mine. "Please," I beg.

"I—I'm sorry... I don't have any other choice. You *know* him." Her eyes plead with me to understand, and I choke back my tears because damn it all to hell, I do.

We don't speak as she helps me shower and get dressed. As I'm putting my shirt on, the sleeve catches my swollen pinkie and I whimper, drawing her attention. Her hands cradle my own as she examines the tender flesh. "He do this?"

I nod. "I spoke without permission."

Her face drains of color. Wordlessly, she goes about setting my finger in a splint. "It's not much, and the bones aren't set right, but without a sedative…" I nod helplessly. In other words, it would freaking hurt, and it's in everyone's best interest that I stay quiet.

I'm just lowering into the wheelchair when I hear Vince's footsteps approaching behind me. "Everything alright in here?" He grips my shoulders, fingers biting painfully into my tender skin.

Lowering my eyes, I nod, not trusting myself to speak.

Vince grips the handles of my wheelchair and pushes me toward the door. "How do I get her out of here… undetected?"

"Th–there's an employee entrance. It will be empty this time of night," Doris whispers.

I watch confused as Vince nods and holds his hand out to her. *The heck does he want? A freakin' congratulatory handshake?* My question is answered when Doris withdraws her hand from her scrubs pocket and holds out several unlabeled medicine bottles.

My stomach hollows out. Those pills… they're either for me, or for him. Either way, they do not mean good things for what's to come.

We make it out of the hospital undetected, and as Vince shoves me into his car, I look out my window,

233

my heart breaking at the sight of Doris standing alone, defeated tears soaking her top. "I'm sorry," she mouths the words. All I can do is nod and hope she knows that I forgive her.

After hours of driving, exhaustion settles in and fear takes over, sending me into a strangely peaceful sleep. It's still dark when I wake and I have no idea where we are. I search the darkness for signs or landmarks that may give me a clue, but there's nothing. Just the glint of moonlight that illuminates the trees and scatters light across the empty land.

The red numbers on the dash show it's nearing 3 a.m. My bladder spasms and I squeeze my legs together. "Vince—" I whisper.

The blow to the side of my face causes my head to bounce off the glass window with a painful thud. My ears hum as the world around me spins.

"You will address me correctly, or you will suffer the consequences," Vince spits at me. "You always were slow to catch on. Fucking pathetic."

I cradle my face in my hands, careful of the split skin around my eye. It swells almost immediately, and it won't be long before my eye is swollen shut. Blood trickles from the corner of my mouth and my tongue darts out, craving the metallic tang.

The car slows as the road comes to an end. A dead end.

HA! Dead end.

I'm sure that's literal in every sense, at least for me.

An old, abandoned warehouse comes into view. Shack may be more of an appropriate word due to its appearance, but its size says warehouse.

Vince pulls up next to the building and puts the car in park before exiting. As he walks around to my side the reality of my situation sinks in. *I'm going to die here.* A sob breaks free from my chest. Oh god. This is it. I've fought my entire life to get to this point. Years of beatings and abuse, and it's all come down to this. I *survived* for *this.* To be slayed like an animal at a seedy chop house.

Outside the window, I watch as Vince swallows a handful of pills from the bottle Doris gave him. When the door is wrenched open, I jump, a scream bursting from my throat. My fight-or-flight kicks in and I scurry, attempting to crawl over the center console, but Vince grabs my feet and hauls me back. I kick wildly, looking for purchase anywhere on his body. Behind me, Vince grunts, losing his grip as my feet finally connect. I make it far enough to reach the handle before his door flies open. I only have a moment's satisfaction when I see the blood dripping from his nose before his closed fist pulls back and releases.

Then, it's lights out.

WASHED IN BLOOD

CHAPTER 22

PRIEST

The sunlight pours through my bedroom window, and on its heels, a massive hangover. *Fuck! How much did I drink last night?* On the way to the bathroom I rub my hands over my face and groan at the pounding headache that begs me to go back to bed.

In the bathroom mirror my reflection stares back. Christ, I look like shit. *At least the outside matches the inside now.* When I pull open the bathroom drawer, I'm relieved to find a bottle of ibuprofen. After downing two tablets and freezing through a cold shower to wake myself up, I head to the kitchen.

As I relax onto the barstool with a mug of coffee, Demon walks in. "You going to see Willow?"

I kick a barstool out and offer him a seat. "Yep."

He sits, his eyes on the floor for a long minute before he finally speaks. "I ah... heard she's pregnant."

My hackles rise and I narrow my eyes, he *does not* want to fuck with me today. "Seems that way..."

When I hesitate, he continues, "Yours?" His eyes roam my face.

A mixture of disappointment and resolve settle on my chest. That baby may not be mine by blood, but it's mine in every other way that matters. If there's one thing I know, DNA does not make a family.

I stand and dump the rest of my coffee in the sink. *I need to see her, now.* "It will be."

He gets to his feet and pats my shoulder. "Happy for you, brother... and Priest," he says, "sorry about—"

I cut him off. "Forget about it, brother."

He nods gripping my shoulder one last time. "Go get our girl."

The ride to the hospital is quick. There's not much traffic on Sunday mornings thanks to Church folk getting their weekly confession in. Taking note of the storm clouds rolling in, I park my bike close to the door in case it's raining when I leave. I take the elevator to the third floor and head straight to Willow's room. I pause outside her door knowing full well she's not going to make this easy on me. Knocking lightly, I wait a second before pushing open the cracked door.

I stop when my eyes meet an empty bed, its sheets and pillows stripped. A sinking feeling sits in my gut. *The fuck is she?* "Willow?" I call out, pushing the bathroom door open. The lights are on but like her room, it's void of any sign of her. Surveying the room, I take stock of everything. The clothes she was wearing yesterday when we arrived are no longer stacked on the vanity. The flowers and teddy bear Angel told me he had sent from the gift shop are nowhere to be seen. The bassinet that sat in the corner is also gone. My stomach lurches. Fuck, what if something happened to the baby?

Stalking to the nurse's station, fury and dread compete for the leading emotion. I slam my fist against the counter causing the young nurse sitting at the computer to jump.

Starting at my head, the woman's eyes peel my clothes off from top to bottom. Leaning forward, she presses her breasts out before wetting her lips. "Can I he–"

I cut her off. "Room three-two-seven. Where is she?"

She taps on her computer while mumbling under her breath, but I don't give a shit. Bitch is

238

wasting my time and I need answers. "Looks like she checked out early this morning," she chirps.

"Checked out? No—That's not possible. Check again, they must have taken her for testing or some shit." I point at the computer screen.

Her fingers click against the keyboard again, each click winding the tension inside me tighter and tighter.

The clicking stops and the nurse looks at me warily. "Sir, I'm sorry but she's not here."

I slam my fist against the counter causing several nearby nurses and doctors to stop in their tracks. An older nurse approaches; I recognize her as the one assigned to Willow yesterday.

"Is everything alright here?"

Is everything alright? I glance at her name badge hanging from her pocket. No, *Doris* everything is not alright. I'm about to claw out of my fucking skin if someone doesn't tell me where the fuck my woman is. "Willow Jane, room three-two-seven. Where is she?"

"Sir, I'm afraid I'm going to have to ask you to leave."

"Please," I beg. "Just tell me who checked her out. She has—" I look down at my boots as the reality of the situation crashes on my chest. Lowering my voice, I beg the older woman to give me what I need. "There are men after her who want to hurt her. Please, I'm trying to keep her safe."

The woman's face pales and my eyes catch on the slight tremble that takes over her hand. A thread of doubt flickers into her resolve. Lowering her gaze, she glances at the nurse who's watching us with rapt attention. "I—I'm sorry, sir. It's against policy for us to give you any further information on Ms. Jane, or her release."

I stare into her wise eyes trying to read everything she's saying without words. *She fucking knows something.*

I don't know who took Willow, but when I find them, it will be me who escorts them to the gates of hell.

My mind is tortured the entire ride back to the clubhouse. Plagued with the words I spat at her in the heat of the moment. *"Always think before you speak, my boy. One day you're going to open that mouth and something is going to tumble out that you can't put back in."* My mom's words filter through. She had no idea what she was getting into with me, and I didn't make those first few years with her easy. Anger at my situation manifested to hate and resentment. And though it wasn't hers to bear, I took it out on her. It took me years to harness the control I now hold over myself. But in a single breath, I did just what my mama told me I would. Numerous times I've paid the price in blood, this time I'm paying with everything.

I pull up to the club house so fast the brothers rush out with their guns raised.

Angel glowers at me, chest heaving. "The hell, man, you gotta shit or somethin'?"

My men chuckle as they put away their pieces and I swing my leg off my bike. Once I have both feet on solid ground, I face the thundering clouds above our heads and release a guttural roar. Everyone around me freezes. My eyes squeeze, hands clenching and unclenching as I let the fury envelop me fully for the first time. Breathing deep, I let it consume me.

When I open my eyes, Demon is there. "Priest?"

I don't answer him, instead I look to Bullet. "Find her."

Bullet takes a hesitant step forward. "Find who? Willow?"

Any semblance of control snaps and I charge him, clenching his shirt in my fists. "Yes Willow! Who the fuck else would I be talking about?"

Bullet holds his hands up in a placating manner. A hand grabs my shoulder and I turn, fists raised. Concern is etched on Patch's face. *Fuck. I need to calm down.*

My voice cracks, "Willow's gone."

Angel breaks through the group and turns me to face him. "Gone? The fuck do you mean she's gone?"

"Priest." Willow's voice filters through my thoughts and I shake my head. We don't have time for this. Turning, I start for the clubhouse. The men follow behind me and I fill them in on what I know. "I got to the hospital this morning to find Willow's room empty." Standing at the head of the table, the rest of the men follow my lead while Bullet sits at his computer, fingers moving across the keys. "When I approached a nurse to ask where she was, they informed me Willow had been checked out. I tried to get more information, but they wouldn't budge." I shove my fingers through my hair, tugging harshly.

Patch steps forward. "I'll head to the hospital and see what I can find." He turns for the door. Fuck, I completely forgot about Patch being able to login to the computers.

"Bullet?" Demon prompts.

Bullet's fingers stab the keys, his lips pinched tight. "One sec," he mumbles. Several seconds pass before he pounds his fist against the table. "Fuck!" He scrubs a hand over his face before his eyes grow wide and he begins tapping again.

"Bullet," I warn. *Fuck, how long is this going to take?*

Eyes darting to mine, he stops typing and draws in a breath, releasing it before speaking. "I'm trying to log in to the cameras at the hospital. They have them placed every few feet in the hallways, outside and inside the elevators. It's impossible to walk through that hospital and not make it on one of the cameras."

Demon and I both move to stand at Bullet's back, watching the screen. I don't understand any of what I'm seeing. Computer codes and red flashing alerts say denied.

"Damn it! Come on stupid piece of shit," he growls. He stabs the enter key, but the screen goes blank before flashing denied again.

Bullet's shoulders sag as his head drops. "I— I'm sorry. I'll keep trying. I won't stop until I get in," he vows.

I grip his shoulder. "S'okay, man," I mutter and drop my hand.

"Davis." The three of us turn to face Angel who's been silent up to this point. He's sitting in the corner with his elbows resting on his knees.

"Who?" Demon asks.

Angel looks up at us, his brows creased. "One of our last sinners. Myles Davis."

Myles Davis. The fucker was paid to get us away from Willow. "Shit."

I hunch over Bullet's back, searching the computer screen. "Bullet, pull all of Myles Davis's financials. Show me any deposits larger than five K."

"What's going on?" Demon asks as Bullet begins clicking.

"Myles Davis admitted he was paid by an anonymous source to distract us from Willow. Whoever paid him, wanted her isolated," I say absently. My mind zones out as I furiously search my brain.

"Please—I…" her voice cracks from the full body tremors. "I won't tell anyone. I swear… I didn't see anything."

Fucking shit. "The cartel," I murmur.

Demon, Angel, and Bullet are still crouched over the computer when I turn to face them. Bullet's fingers still moving at warp speed before they stop completely. Eyes wide, he turns and looks at me—my suspicions are right.

"Cartel?"

He nods once.

Anguish hits me so hard my knees threaten to buckle under my weight. *How the fuck did I miss this?* Willow confessed what she'd seen, admitted her fears to me, and I failed her. Only it's not just Willow I failed. *The baby.* My stomach clenches at the realization that I failed her the same way I failed Doe. Seems the mistakes of my past are repeating themselves. But I refuse to lose Willow. She breathed life into a corpse. Brought me back from the dead, and I'll be damned if this has the same ending as before.

Calm envelops me like a thick blanket. A war is coming, but lucky for me, my soul finds peace within the chaos.

WASHED IN BLOOD

CHAPTER 23

PRIEST

For years we've avoided war with the cartel. Tonight, we will end this war before it has a chance to begin. Obtaining Willow is our main goal. Our second; not leaving a bloodbath in our wake. We've painstakingly planned every element for the next few hours and now that nightfall is here, it's time to put our plans into action.

Bullet and Angel are mapping out exit routes and I'm putting hollow points in spare clips for my 9mm. Patch is already stationed outside the cartel compound which rests on the other side of the mountain.

Demon has been fuming since I first laid out my plan. "You know I'm not okay with this. It's a fuckin' death trap." He leans against the wall, hands shoved into his pockets and a snarl on his lips. I'm surprised he lasted this long before confronting me. Demonio de Helio is the same cartel responsible for his sister, Sara's death. The days after her death were spent damn near keeping Demon shackled so he didn't go on a killing spree. Of course, we wanted those fuckers to pay too, but Demon wasn't in his right mind. Had we let him do what he felt needed to be done, the consequences would have been catastrophic.

Sick to death of his bitching and moaning, I continue prepping my weapons. "I don't give a fuck, D. You're not down, that's cool, brother. But the way I see it, you got two choices. One, you can back me up not because I'm your Prez and it's your duty, but because I'm your brother. Or two, step back and get the fuck outta my way, because I'm doin' this with or without you." I shove a hand through my hair. "I've had your back more times than I can fuckin' count..." I shake my head hard before fixing my eyes on his. We stare each other down. For a brief moment, I think he's going to split.

With a grunt, he stalks to the table where our ammo is laid out and starts loading up.

"That goes for all of you," I say, meeting the eyes of each of my brothers before tucking my two 9mm in my back holster. Demon's concerns *are* valid, but this is the only option I figured would lead to the least amount of bloodshed.

Two hours ago, I reached out to Manuel Santos, head of the Demonio de Hielo Cartel, and arranged a sit down. Getting the man on the phone was damn near impossible. Lucky for us, we have several informants on the streets who will do anything to make a quick buck. A couple crumbs whispered in the right ears and we had a number. To say Manuel was surprised to hear from me would be an understatement. I've taken considerable measures to never cross paths with the man; now I'm leading us straight to his lair.

With me in the lead, Demon, Bullet and I maneuver our bikes along the winding roads of Blackheart Mountain. It's a two hour ride that takes us through some of the best scenery Colorado has to offer. While I take it in, I think about Willow and how her eyes would light up in awe at the beauty surrounding her. I fucked up big time. I know damn well she loves me, and fuck I love her. I promised her I'd keep her safe—protect her. If I die here tonight, Willow's last memory of me will be the venomous words I spewed in a single moment of unkempt rage. Words that will hold her hostage for the rest of her days. The same words I now regret with every fiber of my being.

As we head along the narrow road that leads to the compound, I can't help but wonder if I made the right decision. I could be leading us all to our deaths.

Fuck. Nerves eat away at my stomach as I consider what's at stake. My brothers would follow me into the pits of hell if I demanded it, but it's my job as President to protect them. *I cannot fail.*

The ornate, gold encrusted gates at the entrance to the compound, tower over us, and in the distance, the top of their multimillion-dollar mansion is visible. Damn, looks like I got into the wrong profession. Guards patrol the fence line from both sides, and as I swing my leg off my bike, I'm flanked by two goons with assault rifles.

On their hips, their two-way radios crackle as the gates open and we're led through. Bullet and Demon follow behind as we make our way into Manuel Santos's mansion. Throwing a glance at Demon over my shoulder, I take in his clenched fists and rigid posture. *Christ.* What the fuck was I thinking letting him come? His eyes meet mine. I narrow my gaze on his hands before I give him the barest shake of my head, and I plead with my eyes. *Do not fuck this up.*

The goons lead us through the foyer and across the marble finished floors before we continue up a winding staircase. When we stop outside a massive, solid wood door, movement in the corner of my eye causes my body to tense.

Three armed men step out from a nearby room. I instinctively reach for the gun tucked into the waistband of my jeans. Before I can blink, beefcake number one shoves his gun against my chest and pins me to the wall. In that moment, all hell breaks loose. Mere seconds pass before we're surrounded by armed men, their guns trained on Bullet and Demon, both of whom have theirs raised toward the man holding me against the wall.

"Back the fuck up!" Demon's body is shaking, the already sparse grip on his rage is slipping. Bullet is the picture of calm. The ease in which he filters out the surrounding chaos is one of the reasons he's here. He has the uncanny ability to stay calm in the face of anarchy. His finger tightens on the trigger. "Back up," Bullet warns, repeating Demon's words.

Fuck. This is it. Before he can get a shot off, the doors behind us swing open.

Manuel Santos doesn't blink at the sight of his men surrounding us. "Priest!" he calls. He waves a hand at his men and they step back, but none drop their weapons. Grabbing my hand like we're old friends, Manuel gives it a firm shake. "I do apologize for this, Raul simply meant to retrieve your weapons before entry. You understand, yes?" His English is heavily accented.

The thought of turning over my guns to these men makes me sick, but Manuel's face—and the armed men surrounding us—says there's no room for negotiation. With slow, controlled movements, I reach under my cut and pull out my matching 9mm Glocks from their holsters. I place them in Manuel's outstretched hand and casually cross my arms.

He raises an expectant brow. "You don't want them to search you, no? Surely you are more prepared than what you present to me."

"Can't blame me for tryin'." I shrug as I retrieve my Beretta hollow point from the waistband of my jeans.

Manuel passes my guns off to a thin man holding a black briefcase. The man, who I assume is Raul, places my guns inside. My eyes are locked firmly on Manuel throughout the entire exchange. A shiver crawls up my spine at the manic smile he sends my way. *Something is not fucking right.*

A scuffle behind me has me turning away from Manuel. Beefcake number two has his brawny arm wrapped around Demon's neck from behind. Demon is a big fucking dude, but the man behind him towers over his 6"3" frame a couple inches.

"No. *Fuck no.* Over my dead body," Demon seethes, the muscles in his neck bulge as he bucks against the man's hold.

"That can be arranged." Mr. Beefy raises his free hand and holds the barrel of his pistol against Demon's temple.

Fuck. This is what I was afraid was going to happen. Bullet steps to the side, his empty hands clenched into tight fists. *Shit, he already gave up his weapons.*

I raise my hands and take a tentative step forward. "Demon, give him your guns." It's a beg and demand all in one. Because fucking hell, I do not want to die tonight. If Demon goes down, the odds are not in mine and Bullet's favor for making it out of this place alive.

Demon stares at me, all the hate in the world burning in his eyes. He may be my Vice President, and I knew bringing him here was a mistake, but there's no way I could do this without him.

The decision to leave Angel at the clubhouse is almost laughable, but I couldn't risk Willow turning up and someone not being there. I know how close she and Angel are, so he was my first pick to stay behind. Patch is stationed up the road ready to jump into action if we need him. If I don't get this movin' and get Demon the fuck out of here, the whole plan could blow up in our faces.

Demon extends his arms and Beefcake steps back before Raul relieves Demon of his guns. Demon smirks at me over Raul's head. *Fuck.* They didn't check him for knives which I know he has strapped around both ankles.

I turn back to Manuel in time to see what I've imagined of him all along. He stares openly at Demon, disgust dripping from his curled lips. His attention turns to me, the mask from before slips back into place with a sly smile. "Come, come!" He ushers us inside his opulent office where white marble floors are polished to a mirror-like sheen. Chairs and couches are finished in rich shades of red velvet, and an open fire burns on one side of the room. On the opposite side, Manuel's enormous desk holds a state of the art computer and a security screen that shows various areas of the mansion and its extensive gardens.

He sits in a plush leather desk chair, his hands steepled on his desk. "I must admit, I was surprised when I was informed of your intent to make contact. My mind turned itself over wondering your play. My men told me you were not to be trusted, but curiosity got the better of me I'm afraid."

Looks like our men had the same concerns. I glance at the two men who escorted me inside and are now standing guard at nearby windows. The smaller of the two uses the tip of his rifle to peel back the curtain and assess the grounds below. The giant who fucked with Demon, is staring at me.

A young man—clearly Manuel's son—wearing a crisp black suit and black shirt and tie, steps forward. "Ah, gentlemen. I forgot to introduce you to my son and successor, Diego Santos." Manuel recites the words as though it's an honor for us to be seen in his son's presence. Diego, a damn near clone of his father, nods to each of us as Manuel continues, "I have been teaching him the ropes for several months. Though I plan to be around for many years, you can never be too prepared, no?" He stands and wraps an arm around his son's shoulder. "You asked for a sit down and I say to myself, this is a perfect time for Diego to prove all he's learned." He extends his arm toward his chair as if offering his son the throne. "Today, you will lead."

Diego takes a seat in his father's chair mirroring the position his father was in only moments ago. He clears his throat before draining the amber filled tumbler that sits on the desk. "Could I offer you something to drink, gentlemen?" Unlike his father, his English is smooth and clear.

Before we can answer he barks out harshly, "Isadora."

A gaunt, gangly woman steps out of the shadows at the back of the room and rushes to the desk. She bows her head slightly. "Yes, sir."

Diego thrusts his empty glass at the woman. "Get them bourbon." Diego lifts his arm gesturing to us. Isadora jumps at the movement.

My gaze narrows on what can be seen of her body. She looks sick, and her face is thin and pale, but her long sleeve shirt and pants obscure most of her skin.

Beside me, Demon's hands curl into fists on his thighs. A muscle jumps in his cheek at the force of his clenched jaw. When I follow his hardened gaze to the woman, I notice the tinge of purple bruises that mar her left cheek.

Isadora scurries away and a heavy silence lingers in the air before she returns moments later. A tray, laden with five glass tumblers filled with bourbon sits in her hands. She sets the tray down on the edge of the desk and serves Diego first. Her hands shake and the glass slips from her grasp. Everything else happens in slow motion.

Diego stands, his chair tips over behind him as he rushes backwards to avoid the stream of bourbon heading toward his lap. Isadora's face drains of color as she lifts her frail arms to block her face, but she's not fast enough. Diego's open fist backhands her; the force of the blow takes her to the floor.

His screams are a muddled mix of Spanish and English, "Fucking... *puta*... stupid fucking bitch." Diego rears his leg to kick Isadora, and at the same time, I grab Demon's arm as he jumps from his seat.

"Suficiente!" Manuel barks. Diego pauses, rage pours off his body in waves, but he obeys his father's command.

Isadora pushes herself up on shaky hands and knees, tears stream down her face and smear her mascara. I tug on Demon's arm, but he rips it from my grasp and stalks toward her before placing his body between Diego and Isadora. He kneels beside her, his massive hands known to inflict so much pain, touch her as if she is made from spun glass. He speaks to her in a low, rumbled voice. I can't make out what Demon says, but I don't miss her whispered plea, "Please... don't."

Manuel continues, oblivious to the fact that Demon is seconds away from disposing of his son, consequences be damned. Demon scoops Isadora against his chest and I'm momentarily thrown by the jarring change in his demeanor.

Manuel shakes his head. "Ah, leave her. The only time I see any strength from that one is when she has to get off the floor." Manuel glares at Isadora with disdain. "Pray you have better luck. After Diego, I ask for more sons, and look what I get…"

Holy fuck. I barely manage to swallow down the bile rising in my throat. Isadora is Manuel's daughter. His fucking *daughter.* Ignoring Manuel, Demon helps Isadora to her feet. She mumbles a meek thank you and resumes handing out drinks as if she wasn't just beaten to the floor by her own goddamn brother.

Diego rights his chair and takes his seat. "Get this shit cleaned." Isadora nods and scurries away. "Now, gentlemen. What can we do for you? It's not every day the local motorcycle gang reaches out to you."

His smartass smirk tells me he knows good and fucking well we're not a gang. And as much as I want to school the little fucker, I take the high road and put on my best fuck you smile. "I can say the same. I didn't wake up this morning expecting to have my nightcap with you, so I guess you can say we're even."

I'd rather rip off my fingernails than say my next words because I know what they mean. Men like this don't do anything for free, and I expect to leave this room in their debt. Demonio de Heilo is not someone I want to owe a marker to.

"I was hoping you could help me." Diego's brows raise in surprise. "Two nights ago, our clubhouse was broken into. My woman was alone at the time and fled in fear for her life. When we finally found her hours later, she was hiding in the forest, hypothermic and cut up to hell from running through the elements." I study Diego's face with every word I speak, searching for any sign of familiarity with my story. When I find nothing, I continue, "Once we got her to the hospital, she was able to let me know it was two men who broke in and targeted her."

"I am sorry to hear that," he says robotically. "No permanent harm came to your woman?" he questions.

"Thankfully, she was fine. Only a few bumps and bruises."

"Of course." Diego nods. "Pardon me for asking, but I'm afraid I don't see what this has to do with us."

"Maybe I should start at the beginning then." Feeling cagey, I stand and pace behind the chairs where Demon and Bullet are seated. "About three months ago, a man, Robert Guidelli and his wife Frances were murdered. Robert was gunned down in the alley behind his deli. Frances was found dismembered, her remains scattered throughout their home—"

He cuts me off, "Ah, yes, I remember hearing about this. Such a torturous way to go."

"I imagine it would be. I'm bringing this up because what no one knows is, my woman was there that night. Wrong place, wrong time sort of thing. Her immediate reaction was to run and hide. In her attempt to do so, she alerted the men who murdered Mr. Guidelli."

He leans back in his seat, his face a picture of indifference. "How unfortunate."

I chuckle darkly. "Yeah, I guess you can call it that. She stayed hidden in the woods for days until we found her on the back of our property. When she finally opened up about what she saw, she was terrified. I pressed her for details, but all she knew was that Mr. Guidelli had been loaned a sum of money, that of which he could not repay. So, they took payment in the form of both his and his wife's lives. She had no physical markers or names, nothing concrete for me to go off. Other than keeping a close watch on her, there was nothing more we could do."

"Mr. Priest, I can assure you that we have no dealings with a… *Mr. Guidelli,* and we certainly did not murder he nor his wife." Diego clasps his hands together on top of the desk, growling when his hands meet the spilled bourbon that is yet to be wiped clean.

Either he has one hell of a poker face, or this man honestly has no idea what I'm talking about.

"See, I myself would have never thought you to have any ties to them either. It's one of the reasons I never looked into the cartel when she first shared her story. But the funny thing is... the night those men broke into our house, my brothers and I were handling club business. It wasn't until our *business* revealed that he had been paid to distract us, that we realized we'd been set up."

The door to the room opens, interrupting my train of thought. I pause as Isadora peeks her head inside.

"Fucking finally," Diego mutters and scoots his chair back while waving an arm toward his desk. Reading his command, Isadora hurries to clean the spilled bourbon. I stay silent, intending to wait until she leaves before continuing, but Diego seems to have other ideas. "Continue, continue. She's fairly simple, pay her no attention." The tightening of her jaw says otherwise, but I continue and hope she finishes and leaves quickly.

"So, here's how it all comes together. This morning I went to the hospital intending to check my woman out and bring her home. You can imagine my surprise when I was told she had already been checked out. So, I started piecing things together. When we tracked the payment deposited in the account of the guy who was supposed to distract us… Well, it led us here."

Diego watches me over his sister's head where she's still wiping down the desk. From the corner of my eye, I see Manuel step closer. I wonder who will be the first to break. Father or son. Diego questions, "What do you mean it led you here? Here to this exact location? You'll have to spell it out I'm afraid."

I must admit, I thought Diego's tough exterior would crack as soon as I mentioned tracking the payment, but he's still the picture of calm, other than the glare aimed at his sister.

Isadora is finally finished wiping down the desk and goes about righting the objects on top and putting them back to their original place.

"Do you employ a man by the name of Santiago Guerro?" I ask point blank. Almost immediately, I have my answer. But it's not from Diego or Manuel. As soon as I mention the name, Isadora's body goes rigid and her head turns toward none other than Beefcake, the goon who fucked with Demon.

A wide-eyed Diego turns his chair toward a pale faced Santiago who is now standing with his palms raised. "It's not what you think… I—I can explain—" he rushes out.

"Oh, you will be explaining. Of that I am certain," Manuel cuts in.

Santiago's eyes go wide as he agrees with his boss. "Six months ago, Robert Guidelli came to see you about a loan—"

"And why do I have no memory of this meeting?" Manuel questions with a raised brow.

Santiago hesitates and swallows, visibly shaken. "I, ah—intercepted him."

"You fucking what?" Diego paces across the room and stops in front of Santiago.

Santiago is easily a foot taller than him, but the way he wilts in front of the man, proves who holds the power in this room. "You take business from my family?"

Santiago shakes his head. "No. No, no... I would never do that. I knew there was no way you would do business with Guidelli. The loan he requested was too small, I was saving you the trouble—"

His tirade is cut off when Diego reaches under his suit jacket and pulls a gun from the waist of his pants. It dangles in his loose grip by his side. "And I am to believe you worked alone? What your body has in excess of muscle, it lacks in your brain."

Santiago's submissive exterior cracks when the insult penetrates. A muscle tics in his cheek, and I wince at the force of his teeth grinding together. "I worked alone, no one helped me."

Diego raises his arm, resting the barrel of the gun between the man's eyes. "And yet, I do not believe you."

"Wait!" I turn my head toward the voice, surprised to see beefcake number two step forward.

"Ahh, Reuben. I was wondering how long you were going to stand there and watch your brother take the fall." Diego smirks.

"Shut the fuck up, Reuben," Santiago growls as a bead of sweat drips from his hairline and trails down his clenched jaw.

"No, fuck that." Reuben's gaze darts from Diego to Manuel. "It was my idea. Tiago just went along with it—"

"The woman?" Manuel cuts in.

Reuben shakes his head. "We chased her into the woods; she fell down a ravine. We left her there, figured if the wolves didn't get her, the elements would." He shrugs. "About a week later we saw her in town. Only she wasn't alone." He glances at me.

The day outside Aspen General comes back to haunt me. The way Willow's body trembled when I found her outside the store. The bags filled with her new clothes, spilled out on the ground at her feet. *Mother fucker.* They were there… she saw them and never said a word to me. *Why?*

Reuben continues, "We made an idle threat. Didn't need her running her mouth off to anyone. Time went on, we figured we were in the clear, but we needed to make sure. We paid some punk kid to get Priest's attention. Fucking greedy ass shit, all he cared about was the payday. The night you took him, we put our plan into motion."

"Which was?" I interject.

Reuben shrugs. "Scare her quiet, however that meant."

The fucker must have a goddamn death wish because he smirks like he's bragging about his latest fuck, completely unaware I'm seconds from draining the life out of his eyes. I know how the rest played out; I don't need to hear it. All I need now is Willows location.

"Where is she?" I stand and walk toward him. His finger moves to stroke the trigger of his rifle. A challenge shines in his eyes, but this motherfucker doesn't know who he's dealing with. I've stared death in the eyes—literally—*and* lived to tell the tale. If he thinks he's going to scare me, he has another thing coming.

A sly smile plays across his thin lips. "Sorry to say we had nothing to do with your woman's disappearance. Last time I saw her she was running into the wild, teasing my cock with a sexy as fuck nightie." He grabs his dick, squeezing through the material of his pants.

Before I'm able to wrap my hands around his throat, Diego grips my arm, stopping my advance. He looks at Reuben and tsks. "Family... Such a fickle thing, is it not? How they can be the cause of your rise, and also your fall. Shame yours was the latter."

Reuben's brows scrunch. "What?"

"Oh no, I wasn't talking to you." Diego turns and the deafening sound of the gun discharging reverberates off the walls of the room.

Santiago's lifeless body hits the ground with a jarring thud. From somewhere in the room, Isadora screams. Reuben charges Diego, the impact sends them both crashing to the floor, a mass of grunts and fists. Diego pulls his gun but Reuben swings, and the gun sails across the floor. It spins then comes to rest at my feet. *Well, would you look at that.* I crouch down and grip the gun, testing its weight in my hand as I watch the brawl, wondering how this will turn out.

I glance over my shoulder to find Bullet still seated, arms behind his head staring at me expectantly. His gaze drops to the gun and he quirks a brow. I shrug. I haven't made up my mind yet, so sue me. Demon's at the back of the room, his hands caged around Isadora's puffy, tear-stained face, blocking her view of the impending death match.

Manuel sits in his leather chair, one leg crossed over the other, a glass of bourbon in his hand, and his gun on his desk in front of him.

Reuben straddles Diego, his brawny hands closed around Diego's neck. Veins protrude from his forearms as he drains the life from the heir to the Demonio de Heilo throne.

Fuck. Time to make a decision, Priest. What are you going to do? Reuben turns away from Diego's mottled blue face, his eyes lock onto mine. He tosses me a wink, and my decision is made. For the second time tonight, the room shudders with the ear-piercing crack of the gun firing.

"Thanks," Diego groans through clenched teeth.

I smirk and turn to him. He doesn't look at me, his eyes are on the snow covered courtyard in front of his father's mansion.

After I shot Reuben, Manuel suggested we move our meeting to another room, but it's time for us to go. For them, the night is over. For me, it's just getting started. Though Willow no longer has to worry about any repercussions from witnessing the murder, I'm leaving here without her, and that was not part of my plan. We're back at square one, no closer to finding Willow than I was fourteen hours ago.

We continue through the foyer and out the front door of the mansion. "Don't mention it," I grunt back, but I mean every word. No doubt this incident will come in handy in the future. It's not every day you save the life of the cartel boss's son. They owe us now.

Diego extends his hand to shake mine. "Sorry you didn't get the answers you were looking for."

It's strange to be having a relatively normal conversation with the man. For years, we've hated them on the principle that they were responsible for the death of Demon's sister. But based on his age, Diego couldn't have been more than a young boy when Sara died. Logically, I know he's not the one who took her life, but the blood of the man who sentenced her to death, runs through his veins.

"I've heard about what you do," he says when I don't respond.

"Yeah, pretty sure everyone 'round these parts have heard of the club, or had their car serviced by us a time or two."

"That is not what I'm referring to... but you know that."

"It doesn't exactly jive with your line of work." I shrug.

As the gold encrusted gates open, Diego stares at me, a war brewing behind his onyx eyes. He glances over his shoulder and I follow him when he strolls over to my bike.

"What if it did?" he asks. His eyes are on his father who stands nearby, barking orders into his phone.

"Come again?"

He lowers his voice. "I said, what if it did... jive with our line of work?"

I stare at him several seconds. The fuck is he talking about? They sell sex. No, no. They sell *people* for the sake of others getting sex. In no world could that jive with what we do. We live to kill motherfuckers like him. Erasing them from existence is our end game.

"I know what you're thinking—"

I cut him off, "I'm positive you don't."

"I am not my father," he says. His dark eyes dart to the man in question.

"No? Because the man I saw beat his own fucking sister to the ground earlier, begs to differ. That man is exactly the monster everyone has made your father out to be."

Diego winces when I mention Isadora and the beating rained upon her by his own two hands.

"I'm expected to uphold a certain image. That image reflects that of a man who believes women are beneath him. Flesh and blood included," he says. "It does not mean I agree."

I shake my head and swing my leg to mount my bike. "You've got a decision to make then, Diego."

"And what is that, *Priest*?"

I reach behind me and grab my helmet from the back before slipping it on. I raise my facemask and focus on him through the opening. "Is your family going to be the cause of your rise... or your fall?"

I start up my bike and with a wave, we pull away from the compound, leaving the cartel prince with his own words ringing in his ear.

WASHED IN BLOOD

CHAPTER 24

PRIEST

It's past two in the morning when we finally make it back to the clubhouse. Since I don't know what time Willow was taken from the hospital, I have to go by when I first discovered she was missing. And based on that, she's been missing for at least sixteen hours.

As we park our bikes and remove our helmets, Angel comes out from the clubhouse. He approaches Patch who gives him a slight shake of his head before gripping his shoulder and talking in low tones. Angel's shoulders drop in defeat.

Demon stands beside his bike, his haunted eyes meet mine before he turns and strides inside. I don't know what the fuck just happened, but Isadora triggered something in him. Never in all the years that I've known him, have I ever seen him react to a woman the way he did with her.

Bullet's hand closes over my shoulder. "What's the plan brother?" I study him, taking note of the dark circles hanging beneath his eyes. My men are tired. *I'm tired.* And I have no fuckin' idea where to start or what to do next. Bullet reached out to an old military contact, but he's yet to hear back. Right now, we're completely blind and until we have direction, there's nothing more we can do.

"Sleep." I grunt, standing from my bike and dropping my helmet on the seat.

Bullet nods and heads inside; Patch and Angel follow behind. I raise my head to the crystal clear, star filled sky and release a shuddering breath, the heat from my chest shows in the cold night air. How the fuck am I supposed to go in there and sleep not knowing where she is?

For over twenty years I have believed in and followed Azrael's prophecy for me. I found my brothers and saved them. Together we avenge and save others from the filth of the world. I waited patiently for a reward unknown to me. I can't count the nights I would lie awake imagining the possibilities. When I was younger, I would dream about winning the lottery, or having a garage filled with the world's most exquisite cars. Yachts, parties, and endless women in bikinis, the world at my fingertips.

As I got older, my dreams changed, evolving to fit the man instead of the boy. The dream of wealth was futile after we opened the garage and club, both far surpassing anything I could have hoped to achieve. But there was a part of me that no amount of money or sinners could fill. For years, my soul was gasping for breath, desperate for anything to take the ache away. It wasn't until Willow that I found the sweet relief I had spent so long searching for. Willow thought she was broken, but it was her jagged pieces that filled the void in my heart and soul.

It feels like I've just closed my eyes when someone comes beating on my door. "Priest... you better get out here man... Priest." The pounding continues as I snatch the covers back, growling low in my throat as I shove my legs into my jeans.

I throw the door open to a pale faced Angel. "The fuck is going on?"

He yawns and rubs his head. "You have a visitor."

A hundred faces run through my mind, but I never would have guessed my visitor to be none other than *nurse ratchet* from the hospital. The same one who had a look in her eyes that set off every radar I have in my body. But the put together woman from yesterday, is nowhere to be found. In her place is a woman who looks like she's aged ten years overnight. Her face is pale but for the dark bags under her eyes.

"Ma'am." I greet her. stopping several feet away.

"I'm sorry to show up like this." Her hands nervously wringing her fingers. "I remembered the name on your vest... so I—I asked around and found out where to find you." She takes in a shuddering breath as her eyes roam my body, taking in my own haggard appearance.

"I—I ah... I made a mistake," she whispers. Her eyes well with tears before they spill over and course down her wrinkled face. "I—I shouldn't have let her go... with him. She *begged me* not to let him take her. But, but you have to understand, I had no choice." Her knees give way and Angel rushes forward to scoop her into his arms before he helps her to the couch.

"Ma'am—" I start.

"Doris... my name is Doris."

I nod and give her a small smile. "Doris, can you tell me what you remember about the man?"

She nods as Angel hands her a box of tissues. "There was a call at the nurse's station that the patient in room three twenty-seven needed assistance. Since it was so late, I was the only one at the desk at the time. My co-worker had gone on a coffee run, so I walked to her room to check on her." She wipes at her nose with the tissue and her eyes raise to mine. "I smelled him as soon as I walked in the room." Her body trembling.

The fuck? She could smell *him?*

"At first, I thought I was dreaming. That's the only place I see him anymore you see, the devil of my dreams. I—I wanted to run away, but I was frozen. I just stood there, even if I had run, there is no escaping him."

"I'm sorry, I seem to be missing something. Are you saying you *know* the man who took Willow?"

Doris nods. "I used to live in Santa Fe, New Mexico. I worked at the local hospital. I'm a single mom with three kids, and I'm also the primary caregiver of my elderly mother," she explains. "My mom, she has a medical condition and requires medication every six hours, round the clock. Everything was fine until she was cut off from her insurance. The day I went to pick up her prescription and was told it was no longer active, I vomited in the middle of the pharmacy. I didn't know what I was going to do. I applied to dozens of agencies, but no one would insure her due to her condition." She averts her gaze and wraps her arms around herself. "So I did what I had to do."

"Which was?" Angel cuts in.

She turns to him, but I answer for her, having already put some of the puzzle together. "She started stealing it from the hospital."

Doris turns back to me and nods. "I did. My— my mother was going to *die*. My *mama*," she cries. I sit on the coffee table across from her before reaching over to pat her hand.

"It wasn't long before someone noticed. I should have been more careful. Taken them from different floors, different shifts, but I wasn't thinking that far ahead. The hospital launched an investigation. That's when I first met Vince."

Vince. So that's who has Willow. But how does she know him?

"And what happened when he found out?"

"He propositioned me," she says, and I tense.

Demon growls and the nurse jumps and rushes out. "No, no. Not like that." She shudders. "He told me he wouldn't report me, but there were conditions."

"You started supplying him," Demon says from behind me.

"It was my only option. At least in my mind it was. My mom depended on those medications, and that was my only way of providing them. So I did what he asked. Every week I would meet him at an old gas station across town and drop off a paper bag. He got the drugs, and I was able to keep my job and continue to supply for my mom as well."

"Sounds like you had it made. What made you quit?" I ask.

Her body tenses, eyes flashing with fear. "One night I stopped at our usual spot, but he wasn't there.

After a couple hours, I went home. It's not the best part of town to be in that late at night, and I needed to get back to my kids. I figured he would text me with a new time and that would be that."

"But it wasn't that simple," I say.

She breaks down, shaking her head. "He broke into my house. Came into my bedroom and demanded to know why I didn't show. I tried to explain that I'd been there, but he was out of his mind. There was no reasoning with him, he was just… gone. My kids heard the commotion and came to my room… they—" She chokes on the force of her sobs. "They watched as a policeman beat and raped their mama."

Mother fucking Christ! My stomach rolls and the hate I previously held for this woman melts away. The back door slams and I turn, seeing everyone but Demon. *Fuck.*

"Doris, sweetheart. Where did he take her?" *God, give me something. Fucking anything.* She's my last thread of hope and I'm desperate for anything she can tell me.

My heart sinks when she shakes her head. "I don't know. I helped them get out a back employee entrance, but I don't know where he was taking her."

My head drops, shoulders sagging with defeat.

Doris is still babbling almost incoherently. "She was so scared… she grabbed my arm and begged me to help her—" She sobs. "I couldn't get her face out of my mind. Then you showed up and—and I thought if anyone could stand up against him, it would be you. "Save her," she begs while clutching onto my arm.

I stand to leave and Angel takes my place, holding the broken woman.

"Wait! You should know... I gave him pills. Before he left, I knew he wouldn't leave without them. There's no telling what kind of state he's in by now, but he's volatile when he's on them." She reaches for me, a piece of crumpled paper clutched in her hand.

I take it and smooth the wrinkles before reading the scribbled name. *Vincent James.* And just like that, we have the name of our next sinner.

"What have you got?"

Bullet is at his computer searching the name of the man we now know took Willow. *Vincent Reginald James,* husband of Willow Jane James... *Husband.* I force back the vomit that rises every time I say the word. I think of the weeks spent retraining her body not to flinch at loud noises, or cower down when I reached for her. I can't imagine the kind of life she must have lived with him for those reactions to become so ingrained. And now, he has her.

"Vincent James, thirty-seven years old. Lives in Santa Fe, New Mexico and—fuck."

"What?"

275

Bullet grimaces "Doris was right, he is a cop… a narcotics officer."

Everything clicks into place. It all makes sense now. Willow told me that when she first got with her ex, things were different. She said they lived a happy, normal life for years. Until one day they didn't. Sounds to me like good old Vince started dipping his hand into the honey pot. The pull of temptation… or in this case, the drugs he pledged to fight against, were too sweet to be refused. Drugs will change any man. But a man who's lived his entire life on the straight and narrow? I imagine the difference would be night and day.

Bullet continues scrolling and clicking until several pictures fill the screen. My breath stalls in my chest. *Mother fuck.* This must have been taken several years ago. The Willow on the screen is younger and still has an air of innocence to her. Her face is beaten to hell, both eyes swollen almost completely shut. Her busted lip has several stitches closing the skin together. The next picture is dated six months later. A broken arm in this one. Picture after picture, years of documented abuse are put on display.

"Where are you getting these from?" I ask as yet another picture of a beaten Willow shows on the screen.

"It's all on file at his local precinct. Not like it was out there in plain sight. Whoever did this, wanted them to stay hidden while still being accessible," Bullet says.

"The fuck?"

"Nurses are required to call in all cases of suspected abuse so they can be investigated."

"But it wasn't?"

Bullet clicks his mouse several times before zooming in on what seems to be a scanned hospital document. "Oh no. It was definitely investigated." He lifts his hand and taps his finger against the screen.

I lean down, squinting to make out the pixelated image. "Son of a bitch," I growl, white hot rage flowing through me.

Right there in black and fucking white is the signature of Vince James. *Mother Fuck.* Determination settles in my gut. Every ounce of pain Willow endured at his hands, I will force him to relive with mine.

Several times I asked her why she didn't leave. Pack her bags and go. Her answer was always the same—there was no way out. If this guy's a cop, Willow would have felt like there was no one she could turn to. Hell, if she couldn't trust her cop boyfriend, who *could* she trust. Then to find this… hundreds of pictures, evidence of the times she was so close to freedom only to have it cruelly ripped away. *Christ.*

"Where is he?"

"Priest, you know this chang—" Patch cuts in.

"Are you fucking kidding me? This changes nothing." I snarl. "This mother fucker will die by my hands. Any one of you have a problem with that, get the fuck out... NOW!"

277

Demon steps forward and leans down to get a better view of Bullet's computer screen. "What's his last known location?"

"Looks like he took an abrupt leave of absence from work yesterday morning. Charges to his credit card show he took a flight out of O'Hare International; it landed in Aspen a little after midnight."

Mentally, I calculate how long it would have taken him to drive from the airport to the hospital where Willow was, and I curse. "That means he's had her almost forty hours."

"Have there been any more charges on his credit card?" Angel asks.

Bullet shakes his head. "No. He has one credit card to his name, and it's the one he used to reserve the plane ticket."

Fuck! We did not come this far only to reach another dead end. This is a cop we're talking about, so we need to think like cops. Obviously, this guy is smart, or he thinks he is. If he plans on killing Willow, he'll want no records of him ever being here, but he would have needed a valid credit card to book the flight. "Cash. What about cash? Search large withdrawals from his checking account."

Bullets fingers move across the keys before he shakes his head. "Nope, nothing from his checking. But… he did put in a rush withdrawal of fifteen K from his retirement fund about an hour after he requested leave. Looks like funds were disbursed just hours before his flight out of O'Hare."

Okay, now we're getting somewhere. "Bullet, search car rentals within a five mile radius of the airport. Pull up the closest three. I want the names of anyone who rented a car within the last twenty-four hours."

Angel cuts in, "Places like that usually require a valid credit card. If he's looking to pay with cash, I doubt that's where he'd go."

I thought about that myself. He only had three options: buy, steal, or rent. My first thought is he'd try to buy something, but that'd cut too much into his stack of cash. He wouldn't consider stealing, he's too smart to come this far only to get arrested for trying to jack a car. He gets caught doing that, it would seriously fuck with the cushy job he has waiting for him at home. By renting, he's covered all bases. It won't cost him much cash to grease the pocket of some rent-a-car employee. When he's finished with the car, he brings it back to the rental center where it's cleaned from top to bottom. Then he's on his merry way.

"I want a list of the people who paid with a card registered to a different name than the one listed on the rental agreement. Show me any that don't match or have a similar variation."

Bullet continues clicking, and understanding hits Angels eyes. "You think he stole someone's card?" he asks.

"No. I think he greased some greedy fuck's pocket and used their card, while they pocketed the cash... *plus* a hefty tip."

"Got it," Bullet says as a list of less than ten names and rental information shows on the screen.

I lean over his shoulder to scan the screen, but it seems like good old Vince used a fake name. "Cross reference the names on the cards with store employees."

Bullet types in the new variables and clicks enter. The computer beeps once before the list disappears. All but one result. John Smith rented a black Land Rover from Equipment Vehicle Rentals (EVR). Card used was that of an Alaska Watson, who... surprise, surprise, just so happens to work at EVR.

"Look at this," Angel says, reading something on the screen of his phone. "All of our vehicles are top of the line Utility Equipment Vehicles. Therefore, they shall be treated as such. Each vehicle is outfitted with a tracking device so that EVR are aware of the location of our vehicles at all times."

"Bul—"

"Got it," he cuts me off as each of our phones ping with a text. "Looks like they're about two hours from here. I sent the location to our phones." He gets up from the computer. "Let's go."

WASHED IN BLOOD

CHAPTER 25

PRIEST

The ride to the location of Vince's rental car passes in a blur. Visions of what we could walk into plague my mind. Fear is not an emotion I'm familiar with. But instead of shying away from it, I embrace it. I breathe it in as it settles in my bones. I let it fuel my rage as it feeds the monster within. In the dark of the night, I find fear is my ultimate source of power.

The road comes to a dead end at a dilapidated warehouse. I pull over and shut off my bike. My brothers pull up beside me to form a blockade across the road with their bikes. It's more of a statement than a preventative. This fight won't make it outside the crumbling walls we're standing in front of.

"You got a plan?" Demon asks.

I nod, eyeing the small flickers of light that escape the board covered windows on the abandoned building. "Get Willow out alive."

"And Vince? He dies here?"

"No," I say meeting his shocked expression. "He dies a sinner's death," I explain as an evil smirk forms on Demon's face.

Vince will not die here tonight. I will do everything in my power to ensure he survives long enough to experience nothing less than the torturous death he deserves.

"Angel, Patch, I want you covering exits. I don't anticipate him making it that far, but we're going in completely blind. If the situation arises, do what it takes to *detain* him. He dies by my hands." They nod before taking off toward the warehouse.

I glance at Demon and Bullet. "You're with me." Together we walk the remaining distance and meet up with Patch at the front door.

"You scout?" I whisper.

He nods. "Only this exit and one at the back that Angel's guarding. Windows are all either boarded up or too fuckin' dirty to see inside. Lights are on in a few rooms, no way to tell where he's at, or where she's being held."

Fuck. Unease prickles my spine like a thousand fire ants burning beneath my skin. We're going in completely blind. For the second time in less than twenty-four hours, I could potentially be leading my men—my brothers—to their deaths.

Demon grips my shoulder. "You good?"

"What if this is wrong?" I ask, giving voice to my fears. "What if I'm leading us to die? What if she's already de—" I choke, unable to finish the thought.

"And what if she's not?" he throws back. "That a risk you're willing to take. Walk away now and never find out if you could have saved her or not. Find another woman, move on as if Willow never existed for you..."

My chest is heaving by the end of his tirade. *Fuck no.* There is no turning around for me. Not now. But there could be for them, this doesn't have to end like this.

"No. *Fuck no,*" Demon spits. "Get that fuckin' thought outta your head. We're in this together. Every one of us would willingly follow you to the ends of the earth. If that means our death, so be it. It'll take a lot more than death to break my loyalty to you. Come heaven or hell, I'll follow you in this life, *and* in any life after."

I hold his stare and nod, not trusting myself to speak. My gaze flickers to Patch and Bullet and I see the truth in Demon's words reflected in their eyes. I drop my head and stare at my boots for several seconds, shoulders heaving. *God, give me strength.*

I raise my head to meet my brothers' eyes. "Let's go."

Surprisingly, the door to the warehouse is unlocked. We enter, guns raised, completely undetected. The inside of the building matches the decaying exterior. I glance up and narrow my eyes at the second story of the warehouse. Offices line the perimeter connected by a narrow walkway which at first glance seems to be suspended midair. A dim light shines beneath a closed door in the corner farthest from us.

I snap, getting Bullet's attention before directing his to the light. He nods and takes off, his Delta Force training takes over as he scans his surroundings, eyes focused through the sight of his rifle.

I motion for Demon to follow me as I approach the first closed door on our level. One by one, we clear four rooms in a few short minutes. With each barren space, my faith dwindles. The knife that appeared in my heart the moment I realized Willow was gone, twists deeper. With each turn, it shreds my delicate flesh, decimating it beyond repair.

Ahead of me, Demon opens the fourth door and steps inside before his body goes solid. He looks back at me over his shoulder, his face tells me all I need to know. *Willow.*

I move to push past him, but he turns his body, blocking my advance as he grabs my arm. "Priest," he chokes out.

No. No fuckin' way am I too late. Fuck that shit. That's not how this was supposed to go, goddamn it. I plant both fists in his chest and shove him like a battering ram. Demon staggers back several steps, and I rush into the room.

My breathing stalls as my brain struggles to process the images my eyes are feeding it. This isn't the first time I've been in this room. But unlike twenty years ago, Azrael is not sitting in the chair in the corner... it's empty. The rusted metal bed which was also empty, save for a bloodied mattress, now holds the very reason my heart beats, handcuffed to its bedposts.

I push back the bile threatening its way up my throat as I rush to the bedside. My eyes track over her injuries. A dozen bloody stab wounds mar Willow's exposed skin. Several have begun to scab over, while others still drip with her precious lifeblood that pools beneath her on the filthy floor. Based on the way her clothes are caked to her skin with a crimson paste, I'd bet the covered flesh looks much like the rest. Her pale creamy skin has been replaced with a grey ash.

When I reach her side, I drop to my knees, my hands hover above her broken body.

"*Fuck. Fuck. Fuck!*" When my fingers touch her neck, I almost cry out at her pulse thumping against my touch.

"Willow... baby, can you hear me? We're gonna get you outta here, okay? It's gonna be alright."

Demon works to free the handcuffs from her ankles, while I free her hands. Her fingers are blue and cool to the touch, and I worry about the permanent damage she could be facing. I bring her arms from their prison over her head and rest them by her sides. When my gaze catches on the slight swell of her stomach, my face pales. I stare at the saturated shirt covering her baby bump; my stomach bottoms out as I reach for the hem.

Please. I'll fucking give you anything you want. Don't take this... not this.

With slow, steady movements, I raise her shirt, baring the skin of her abdomen to my eyes. Bunching the shirt, my hands stop when I reach her breastbone.

"*Mother fucker,*" Demon growls as my eyes land on the space where Willow's baby—*my baby*—lies safely inside her, oblivious to the torture its own flesh and blood has put its mother through.

Pulling back, I narrowly miss Willow's body as the vomit which had been threatening, finally erupts, mixing with Willow's blood on the grime covered floor.

I take pleasure in the knowledge that I will be the one to punish Vince. In his pain, he shall repent, but he will not find forgiveness. They call me Priest, but I will become his devil.

I stand and place my arm under Willow's knees, preparing to pull her against my chest when the unmistakable sound of a gun cocking cracks through the air.

My body freezes as his shoes drag across the floor. "I'm afraid I can't let you do that."

Hands raised, I back away from Willow before turning around to face Vince. I'm barely able to contain my sneer at the sight of the man in front of me. His greasy black hair hangs over his crazed eyes, his blown out pupils confirm my suspicions. Vince is an addict. He's also huge. Standing at least six foot two, the sheer size of his hulking muscles make me wonder if drugs are the only thing he's been injecting into his body.

Where the fuck did he come from? My mind races as I try to come up with the best course of action. I need to keep his attention on me, and the fuck away from Willow.

Movement from my left has my eyes darting to Demon.

Vince notices and pulls another gun from his back before raising it to Demon. "Guns on the ground."

Demon tosses his weapons on the ground in front of him before coming to stand beside me.

"You too," Vince says.

I toss my guns on the floor with Demon's. "This doesn't have to go down like this. Let us take her and we'll leave," I say while taking deliberate steps to move my body toward the door. Just as I'd hoped, Vince's body mirrors mine.

Vince sniffs and wipes his nose, his crazed eyes dart over the room.

Jesus Christ. He's high as fuck. Completely coked out. His movements are erratic, unpredictable.

"Oh no. That's where you're wrong. This is exactly how this has to go down. It was always going to come to this. I picked her on purpose, you know? A meek, broken teenager who wanted nothing more than to be loved. Been treated as nothing her entire life. All I had to do was throw her a bone, and the bitch was panting over my dick," he sneers, crudely palming himself.

It takes herculean effort not to kill this mother fucker right now. But with his gun already pointed at me, and mine on the floor, he'd get his shot off before I'd get the chance to dive after mine.

I have to be smart in playing this. I don't know what, or how much Willow could have revealed in the time he's had her, so I take a risk and play it, hoping he has no idea who I am. "Sounds like you had it made, bro. She's a fine piece, thinkin' I might need to try your methods." I smirk, but the words taste like acid on my tongue.

Vince laughs. "Fuck yeah. It was all good... until it wasn't. Bitch started to grow a backbone. That's not how I like my women. I prefer a mouse to a wildcat, you know what I mean?"

I laugh with him. "Hell yeah, man. Bitches need to learn their fuckin' place."

Vince nods, getting excited. "See man! You get me. I mean, I don't think it's too much to ask, you know? I get home from work and I want a beer waiting for me, and my dinner ready. And when it's time for bed, I want her to spread her fuckin' legs while I take what I want, and she keeps her mouth shut while I do it."

Apparently, Vince has a loose tongue when he's high, because surely he would shut the fuck up at the murder in my eyes. How the fuck do the people he works with not see this? The man standing in front of me is not a respected narcotics officer, instead, he resembles those he has been charged with disposing of.

I vow that his death will not be quick. By the time he takes his last breath, he could have died a thousand deaths and it still would not be justice enough.

"But like all bitches, she got too fuckin' needy. Always talkin' about the future and shit," he spits.

Distracted by his tirade, I've managed to pull him out of the room and into the open warehouse. Discreetly, I search for Bullet on the level above us—he's nowhere to be seen. Christ, I hope he's trying to get into place and stay hidden and not lying up there knocked out or worse, dead.

"Well, good thing you got clear of her, dude. Sounds like you lucked out." But it's the wrong thing to say. The change in Vince is immediate.

"Got clear of her? No. No, no. You're wrong about that. See, that little cunt in there thinks she can play me for a fuckin' fool. Tryin' to trick me into believin' I knocked her up. I ain't raising no bastard. Figured a coupla well placed kicks and that runt would be nothing more than a memory," he boasts as if he's bragging about winning an Olympic gold medal.

"But apparently, this bitch doesn't fuckin' learn. No matter how many times I broke her down, she managed to find her legs. After her beating, I went out to celebrate. Figured I'd pull an all-nighter. She managed to slip past my boys on watch and get away. At first, I was gonna let her go, you know? But then I got to thinking. She may be a bitch causing more trouble than what she's worth, but she's *my bitch.* My cunt to break, again and again until *I* decide she's had enough." He ends with a roar before pacing back and forth muttering beneath his breath.

My fists clench as he recalls the sordid tale. I want to feel the bones of his face crumble beneath my hands. I want to watch as he struggles to breathe for the blood choking his airways.

Demon taps the toe of his boot against the concrete to get my attention. Bullet is crouched on the walkway of the mezzanine. His hands move as he points out where he needs Vince's body for a clear shot.

I nod and clear my throat to get Vince's attention before moving again. "So what's the plan here, man? I mean, if you kill her, there's no one else for you to break. Seems like a lot of work having to stake out a new bitch, you feel me?" I don't give a fuck what his plan is. Willow is leaving with me, and this sick fuck will never have the chance to prey on another woman again. I just need to keep him talking.

"Yeah, it was a lot of work. Months of stalkin' her at the piece of shit diner she worked at. Pretending to actually enjoy the shit they served. While I was watchin' her, noticed one of her slut friends always makin' eyes at me, so I took advantage." He grins. "Bitch was so hot over my dick she didn't hesitate to answer my questions."

"My man," I chuckle, congratulating him. "So what'd you find out?"

He laughs. "Bro, you will not believe my luck. First time I followed her, she was walkin' to the bus stop. There was something about her that called to me, you know? Instinct." He smirks. "And I was right on the fuckin' money. So this bitch apparently has no family. And when I say no family, I mean *none*. Her mom was some teenage slut who got offed before she was born, but she managed to push her out first. Ended up growing up in the system. No friends, no family, no one to call and check in on her wellbeing. Was like she was made for me."

A thousand thoughts run through my mind as more pieces of Willow's puzzle click into place. She was raised in foster care, like me. Yet she never mentioned it. But something he said sticks out. *Her mom was some teenager... Got offed before she was born. Managed to push her out first.* No. Fuck. No. There is no fucking way.

"But you're exactly right. Busted my ass to make her into the bitch she is today. Which is why it's gotta be me who teaches her this last lesson." His body twitches violently as the rush of drugs and excitement floods his system.

"And what's my last lesson, Vince?" a soft voice croaks.

CHAPTER 26

PRIEST

My world catches fire as Willow scampers out of the protection of the room. Her arms cradled protectively around her belly, a hitch to her step as she favors her right leg.

Goddamn crazy, stupid woman. I watch helplessly as she destroys everything I've put into place. She refuses to meet my eye, instead she focuses her attention on Vince.

"I asked you a question. What. Is. My. Last. Lesson?" she repeats through clenched teeth.

Pulling my gaze from Willow, my stomach bottoms out when I see that Vince's gun is no longer trained on Demon and I, but now rests on Willow. My eyes track Bullet as he moves silently above us, but he shakes his head. *Fuck!* He doesn't have a shot, and right now, Vince is moving *away* from where Bullet needs him to be.

"See here? This is exactly the kind of shit I was telling you about," Vince says to me before looking back to Willow. "That backbone is going to be the death of you," he taunts. "As for your question, deep down, I think you already know the answer. Don't you, babe? It's part of the reason you ran."

Willow nods as tears streak through the dried blood on her face.

"I ASKED YOU A FUCKING QUESTION! ANSWER ME, BITCH!" All traces of the fucked up drug junkie have disappeared. In its place is an unpredictable man.

Willow's chest heaves with the force of her cries, but still she answers him. "Yes, sir."

"Yes, sir, *what*? Why don't you explain to our guests, Willow?"

Willow's haunted blue eyes come to me, her voice toneless and robotic when she speaks. "I belong to him. He is master of my body, and I am his to control. He gave me life and he shall also take it. The beat of my heart rests in his hands."

God, baby. What the fuck are you doing? My stomach rolls with each word that comes from her mouth. My view of her goes blurry as tears distort my vision. *Come back to me, baby. This isn't you… this isn't you.* Vince watches her, a satisfied glint coming to his eyes as he nods, agreeing with her words. His grip on his gun tightens as his finger caresses the trigger.

I'm running out of time. One last look at Bullet confirms Vince still is not in a clear position and my mouth moves before my brain has a chance to catch up.

"Now, Willow baby. That's not what I remember you telling me," I say meeting Willow's stunned gaze. She shakes her head frantically, begging me to stop, but it's too late. I have to get his attention off her. And this is the only way I know how.

Smirking at Vince, my insides die as I attempt to fuel his rage and turn it on me. "So you see Vince..." His brows furl at my use of his name. "Funny thing is... I also targeted Willow." Arms crossed, I shake my head as my feet move me closer to where she stands.

"The fuck are you talking about?" Vince seethes as his gaze darts between me and Willow.

"I came here tonight after finding out *my woman* had been kidnapped from the hospital. It was a lot of trouble to go to, but like you said, bitch is worth the effort."

I hate the way Willow's body flinches at my cruel words. I hate even more that I'm just getting started. If I want him to forget about her, I have to become all he can see.

"That pussy, man..." I trail off on a groan. "*So* fuckin' sweet. 'Course I'm not telling you anything you don't already know, but *damn.*"

Vince's face is mottled red, the grip on his control slips as I chip away at it with each word. Chills break out across my skin at the sound of his teeth grinding together, but I've done exactly what I had to do. I'm standing directly in front of him, my body blocking Willow from his sight. Behind me, she begs, whispering my name under her breath. My heart aches at the terror in her voice.

Time slows as I embrace the last minutes of my life. God, I want to hold her. I want to feel her curl up against my chest, her hair teasing my arm as her fingers dance along my skin. I want to promise her everything is going to be alright. I want to argue with her as she disagrees that without me, nothing could ever be right. And then I want to make love to her as I promise her with my body and soul, this is not the end. Pain is temporary. It's a fleeting wound that only time can mend, and time is what I'll give her. As much as I wanted Willow's future to be mine, I'll rest peacefully knowing that she has one.

I look over my shoulder, pretending to give her a snide grin. But the reality is, I need to see her face one more time. I need to burn the beauty of it into my soul, branding it in such a way that it will stay with me from this life into the next.

Her mouth is hanging open as she struggles to take in air. It's the pain filtering in. The despair is taking over and she's helpless to do anything but let it invade.

I love you. I mouth the words to her before turning back to Vince. My next words will push him over the edge and seal my fate. "You want to know the real cherry on top, *bro*?" I taunt. Vince stands motionless, a prisoner to his rage.

"That baby in her belly... It's mine."

A flash of golden blonde has my head turning as two simultaneous gunshots crack through the vacant warehouse. My body is prepared for the impact of a bullet that never hits its mark. I watch in horror as Willow jumps, placing her body in front of mine. Her tiny frame jerks as the hot metal pierces her skin, shredding its way through flesh and muscle. She hits the floor before my brain can process her fall. My stomach rolls at the sound of her head cracking against the floor. I dive on top of her to protect her from the impending spray of bullets, but they never come.

The sound of flesh pounding against flesh reaches my ears, followed closely by grunts and groans. In the corner of my eye, Vince goes down, crumpling under the weight of Demon slamming into him. Vince screams, but my focus is on the crimson flow pouring through the cracks of my fingers where I grip Willow's thigh in my hand. She coughs, pulling my attention from the growing pool of blood. I can't contain my guttural moan when I see a second pool of blood growing under her head. She coughs again and fresh blood spews from her mouth.

No. NO! This isn't how it was supposed to end... She's my reward dammit. SHE'S MY REWARD!

I don't know where or how to hold her. Thankfully, a pair of hands cover mine and I'm relieved to see Patch. His mouth moves as he barks orders at someone, but the sounds around me are distorted. I focus on his mouth as it moves, trying my best to read what my ears aren't hearing.

"Priest... PRIEST! You can let go now. I've got it, you can let go."

I release Willow's leg, one hand moves to cradle her face, the other searches for the source of the blood flowing from her head. Her eyelids flutter and the sight has me finding my voice.

"Willow... Willow, open your eyes for me, baby. I need you to keep your eyes on me, okay? Just keep them open." I smooth her hair from her face. Blood coats my hand and leaves a path of crimson in its wake.

She coughs again before a sweet smile forms on her lips. Her eyes are fixed on me. "Hi," she whispers.

I lean down to press my lips against hers. "Goddamn you, baby. What the fuck were you thinking?" I scold her while peppering kisses along her face.

"I thought it was time," her voice is weak.

I clutch her to me as she drifts. "And what exactly was it time for? Last I checked, I was the one playing hero." I laugh even though I'm dying inside.

As the light fades from her eyes, her chuckle becomes a harsh cough. I cling to her body wanting to be tethered to this moment forever. Blood coats her teeth when she grins, but I commit every inch of it to memory.

"It was time someone saved you."

What's left of my heart dies in my chest as her eyes flutter shut. "Willow. Baby, you gotta open your eyes for me, you hear me?" I shake her. "Goddamnit, Willow! Open your fucking eyes RIGHT NOW."

Next to me, Patch has gone still, his hands no longer work to stop the blood oozing from her thigh. Beside him, Angel's hands are shoved into his hair as he rocks back and forth. Demon and Bullet stand over us, watching with solemn faces.

"KEEP WORKING!" I bellow at Patch as my body falls into a soothing, rocking motion. I tell myself it's for her... a vain attempt to soothe her pain. *It doesn't matter anymore. There's no more pain for her now.* I pull her tighter against me. Nothing is enough, I *need* her closer. My hand slips, knocking against the swell of her belly.

I cry out. "Patch... Patch, please. Save the baby," I beg. "Just save the baby, okay? You can get it out, right? You can get it out and I'll have a piece of h—WHY ARE YOU JUST STANDING THERE?

GET IT OUT!" I roar as he watches, devastation on his face.

He's not going to help me? Well fuck him. I don't need him, she just needs to wake up. "Willow, baby, please. Please..." I choke. "Don't do this to me, don't fuckin' do this to me! God, take me instead... just take me."

Flashes of red and blue dance across the walls of the old warehouse, and for the second time in my life, I'm left begging death to take me with him.

I'm not sure how long I sit and rock my sleeping angels, but my arms never loosen their hold. An old church hymn flickers through my mind. I close my eyes to block out the pools of blood surrounding us. Mouth to her ear, I whisper death's lullaby,

> *"What can wash away my sins?*
> *Nothing but the blood...*
> *Nothing but the blood of Jesus.*
> *What can make me whole again?*
> *Nothing but the blood..."*

I drop my head and let the tears flow into her hair. *"Nothing but her blood."*

WASHED IN BLOOD

CHAPTER 27

PRIEST

Three months later

"Yo."

I look up from the spreadsheet on my desk as Angel makes himself comfortable in the chair opposite me. I lean back to stretch, but wince when the tense muscles in my neck crack. I groan as I massage my fingers into the tender skin.

"You want me to give you some privacy boss?" Angel laughs.

I open my eyes and glare at the uninvited visitor. "There a reason you're here?"

He relaxes back in his seat, resting his arms behind his head. "Just being a good messenger boy."

He winks. "Patch said Vince has another infection. Worse than the last."

My lips tip up, a rare occurrence these days, but it can't be helped when I picture the emaciated man chained up like an animal at the lodge. Three months ago, we left the clubhouse set on rescuing Willow. I thought I'd imagined every possible outcome, but I was wrong. Nothing could have prepared me for the sight of Willow's body taking the bullet intended for me.

"How long are you going to carry this out, Priest?" His tone holds no judgement. He was there, after all. My brothers had a front row seat to the night my world imploded. They stood by me as I held her lifeless body, begging for a miracle that would never come.

"As long as it takes."

"Priest… you know she may ne—"

"Don't you think I fucking know that?" I seethe. "It'll end when I'm goddamn ready, and not a minute before."

Angel holds his hands up in surrender. "You got it, Prez. I'll let Patch know to start his meds." He stands and walks to the door before turning back. "Me and Bullet were about to head to Corrupt, you want to come?"

"Nah." I push back from my desk. "Think I'm gonna go for a ride," I say as I grab my helmet and follow him out.

Angel stops me in the hall as I'm lifting my helmet over my head. "Priest, listen... you know if you ever want to talk—"

"Don't," I cut him off. "Just don't." I pull my shoulder from under his hand and strap on my helmet as I mount my bike. There's nothing he can say that will change anything anyway.

For years the cemetery has been a sacred place to me. A place to be alone and away from the chaos of the world. A place to pray and hope to hear God's whispers in the wind. But today, the marble bench doesn't bring me the relief I seek. Instead of answers, I'm plagued with more questions.

I sit in front of the tiny headstone where the concrete angel stares at me, mocking. The inscription haunting me more than ever.

Baby Doe.
Precious baby, nameless soul.
Claim your wings, it's time to come home.

The metal gate surrounding the children's cemetery creaks, and I startle at the noise.

"Thought I might find you here," my mom says as she bends to press a kiss against the top of my head. She takes a seat beside me.

"Hey, Mom." I scoot over and wrap my arm around her, my soul finally finding, and clinging, to the peace she's always given me.

"What do you think happened to the mother?"

I turn to the headstone I've memorized by heart. "I'm not sure. I asked the groundskeeper once. He checked the office records, but there was nothing of any use."

Mom reaches over and places her wrinkled hand over mine, squeezing my fingers tightly. "Why do you come here, Kingston?"

I take a deep breath as I glance around the cemetery. The grounds span for miles... the home of bones and ash. In a forgotten corner at the back, is a section not many know exist. The faded sign hanging on the gate deems these *The Lost Children.*

Why do I come here? Because *I* was a lost child? Because my heart aches for these children tossed in the back. Forgotten in death as they were in life. "I don't know. Just like the peacefulness here, I guess."

"You've always had a thing for the cemetery, Kingston. I mean why do you come *here...*" She pats the bench before tipping her head toward the headstone. "To this grave?"

My heart aches when I turn back to the stone. *Baby Doe.* She didn't even have a name... *Precious baby, nameless soul.* "I don't know what you want me to say, Mom. I don't know why, maybe because there's a seat. Maybe because in the summer, I'm shaded by the trees."

Mom's brows narrow with her glare. "Don't sass me, boy. Just because you came to me almost a man, does not make you too old for me to switch over my knee."

I look down so she doesn't see my grin. "Yes ma'am."

"Kingston, you know—"

"I know it's not her." I look back to the grave that bears the name of the first girl I ever loved. "But being here... it's where I feel closest to her."

Doe Smith's remains were never accounted for. No matter how much money I threw at the hospital staff or private investigators, I was never able to track down where she was laid to rest. My heart aches at the thought of her body burned and scattered as if she never existed.

"What am I supposed to do?" I ask my mom, voicing every fear of the lost boy inside.

"Are you ready to let her go?" she questions, no judgement in her tone.

Am I ready to let her go? I don't know how to answer that. How the fuck am I supposed to let her go now? After everything I've learned?

Two weeks after we attempted to rescue Willow from the warehouse, Vince's words were still playing through my head. *"Her mom was some teenage slut who got offed before she was born.*

Managed to push her out first. Ended up growing up in the system."

I couldn't let those words go.

Three weeks and several thousand dollars later, my private investigator, Walter Spivey, handed me a thick manila envelope holding every last detail he could find about Willow. Between the two of us, we were able to complete a heartbreaking timeline of tragedy and devastation that was Willow's life. The contents of that envelope, and what we compiled together, changed my life in ways I never thought possible.

Willow Jane Smith was born twenty years ago on November 20, to sixteen-year-old Doe Smith. After successfully delivering a twenty-six-week-old Willow, Doe succumbed to her injuries from a gunshot wound.

Despite the odds stacked against her, Willow lived in the neonatal intensive care unit for the first four months of her life. Upon release, she was relinquished to the hands of Colorado Child Services where she was placed in the first of thirteen foster homes.

On her eighteenth birthday, Willow was forced out of her last foster home. Her whereabouts for the next six months are sketchy at best. She next resurfaces behind a diner where the owner, Mr. Warren, and his wife stopped a rape in progress. A police report was filed, and Willow was quick to take up the couples offer to work at the diner, earning more than a fair wage while living in their garage apartment.

According to the Warrens, her life takes another turn four months later when she meets Vincent Reginald James. A respected police officer, he sweeps Willow off her feet, and they wed quickly. Immediately following their speedy nuptials, the couple moves to New Mexico after Vince is offered a promotion with the narcotics team.

It seems life can't get any better for the young couple, but things soon take a turn for the worse. Sealed hospital records show countless emergency room visits and unanswered pleas for help. When we first found photographic proof of the abuse, I was stunned that no one stepped in to help her. But after some digging, we found that not only did we recognize Vince's signature, but Doris Vale, the same nurse whom Vince blackmailed, had been doing a whole lot more than supplying him with the drugs he craved. Her signature was also present, answering our questions as to why no hospital staff were alerted.

Those hours we spent in the warehouse proved to be a fountain of knowledge. In the midst of his coked out high, Vince admitted that Willow's baby wasn't meant to survive the brutal beating he rained upon her. That same night, she fled her home. Security footage from a truck stop two hours away, shows Willow getting into the cab of an eighteen-wheeler with an older truck driver. The road ends in Willow's home state of Colorado.

Walter interviewed several business owners in the neighboring town, who after seeing her picture, confirmed Willow had been looking for work. Based on the accounts, she spent about three weeks searching for work and any means to provide for her and her baby.

The next sign of Willow was three weeks later when she was seen in town at Aspen General with me. Everything that had happened since then, I knew, because I lived it with her. Resentment settles in my gut as I think about all I was given, and all I have lost.

When I was sixteen years old, I met Death. That night, he gave me a second chance, but it came with a price. He may as well have carved my heart from my chest for the hole he left me with. For years I debated if it was worth it, and for years I would have said no. But God finally rewarded his servant in the most beautiful way. He made an angel just for me. Intricately woven together by the pieces of my past, he gave the King a Queen.

Then he took her away.

I stand from the bench and pace the grassy space between the small graves. "How am I supposed to do that?" I look to my mom, begging for answers. "I–" I grind my teeth and shove my hands through my hair.

"I just fucking found her! I found her and he took her, but it's so much worse this time. I didn't just lose her, I lost both of them... *again*," I choke out.

My mom stands and walks to me before wrapping her arms around my waist. The top of her head barely comes past my chin, but I feel her hold on me as if I'm a child again, and like a child, I cling to her.

"It's time to let her go, baby," she whispers. "Let her fly."

WASHED IN BLOOD

CHAPTER 28

WILLOW

The familiar timbre of Priest's voice pulls me from the darkness that holds me captive. His breath is hot against my skin, and my fingers ache to thread through his hair.

"Willow… you've gotta wake up, baby. Just give me something, a fuckin' twitch, that's all I need." His lips drag across the back of my hand as he speaks. "I don't know what to do here. It's been months and they—they don't know why you won't wake up. The doctors, they say it's all on you now, baby."

What the hell is he talking about? Wake up? I'm trying to wake up! My freaking eyes won't open! Oh my god. What's happening?

Strong hands grip my face, pulling me away from my internal panic. "Damn it, Willow. You did not survive your entire life to fall at his hands. Come back to me, baby... come back to me." His hands leave my face and I panic.

No, no, no don't go. Don't leave me! I fight to open my eyes, to move my fingers, my toes... *something.* But my body defies. The darkness calls to me, and like a sailor, I heed my siren's call.

I have no sense of time. Darkness is my only companion in my new form of hell. Visitors come and go, completely oblivious to the fact that I'm awake. A prisoner to my own body. I listen to them confess their deepest desires and darkest secrets. My heart cries for them as they give me their truths. These men, the things they've been through... my mind can hardly process.

The biggest surprise has been my current visitor. He's always alone when he comes, and from what I've gathered, the other men have no idea he's been here at all.

"He kicked Angel out of his room, you know? Moved him to the other side of the house with me and the other two. Said he needed that room for a nursery for when you come home. Said he didn't want the baby far, but wanted to be able to be with his woman without his kid watching." He huffs out what I expect is his version of a laugh.

My heart warms; he's not giving up on me. I'm stuck here, and he's at home turning Angel's room into a nursery.

"Angel was fuckin' pissed. I think it had more to do with the fact that he would have to be closer to me than anything." His voice lowers to a whisper, "Christ, I've fucked everything up. This isn't who I used to be—who I *want* to be. Anger and hate have taken over my body. It's like a disease that's infected every inch of me, and now it's seeping from my pores. And there's this… this need. A need to infect everyone around me. Because if I have to suffer, then they should too." My stomach clenches at his words. *He's drowning, and no one has noticed.*

"You gotta wake up for him, Willow. I know I'm a fuckin' bastard, and I got no right to ask anything of anyone, 'specially you," his voice cracks. "But he saved us. King saved each and every one of us, and now he's lost. He's lost and there's nothing we can do. It's all on you now, girl." His chair scrapes across the floor and I'm stunned when the barely there touch of his lips press against my head. "Save him, Willow."

"Why the fuck isn't she waking up? Goddamn it, it's been months. According to you there's nothing wrong, so look at me and tell me why she won't open her eyes."

I'm pulled from the darkness again. Priest's fury fills the room so fully it's almost suffocating. I'm not sure who his words are directed at, but I'm glad it's not me. He is *pissed*—wait! *Did he just say months?*

"Mr. Blake, as I've explained countless times, medically, there is no reason why she has yet to wake up. For all we know about the brain and how it works, there are still things that cannot be explained away."

Priest growls low. "That's not good enough. They said you were the fuckin' best. You've yet to show me a single reason why I should keep those wire transfers going each week. Wake her the fuck up."

"Mr. Blake," the doctor begins. "Though her scans are clear, you need to understand that the brain is a beast all on its own. There isn't always a rhyme or reason, I've told you this. You need to be prepared for—"

A loud clatter has my pulse rising. "No. Fuck no. *Do not* come at me with that shit."

"I—I apologize. I know this is a sensitive time—"

Something crashes. "Get the fuck out."

The doctor must obey because the door opens and closes. For several minutes, I think Priest has left with him because I'm left in silence. Then I hear his boots pace across the room. I don't know where he's standing, but he doesn't touch me, and I don't hear the

313

chair at my bedside move. When he finally speaks, it's muffled, almost as if he's turned away from me.

I strain to hear. "This wasn't part of the deal. Find them, guide them, and be patient. That's what you fuckin' told me. I waited twenty years. I think I've been patient enough."

Who the hell is he talking to? Is there someone else here?

"You gave her to me," his voice cracks. "You gave her to *me,* and now you're trying to take her back when she's not yours to take. There's nothing here for me without her. You want me to do your bidding? Then you need to give her the fuck back, because I'll follow her wherever she goes."

The steady beep of the heart monitor is a sound I'm all too familiar with. But the sunlight filtering in through the window of my hospital room is new. *Oh my god. I can open my eyes. I can finally open my eyes.*

Flower arrangements of all shapes and sizes line the window. I laugh at the humongous motorcycle balloon but quickly grab my middle when the muscles protest. Pain all but forgotten, my focus is solely on the hard mound of my belly forming a mountain under the blanket.

My hands span my growing middle and I sob. *It's been months.*

314

The door to the room opens as Priest walks in and my breath catches in my throat. *He looks terrible.* His focus is on the coffee in his hands, but I can see the dark bags under his eyes and his slightly sunken in cheeks. When I sniffle, his head shoots up, his eyes going wide at the sight of me sitting up in bed. The coffee slips from his hands as he rushes to the bed and clasps my face between his hands.

"Holy fuck... Jesus fuck, you're awake... you're really awake." He presses his lips against mine in a bruising kiss. After several seconds, he drops his forehead to mine, still muttering under his breath. "Thank you, thank you, thank you." When he finally pulls away, there are tears in his tired eyes.

I brush my thumb along the whiskers of his face. "Hey there, handsome," my voice is rough and scratchy. Priest pushes a straw and cup of water to my mouth to help me drink. After several gulps he pulls it back and sets it on the table.

He chokes out a laugh and pulls my hand away before pressing his lips against my palm. "Thought I lost you."

I grin. "It'll take more than that to get rid of me. I've survived his beatings before, this is nothing new."

Priest shakes his head. "Willow, it—it wasn't just a beating... it—" he stops and starts again, "What's the last thing you remember?"

"I remember Vi—" I quiet at the growl that vibrates his chest. "I remember *him* taking me from the

315

hospital. We drove a long time before he stopped at a warehouse. I remember the beatings… the—the things he did. I was scared, scared I wouldn't make it out of there. Scared my baby would die at the hands of its own father."

Priest growls again and my mind goes back to the night he discovered my lies. *Oh my God.* How can he stand to look at me now he knows the truth? Will he let me explain? *No. I don't deserve it.* I let us build a relationship on a foundation of lies. I have no one to blame but myself that I now lie beneath the rubble.

"Priest, I'm so sor—"

"He is *not* his father. *I am.* He will have my last name. The same name as his mother and father. I will provide his wants and needs. I will guide him and give him love and discipline. I will push him to be a better man so that one day he may know and deserve the love of an amazing woman. *I* will do those things, *me.* So, no, Willow, that piece of filth is *not* his father."

My mind is stuck on his words playing on repeat in my head. *He will have my last name… the same name as his mother and father. He… his.*

"It's a boy?" my voice breaks on a sob.

Priest's smile is blinding. "Yeah, baby. We're having a boy."

There's no point trying to contain my tears. Priest climbs into the bed and wraps me in his arms as the echoes of my cries fill the room. But unlike so many other tears that have been shed throughout the years in rooms just like this one, these tears are anything but sad. For the first time in so many years, my tears aren't filled with sorrow or hate. There's no trace of resentment or fear. Instead they're filled with hope for the future.

"I promise I'll tell you everything, but I want you to take it easy. Your body has been through enough for one lifetime." He leans in to kiss me but the door opens.

"What the—who made this mess? You could have at least—Oh! You're awake. You were supposed to come get us immediately if she woke." A perky nurse in bright pink scrubs chastises Priest who growls at her. She ignores him and rushes to the sink where she pulls out several paper towels to clean the spilled coffee from the floor. Once the coffee is cleaned, she turns back for the door. "I'll go let the doctor know you're awake." The door closes behind her.

Priest grips my chin and turns me back to face him before pressing his lips against my head. "Fuck, but I've missed you."

"And I missed you too I'm sure, but *please* stop stalling and tell me how long I've been here." I glance at my body that looks more like *Shamu* than Willow.

His hand moves to my head where his fingers massage my scalp. I moan in pleasure but yelp when his fingertips brush over a sensitive area on the back of my skull. I lift my hand to follow his as I feel the raised, two-inch laceration.

317

"When he shot you in your thigh, you collapsed before I could think to catch you." His hand on my belly fists the sheet. "You dropped so fast there was nothing I could do. Your head cracked the cement floor hard and heavy—" He shakes his head. "You've been here for three months, Willow. This is the first time I've seen you coherent since you were brought in."

Three months?! No wonder my belly is so big. That would mean I'm almost thirty weeks pregnant. A wave of sadness washes through me as I realize how much of my pregnancy I've missed, but I don't dwell on it long, instead, I focus on the fact that my baby is alive and healt—

"Is everything okay with the baby? I mean surely after being out of it that long... there has to be something wrong with him, right? How could there no—"

Priest cuts me off, "Willow, he's fine. He's measuring right on track, bigger actually. He's healthy as a horse. The doctors haven't been able to explain why you were still sleeping. All your scans have been clear. There was no permanent or temporary damage to any part of your brain. Best they could explain it was that you needed the rest. Your body needed to recharge and focus on this little guy." He leans forward and kisses my swollen middle where *our son* is. "It's all going to be okay now."

It's been three days since I woke up and since then, I've been poked and prodded over every inch of my body. I understand their concerns, and I'm sure it doesn't help that I have a hulking biker watching every move they make. I want to smack him half the time because he keeps asking questions, and at his insistence, they run more tests.

When the doctor comes in to give me the all clear to go home, my hand darts out, squeezing Priest's in a death grip the second his mouth opens. He looks at me, stunned. I glare at him before turning back to the doctor with a smile. "Thank you so much again, Dr. Nijaro. I can't begin to tell you how ready I am to get home."

The older man smiles and pats my hand. "It's past time, if you ask me, Ms. Willow. I'm sure you'll be fine, especially with this one watching after you." He jerks his thumb at Priest. "Good luck to you. Both of you." He nods at Priest, then my belly. "You have my number if you ever need anything." He shakes Priest's hand before leaving.

A nurse walks in with a huge smile while pushing a wheelchair toward the bed. "You're going home!" I laugh at her excitement.

"God, I know. I can't wait to be in my own bed again." I groan as she pulls me from the bed and helps me step into my clothes.

The chair rattles on its legs when Priest yanks my bag from where it's hanging on the arm. "I'm going to go pull the truck around," he says as he stalks toward the door.

The nurse turns back to me and cocks a brow.

"Men." I laugh and shrug away his behavior.

Once I'm dressed and seated in the wheelchair, she hands me the last of the flowers and balloons left in my room, and we're off. We make it to the lobby of the hospital where I'm seconds away from freedom. Priest stands by his truck, waiting for us outside the doors, and my smile brightens. He grins back at me, but it dims when his eyes flash over my shoulder. I tense, but relax when an older nurse rounds me, panting hard.

"Oh, thank God I caught you." She leans over, hands on her knees as she attempts to slow her breathing. She finally stands, her eyes coming to me and misting as they scan my face. "God, I can't believe it's really you," she whispers.

"Uhh…" Crap, am I supposed to know who she is? I look her over several times, trying to place her face, but I swear I've never seen this woman before. I open my mouth to ask her just that, but I'm stopped by Priest's domineering voice.

"Can I help you?" He steps up to me and I roll my eyes when he drapes his arm over my shoulder like he's protecting me from the big bad nurse. The nurse seems to trip over her tongue at the sight of Priest, and I smile inwardly. *Yeah, he does cause that reaction.*

"I—I'm sorry. I don't mean to hold you up, I'm sure you're ready to get home. I was just transferred here from Mercy Medical and I saw your name in the computer—" She takes a deep breath before extending her hand to Priest, then to me.

"Let me start over. My name is Marilyn Hanks." She crouches in front of my wheelchair, putting herself on my level.

"I'm sorry Ms. Hanks, you'll have to forgive me, but I'm having trouble placing you." I smile sheepishly but she waves it away.

"Nonsense, Willow. You were just a baby the last time I saw you, no way do I expect you to know who I am."

My heart stops. *I was a baby the last time she saw me?* That's not possible. My mother is dead. I don't know much about my father; that information was always limited when questions were brought up with case workers. The only way she could know me would be if—

"I worked at the hospital where you were born." She smiles sweetly at me. "Actually, I was there the night you were born. I was a nurse in the neonatal intensive care unit at the time. When I saw your name in the computer, I had to come see if it was really you." She grips my trembling hands in her warm ones.

"I've always wondered about you. For years I prayed that God only had good things in store for you, especially after fighting so hard to stay in this world. I tried to ask about you several times, but being a nurse gained me no special access once you were out of our care." Her gaze drops to my belly before darting to Priest.

She lowers her voice, "I see things turned out better than I could have hoped." She winks.

I laugh, even though my mind is racing. Hundreds of questions are begging to pour from my mouth. But before I can speak, Priest grips the handles of the wheelchair and pulls me from the care of the nurse behind me. "It was nice to meet you, but I'm afraid I need to get Willow home to rest now."

I wave at the nurse as Priest pushes me toward the door, but her voice stops us a second time. Priest turns slightly so I can see her as he turns back.

"What did you say your name was?" she asks Priest who stares at her for long, silent moments before answering.

"Kingston Blake."

The nurse's eyes go wide, and a small gasp leaves her lips as her eyes dart quickly between Priest and I. Her lips lift in a grin and she whispers her goodbye. "Well, it was nice running into you. I'm so happy things worked out for you," she says, her eyes on me before moving them to Priest. "*Both* of you."

Both of you? Does she know Priest too? Again, I don't have a chance to ask before Priest is loading me up into his truck. His lips come to mine when he reaches across my body to click the buckle. "Ready, baby?"

I smile and nod. "Take me home."

WASHED IN BLOOD

CHAPTER 29

WILLOW

The guys almost tackle me the second I walk through the door causing Priest to lose his ever-loving shit. "The fuck is wrong with you?" he roars at them. "She just got out of the fuckin' hospital, not to mention she's nearly eight months pregnant."

The others back off but Angel stays, wrapping me against his lean, muscular body. "Glad to have you home, little mama." He kisses the top of my head. "This one's been fuckin' miserable without you." He jerks his head at Priest who's carrying our bags down the hall toward our room.

I laugh at the emphatic nod I get from each of them. "Aw, guys, surely he hasn't been that bad."

Happiness fills me up to bursting as they take turns to hug me and welcome me home. *These men, they're my family.* It took me twenty years, but I finally have the family I've always dreamed of. They start going on about dinner, hinting what they'd each like to eat, and like chastised little boys, their faces drop when they realize I'm not cooking.

"Hell, I guess we better go through the takeout menus," Bullet grumbles as Angel follows him into the kitchen. *Crazy men.*

An arm wraps around my shoulder. I look up at Patch and lean into his warm embrace. "Glad to have you back, girl."

"Thanks, Patch, for everything." My eyes dart to the opening of the hall. "Are you two okay?"

I think back to the hospital when Priest first found out about the baby. The look of betrayal on his face is one I won't soon forget. When Priest hit him… what was left of my bleeding heart broke in two when I saw what I'd caused between them.

Patch's eyes soften at the worry on my face. "Don't worry about us, darlin'. It'll take more than a couple secrets to tear any of us apart. We've been through too much together." He squeezes my shoulder before following Bullet and Angel into the kitchen where I hear their raised voices arguing over Chinese or Mexican.

I glance around the room; my heart sinks when I realize who's missing. *Demon.* I have no idea exactly how long I was able to hear the guys while I was in my 'sleep coma' as I've come to call it. There was no sense of time for me. Each of them confessed things I'm sure they'd be horrified to know I actually heard. But Demon... I don't know how I can convince my heart it didn't hear the things it did.

"Willow." I follow the sound of Priest's voice and find him standing against the closed door of Angel's room. Or what *used to be* Angel's room. Demon's words filter through.

He kicked Angel out of his room... Said he needed it for a nursery.

It takes real effort to keep my features schooled from Priest. He knows me like the back of his hand; he'll be able to tell if I don't pull this off.

"Hi." I go up on my toes to press my lips against his for a quick kiss, but apparently Priest has other ideas. His arms wrap around my waist pulling me tightly against him, or as much as the basketball between us will allow. I giggle when he growls and looks down at my belly.

"Seriously little dude? Already cock blocking." He shakes his head and pretends to wince when I pop him in his toned middle.

"Don't call him that!" I scold, but he only laughs before he sobers, eyes coming to mine.

"You're different, you know? Ever since you woke up... it's almost like you're a different person, Willow."

I know what he's talking about. From the moment I woke up and found out that Vince was no longer a worry in my life, it was like I was able to be the Willow I was meant to be. But even this Willow is one that I've never seen before. And it's all because of the man standing in front of me. My gut churns. What if this isn't who he was waiting on? Does he want the old Willow back?

"It's not a bad thing, baby. You're freer than I've ever seen you. It's like I'm getting the chance to fall in love with you all over again."

"I think this is the freest I've ever been," I whisper, nose burning with tears as the truth of it sinks in. I've found a family in the most unlikely of places. And if I was given the chance at a do-over of my life, I wouldn't change a thing. Because right here with this group of vigilante bikers, is where I would want to be every time. I sniffle when my pregnancy hormones rush front and center.

Priest cups my face. "What's the matter, baby?" His thumb wipes a stray tear away as I shake my head.

"Nothing. Just thinking about how happy I am that I ended up here," I say honestly.

"Fuck, baby. Me too… me too." He kisses me again before he jumps back flashing a bright smile. "Now, no more crying. I have a surprise for you." He rubs his hands together like a little kid about to tear into his presents on Christmas morning.

"Oh yeah? Is that why we're standing outside Angel's door, and not in our bed?" I quirk a brow.

He groans. "Fuck, babe. You can't say shit like that to me when I'm trying to do something nice for you. You'll cause me to put all this on hold so I can show you with more than words just how much I missed you." I moan when he comes behind me and grinds his hardness against my ass.

For a split second I consider how bad I want to see my surprise. These pregnancy hormones are no joke. Happy one second to crying the next, only to end up horny as hell a few minutes later. Jesus. I'm going to need a seatbelt on this rollercoaster, and I'm sure the guys will need one too.

"You ready?" He takes my hands in his. "Close your eyes."

When the door opens, Priest tugs my hands and I follow him into the room. He moves my body, positioning me where he wants me before his hands leave mine. I don't miss his touch long because he comes to stand behind me to wrap his arms around my waist. His hands settle on my belly. "Open your eyes, baby."

Obeying his command, I open my eyes and gasp. I don't have to try hard to mask my knowledge of the nursery, because nothing could have prepared me for this. Angel's room has been completely transformed. I turn in Priest's arms, taking in every inch of the room. Priest steps back watching every reaction as I explore. The entire room is painted in the palest baby blue. White furniture accented with gold fixtures contrast the colors perfectly, and a mini crystal chandelier hangs from the ceiling.

Priest clears his throat, looking uncertain. "I uh—I gotta admit. Once I found out it was a boy, I was going to do it in motorcycles. Phyllis and my mom put a stop to that real quick." He laughs. "They picked a few different themes, but I had the final say."

I walk to the crib and run my hands along the navy velvet bumper, savoring the softness of the material against my skin. Above the crib, a mobile hangs from the ceiling, tiny golden crowns dangling from its ends.

"Priest, it's–" How can I even begin to explain that this room is more than anything I imagined being able to give my son. There was a time I was terrified I would have to leave him in the arms of another woman to love and care for him, because I couldn't. Not long ago, I didn't even have a bed for myself. It broke my soul to think of the things I would need to provide for him, and to realize the chances of that happening would take nothing short of a miracle. Priest talks to me like I saved him, but he fails to see... it's me who's been saved.

"If it's too much, we can redo it. I told them to take it easy, but they said it had to be fit for a king."

"Or a prince..." I whisper. His eyes dart to me. "Come 'ere," he murmurs.

I snuggle into his arms, both of us looking over the details of our son's room. I could say that for the rest of my life, and it still wouldn't feel real. I yawn, my eyes feeling heavy. You would think I'd had enough sleep to last a lifetime after doing nothing but that for the past three months, but apparently not.

"Let's get you to bed."

Our room hasn't changed since the night the Guerra brothers broke into the house. While being in the coma and hearing the guys' confessions was hard, there were definite benefits to it. I finally know every sordid detail that led to me being here. How the brothers were using Manuel's name and money to fund their very own loan shark operation. I know that Priest killed Reuben, I also know that he's struggling with his feelings toward the cartel after what he learned.

I know he wants to believe there's good in everyone, but after hearing what Diego did to Isadora from not only Priest, but Demon as well, I'm not sure if there's any good in that man. Unfortunately, we won't know until Manuel dies and Diego assumes the throne. Only time will tell.

In the bathroom, I step out of my clothes and a sense of déjà vu washes over me. I think about my first shower here all those months ago. It's still strange to think that so much time has passed, and even though I wasn't here, the world still turned. Time still moved on, and in some ways it feels like I was left behind. Lost to my thoughts, my foot slips as I step into the steaming shower stall. I tense, preparing to hit the hard floor.

"Goddamnit, Willow," Priest growls, catching me just before I hit the floor. *Always saving me.*

He pulls the door behind him, putting us both under the spray of the water before he turns his glare on me. "What the fuck were you doing?"

I jerk back. "Um. Taking a shower?"

He turns his back to me, the hot water cascading over the muscles on his back a welcome distraction.

"You have to start taking better care of yourself. How am I supposed to trust that you can take care of yourself out there if you can't even get into the shower without falling?"

We finish showering in silence, both getting lost in the comfort of washing each other's bodies. He kisses me, his eyes begging me to forgive him, but he doesn't have to beg. I'll willingly give him anything he wants. Back in the room, he moves to the closet to get dressed. Several minutes pass in silence, so I go over to check on him.

The scene has déjà vu sweeping over me for the second time today. Priest leans his forehead against the mirror in the closet. This time, it's not anger in his eyes, it's devastation.

"Baby..." I place my palms against his back, but he pulls away from me, avoiding my eyes.

"You gonna tell me what's got you so scared?" I ask.

His body freezes, but I don't know why he seems so surprised. My man may think he's a brick house, but he forgets I'm the mortar that holds him together. I know him inside and out, and lashing out, avoiding eye contact, most people would think those were signs I'd pissed him off. But bikers are a different breed. They face confrontation head on and don't back away until it's resolved. But right now he's terrified, and I need to fix it.

"Fuck," he mutters under his breath. His shoulders tense before he drops his head. "You were safe there… at the hospital." He turns to look at me, his eyes pleading. "We shouldn't have left. What if you fall and something happens to your brain? What if they missed something and we don't find it until you're in labor and—" He stops, his throat moving with the force of his swallow. "I can't lose you again, Willow. I can't do it."

"King, I know you like to think differently, but you can't change fate, baby. I could have just as easily slipped in the shower at the hospital." I cup his face in my hand. "When it's my time to go, it's my time."

He shakes his head and pulls my hand away from his face to press his lips against my palm. "When it's your time, it's mine too."

"Don't talk like that. We're about to have a sweet little boy who's gonna need his daddy." I grin at him.

"And what about his mama, huh? Don't you think he's gonna need her too? You don't understand what the past three months have been like for me, Willow. I've been a thousand leagues under the sea. My lungs burning for air that wasn't there. You're my oxygen. I breathe you in and you infect every inch of me, flowing through my veins, bringing life to the other parts of me." He shakes his head. "You don't want me to follow you, but—what good is a King without his Queen?"

My sweet, crazy man. He doesn't even see what he is to those around him. I've lived my entire life believing I wasn't worthy of the love he so freely gives. And he's right. I have no idea what the past months have been like for him, and honestly, I don't want to try to imagine. I know the feeling that was left in the pit of my own belly when I thought he walked away from me.

My mind wanders to the question sitting on the tip of my tongue. "Priest…"

He twists his fingers through my hair. "Yeah, baby?"

"That nurse at the hospital… she seemed to know you… or us. Did she tell you about me, about my birth?" *Does he know now about the monster that hides beneath my skin?*

He drops his gaze. "I uh—" He swallows hard. "I think it's time I told you the whole story about what happened the day I died."

I nod. *What does that mean? I thought he'd already told me everything about that day...?* I twist my fingers together as unease creeps in. *God, Priest. What did you do?* Secrets and lies almost destroyed us once before, but this time they aren't mine. They're his.

"Willow, what do you know about your mom?"

My mom? What does this have to do with my mom? I want to know how the nurse knew him. He stares at me expectantly, so I shrug. "Honestly, not much. She was an orphan herself. Dropped at the hospital not long after she'd been born. She didn't have any kind of identification, so the hospital named her. She was put into foster care and as far as I know, everything was okay until a freak accident when she was sixteen. She was pregnant with me at the time, but was able to deliver me before she died." I hate the ease with which the words roll off my tongue when in reality, they were pried from my soul. The fact that I don't know much about my mom, and nothing about where I come from, is a pill I swallowed years ago. My heart still longs for the answers it will never have.

Priest takes my hands and presses them against his lips. "I'm going to tell you a story, but first, I want you to know that I love you. I love the way you not only love my monsters, but are so willing to dance with them in the dark. I love the way you feed my soul and breathe life into its darkest caverns. I was told to wait, and I would be rewarded. Well God must want something more from me, because nothing I've done in my life has left me worthy of you. But I'll be damned if he's getting you back now."

"I love you too." I kiss him softly before pulling back. "You gonna tell me my bedtime story now?" I grin.

Priest shakes his head. "I wish it was the kind of story you're thinking of, baby, but it's not. When I was six years old, I was put into foster care. My mom had just died... it was the scariest time of my life. The next few years were hell for me. I hated the world and it must have hated me back, because it fucked me in every way possible. Until one day... it didn't." He smiles fondly.

"I was sixteen when she came into my life. Despite the crap life she'd been given, she was the most beautiful, carefree person I'd ever met. We were young, but we knew what love was, and what it wasn't. That's one of the hardest truths I think kids in foster care have to learn—just how *un*loved they are."

I nod. He's right. Even being a lifer, I learned early on that what other kids and their Moms and Dads had definitely wasn't what I had with my foster parents.

Priest's shaky breath brings my attention back to him. He grabs my hands, squeezing them tight between his. He looks like he's about to tell me he kills kittens. What the hell has he been keeping from me that could be this bad?

"Doe Smith was the first girl I ever loved."

With those words, my world stops. *Doe Smith…* I snatch my hands from his, my mind mentally calculating the math between my age, his, and the age my mother was when she died. *No!*

"Hey. Get that shit out of your head right now. I'm not your fuckin' dad, Willow." He sounds offended that I would even suspect it.

"And you know that… for sure?" I wait while he glares at me.

"We really gonna do this?" he asks.

I nod, standing my ground. *Hell yeah we're gonna do this.* You just told me you were in a *relationship* with my *mother.* You bet your ass you're going to tell me exactly how you know I'm not yours. "We're doing this."

"I was never *with* your mom… in that way. I swear to you, baby. I wouldn't lie about that."

My shoulders sag. "Do you…" *Crap, how do I ask this.* "Did she, uh—cheat on you, or something?" I wince, not wanting to bring up bad memories, but I'm grasping at anything he can tell me about my family.

"She lied to me. Now that I'm older, I'm able to see how she thought she didn't have a choice. That's what hurts the most." I hold my breath when his guarded eyes come to mine. "I know what you're asking, Willow. I don't know who your dad is. I'm sorry, baby." He clears his throat, guilt flickers in his eyes before he drops his gaze.

He knows something. But after everything I've been through, and everything I've put *him* through, I let it go. *I have my own family now.*

"What happened that day, King... the day she died? You were there, weren't you?"

His jaw clenches as my mind begins putting the pieces together. "It was never supposed to happen that way. If she'd have just—Fuck!" he growls, pushing away from me to pace across the room. He stops, his eyes pleading with me to understand. "It was my fault," he chokes out. "It was all my fault. There's no one to blame but me. For a long time, I was furious with her. If she'd have just stayed put, not followed me, it wouldn't have happened the way it did. It took me years to come to terms with the fact that neither of us could have stopped what happened that night. But I still struggled, Willow."

He drops onto the bed beside me and wraps an arm around my waist as he kisses my head. "Until I met you. The second I held your broken body in my arms, it was like I was put back together. You healed me from the inside out, baby. I didn't understand it at first. I mean, how the fuck could this woman who's barely lived, be the answer to a lifetime's worth of pain? But it all makes sense to me now."

He kneels on the floor at my feet, his hands splayed across my belly. "Don't you see, baby? I had to lose her to get you. Twenty years ago, I thought my life was over, but it was only getting started."

My heart cries out when his words sink in. For twenty years, I've carried this pain. The belief that I was responsible for my mom's death. I'd convinced myself that if God couldn't love me, who would? But *He* had plans for me all along. All those times I thought he'd forgotten about me, he was making me stronger. Preparing me, molding me. Transforming me into a woman fit for a King.

EPILOGUE

PRIEST

Six months later

"Willow, we gotta go, babe."

The guys left twenty minutes ago so they could be there to greet the guests. We were supposed to leave with them, but my woman had the sudden urge to try on everything in her closet, even though she picked out her outfit and Leo's, last night.

"Babe," I call from the other end of the hall. *Fuck, we're gonna be late.*

She pokes her head out the bedroom door. "Just grabbing the diaper bag, babe."

Damn she's beautiful. It's been almost a year since I found her in the woods behind our clubhouse, and most days I struggle to believe any of it's real. Not only do I have the most beautiful woman by my side, I'm now a father to a little boy who has my heart in his hands.

Willow rushes from the bedroom, the diaper bag on one shoulder, and Leo balanced on her hip. I extend my hand to take the diaper bag as I kiss her cheek. "You look beautiful."

She smiles and thanks me as Leo grabs the end of her fluffy scarf and brings it to his mouth. Willow tugs it away and his little face drops, but before the tears start, I reach out to tickle his belly. "Look at you little man! All spiffed up." His baby chuckles fill the hall. It's a sound I'll never grow tired of hearing. The sound of happiness, laughter… life. It's all I want to hear for the rest of my days.

Twenty minutes later, we pull into the parking lot of Heaven's Gates Cemetery. I get Leo out of the car and bundle him in a blanket before I wrap him inside my jacket for extra warmth. A handful of cars are parked in the lot along with my brothers' bikes lined up by the gates.

After I told Willow the story about Doe and the short time we had together, she was determined to find her mom's remains.

Our search for Doe's final resting place never amounted to anything. Hospital staff informed us that those without families are often cremated, or left in morgues for months—sometimes years. Alone forever... like unclaimed baggage, or unwanted trash. It made me sick to think of her left there like that.

Willow's words broke my heart. *"All those people... their souls will never be at rest."* She researched ways we could help, and there were a few foundations that caught her eye, but ultimately, we decided to make our own mark. Five months ago, my brothers and I got to work, searching for prime real estate that would best suit our needs. We found a one hundred acre plot filled with Aspen Pines about twenty-five minutes away, and Heaven's Gates Cemetery was born.

In the midst of those trees we built a secret garden for the lost souls of the world. A place for those with no family. A place where the homeless, the orphans, and the unloved could be given a proper burial and be laid to rest. Three days ago, the gates to the cemetery were unlocked. Today, we will dedicate it to Doe.

"Willow!" My mom's voice rises above the gathering crowd, drowning out every other sound as she rushes toward Willow. Leo's arms reach out for his grandma as Mom pulls them both into her chest for a giant bear hug.

"Mom," I say, "you're gonna crush them."

She narrows her eyes and extends her hand to me. "Get over here, boy, give your mama a hug."

Between us, Leo giggles until Mom finally releases her iron grasp. She steps back to take Leo from my arms. "Go on you two, get up there and say your part."

Willow laces her fingers through mine. "I'm nervous," she admits.

I stop and pull her into my chest. "You can do this, babe. You're the strongest woman I know." I brush a kiss over her soft, pink lips.

A heavy hand slaps my shoulder. "Do we need to have you two surgically removed from one another?" Angel laughs and I growl at him as Willow's lips leave mine.

I raise my brow. "Jealous, bro?"

"Nah, she's a few parts short of a Harley for this biker." Angel jerks his thumb toward the fountain in the center of the cemetery. The dedication piece sits in the middle of the flowing water where it's covered in a black sheet, waiting to be unveiled. "Let's get this show on the road so we can eat."

Willow laughs. "Okay, I'm ready." She nods but bites her lip when she glances at the people gathered around the fountain waiting on our speech.

Angel pats her shoulder. "You've got this, Wil."

A small but genuine smile stretches her lips. She's become closer to Angel over the past few weeks, and it's been good for both of them.

"Good afternoon everyone. Thank you for coming to the dedication of Heaven's Gates Cemetery. Twenty years ago, I was born to a teen mother who grew up in foster care. My mom had no family, and only one true friend."

Willow's eyes lock onto mine and I give her a nod, urging her to continue.

"While I survived, my mom didn't, and I was left an orphan myself. Years later, I discovered the heartbreaking news like so many others do, there was no cremation or funeral for my mom. No final wishes, and no resting place for her body. This isn't how it should be."

She glances at me as she grips the string connected to the sheet in her hand. "Today, Heaven's Gates Cemetery is officially open, giving those lost souls a place to rest for eternity. And today, we dedicate the cemetery to my mom and all those who have been forgotten by the rest of the world. Forgotten no more for we hold the keys to the gates... welcome home."

Willow pulls on the rope and the black sheet floats away to reveal the statue. A six-foot, marble guardian angel holding a set of skeleton keys identical to the ones on our club logo. Here to watch over them, holding the keys to Heaven's Gates.

I glance to my right where the first headstone already stands, polished and new.

Doe Smith
Her greatest gift was the one she left behind.

Looking behind me, my eyes land on Doe's gift. My wife's smile stretches across her face. My heart warms when she lifts Leo's little hand to wave at me from across the courtyard.

Her greatest gift was the one she left behind.

Sounds about right to me.

AVAILABLE NOW

Silenced By Sin
Heaven's Guardians MC Book 2

Patch
The smallest caskets weigh the most.
I lost myself the day I buried my daughter.
Her death was only the beginning of my downfall.

I will not play God
As a doctor, the oath I took bound me.
As a father, only blood could set me free.

Pain is my prison.
With guilt my only companion,
I bought myself a life, Silenced by Sin.

Alaska
You are not defined by your mistakes.
I refuse to regret the choices I've made.
I embrace them.

I will bow to no one.
Fear does not make me weak.
In the face of fear, I find my true strength.
I will rise.

With fire in my veins and embers in my soul,
I will give my daughter the life she deserves.

Haunted By Regret
Heaven's Guardians MC Book 3

Haunted (adjective)- Preoccupied with an emotion, memory, or idea; obsessed.

It's what happens to a man that loses his entire family.
The first years that followed their demise were the worst.

Determined to inflict even a fraction of my pain onto those responsible,
I paid them back the same way they paid me.
I was content to live out my days knowing justice was dealt at my hands.

Consumed with rage.
Obsessed with revenge.
Haunted by regret.

Years later, I take in two boys and suddenly it's no longer only about me.

That's where she comes in.
A broken nanny who heals us all.

PREORDER NOW

<u>Betrayed By Beauty</u>
<u>Heaven's Guardians MC Book 4</u>

Mirror mirror on the wall-
F*ck you.
They say beauty is in the eye of the beholder.
I wish it wasn't.
The first time my step-dad raped me,
I prayed for God to save me... he never came.

Instead, my savior came in the form of a Priest.
For years we've done God's bidding.
Blood coats our hands and souls,
Devilish deeds all done in the Lord's name.

But changes are coming and our time is running out.
I'm not sure I'm ready.
Not sure I can face the man in the mirror when the
mask comes off.

I'm drowning in the uncertainty of the future.
I need someone to save me.
I need *them*.

*This is a MMF love story.

COMING SOON

Devoured By Demons
Heaven's Guardians Book 5

AUTHOR BIO

Being the boy mom of a 10 and almost 3 year old, means Ashley Lane lives off Goldfish crumbs and Diet Coke. When her life isn't being ruled by her tiny minions and their endless activities, you can typically find her parked on the couch, Kindle within reach, catching up on the previous week's episode of Grey's Anatomy or Hell's Kitchen.

SOCIAL MEDIA LINKS

Facebook

Reader Group - Ashley Lane's Biker Bitches

Instagram

Amazon Author Profile

Goodreads

BookBub

Website

Newsletter

ACKNOWLEDGEMENTS

First and foremost, to my mama. This is me practicing my please and thank you. _Thank you_ for watching my tiniest heathen while I wrote. Will you _please_ do it again for book two?

To the man and two boys that rule every inch of my heart, thank you for not reporting me as a missing person. My search history would have surely gotten me added to the No Fly List.

Nana, I love you a bushel and a peck, and a hug around the neck. Thank you for all that you do on a daily basis for our family. You're our glue.

To the Grammar Police- AKA my editor, Julie Addicott. No matter the words I put onto this page, they won't amount to even a fraction of what I'm trying to say. After a while, calling you my editor was such an injustice. Because on the long list of things you are to me, an editor is not even close to the top. Soul mate, my other half, keeper of secrets, and vault of my salt. I love you with all the ballsack hearts in the world. Thank you for being you. <3 <3

To my clit circle of trust, my best bitches. Sara and Jill. You two have no idea what you mean to me. If I were to try and explain it, I would say I value our friendship like I value cupcakes. And that's a pretty high honor. Thank you for keeping me around, I love you guys.

My beta: Diane, you read my first words that didn't deserve to be written on a bathroom stall, still the love and encouragement you gave me pushed me to finish. You also deserve a medal for ninja level patience. Hopefully next time I can prove I'm not a total nutcase.

Parker S. Huntington, you were the very first person I ever talked to on this side of the book. You answered my bizarre and intrusive questions with honesty and patience. You have no idea how much it meant to me. Thank you.

Misty Walker, my second friend in this new world, you believed in me from the start. Thank you for everything.

Paige Sayer, thank you for proofreading and making sure my book was a sparkling gem.

To my Biker Bitches. You ladies are the real MVP.

And last but not least, to my readers. Thank you for taking a chance on me and my men. I hope that a piece of each story stays with you when you go.